THE DELIVERY MAN

THE DELIVERY MAN

JOE McGINNISS JR.

Atlantic Books
London

First published as a paperback original in the United States
in 2008 by Black Cat, an imprint of Grove Atlantic Ltd.

First published in trade paperback in Great Britain in 2008
by Atlantic Books, an imprint of Grove Atlantic Ltd.

Copyright © Joe McGinnis Jr. 2008

1 3 5 7 9 8 6 4 2

A CIP catalogue record for this book is available from the British Library.

ISBN: 978 1 84354 731 0

Printed in Great Britain by MPG Books Ltd, Bodmin, Cornwall

Atlantic Books

An imprint of Grove Atlantic Ltd.
Ormond House
26–27 Boswell Street
London WC1N 3JZ

For Jeanine, who deserves more than I can ever give.
And for my mother, Christine McGinniss, who raised me.
And for my son, Julien, I had no idea.

THE
DELIVERY
MAN

Find Yourself Here. Those words are carved into the massive slab of granite that marks the entrance to the Golden Age Court in the Paseos of Summerlin. The Golden Age Court is Phase IV—the most popular Phase, more upscale and modern than the first three master-planned Phases, at least according to the glossy brochure Michele left on Chase's bedside table in the suite at the Palace. The Golden Age Court might just be where Michele will end up—if things work out. *Find Yourself Here*. The words are less an invitation than a punch line: the butt of its own sick joke. Other jokes and other punch lines? How many titanium screws did it take to put Chase's head back together? Twenty-nine. How much lower is his left eye than his right after four reconstructive surgeries? Three eighths of an inch— which doesn't sound like much until you're staring at Chase when he's changing the gauze and you don't know which eye to focus on so you end up looking away. Another: how long will Chase be able to hide from his debts? University Medical Center would very much like the $101,572.92 that Chase owes for all the work

they've done. But that one's not so much a joke as it is the primary
reason Chase finds himself here in one of the bedrooms in a large
suite on the twenty-second floor of the Versailles Palace Hotel
& Casino. There are others. Chase finds himself here—still in
Las Vegas—for a lot of reasons, none of which are admirable.

Chase leaves the wake-up call for seven because the early morning is the only time the suite is quiet, but something wakes him
up at six. (He still clings to the notion that anyone serious about
redemption does not sleep late.) It takes him a while to stand
and when he finally does, the blood drains from his head and
the room spins and he reaches for the bottle of Vicodin and swallows two because he's positive he can still feel the points of screws
and the three steel plates pressing against the bones in his skull.
As Chase grabs the doorknob he suddenly has to lean against
the wall so that he can catch his breath. He's not sure if he'll make
it to the bathroom without fainting. And the suite isn't so quiet
this morning. The throbbing hip-hop beats and what sounded
like a girl shrieking were what woke Chase before the wake-up
call. All the sound comes from the room that he'll need to pass
on the way to the bathroom. It's 6:30 and Chase realizes that the
people in the other room of the suite aren't waking up—they just
haven't gone to sleep yet. It was a private party that would cost
the men in the other room at least four grand apiece. Behind the
bedroom door: the bass fades, hushed voices, bodies shifting on
the king-size bed. Inside: two girls, Brandi and Aubrey, the sweet
smell of weed seeping under the sliding door. Girls find themselves here because this is where you find yourself when nothing else is working. To the girls and their "guests" the sight of

Chase's battered visage sometimes requires explanation. He's the marine just back from Baghdad. He's Bailey's brother who totaled the Escalade. He's the pirate shot from the cannon on that ship at Treasure Island who missed the net completely. But in the end no one keeps track of who Chase really is because no one is ever around long enough to care.

Chase leans back against the wall and watches a man he's never seen before come out of the bathroom, a white towel around his waist, clutching a large plastic tube. The man stares at Chase and gives him an uneasy nod. A slap followed by fake laughter comes from the other bedroom as the man with the white towel around his waist slides the door closed behind him. And in the bathroom Chase's skin is slick and cool and everything is spinning and the shrill ring in his ears that the neurologist says will never go away seems louder than it ever has and when Chase peels the gauze off to change it, the bandage pulls at the stitches and there's a slight yellowish discharge from his eye socket. When he's finished replacing the gauze, he slowly shuffles his way past the room where the men and the girls are making fucking sounds and then he's back in his room in the suite. He leans heavily against the window, looking out at the sweeping vista. The sky is painfully clear and bright. It's a late-summer sky, Chase thinks to himself, noticing the brown haze creeping into view. But how can that be when it's only July? Soon cell phones will start ringing and the men will be calling and then the girls will be fighting for the shower and slathering themselves in body glitter and asking Michele for condoms, extra cash, a ride. And Chase is unemployed and trapped in the suite on the twenty-second floor of the Palace with a girl he just may be in love with even though there had always been a line between them. It was a line that Chase drew for a reason. Two months ago, in the spring, crossing that line was unimaginable. Chase touches the brochure for the Golden Age Court in the Paseos of Summerlin, Nevada—Phase IV, which Michele left on the nightstand. *Find Yourself Here.*

1

It's Tuesday morning and hot and the end of May. Chase calls
in sick to school because he agreed to help Michele pack the rest
of her things—including the massage table—and move her into
the Sun King suite on the twenty-second floor of the Palace
where she will work for the next twelve weeks. When Michele
gets out of Chase's car—her shoulders tan, the Seven jeans riding
low and tight around her slim hips—everyone stares, like they
always do: the bellhops who load her Tumi bags onto a cart, the
valets who no longer care about parking the Mustang, the anonymous white tourists next to the heavy black man with the cane.
Everyone watches the brown hips and the navel ring and the tops
of her breasts. They watch until Michele comes over to Chase
and takes his hand.

Michele's suite has a cream-colored couch pushed against the
wall of the main room and all Chase wants to do is collapse on
it because his head throbs from the heat and insomnia. The first

thing Michele does is order room service. Chase walks past the couch to the window and pulls the curtains open and squints at the huge orange sun. Even though it's only May it feels like the end of July. (Minutes ago the temperature reading on the Sahara marquee read ninety-six degrees.) And it all lies before him: twenty-one stories below is the Garden of Earthly Delights dotted with clear blue rectangular pools and burgundy cabanas, and then it's the Strip and then the pink homes of Green Valley and the surrounding desert and the I-15 that leads to Los Angeles where Chase's father still lives.

"You look like shit," Michele says. "You should sleep."

Chase glances at the couch, then at Michele and tells her he's never felt more alive in his entire life. After a pause they both laugh.

"You need me to come back?" he asks.

"If you want," she says.

"Julia's coming."

"When?"

"Two days."

Michele pulls the faded jeans to her ankles and clumsily steps out of one leg and then the other, revealing the black underwear Bailey bought for her at Victoria's Secret. And then Michele's just staring at Chase. She looks small and too young, standing in her underwear and white T-shirt, the jeans tossed on the bed. "It's going to be weird knowing you're not here anymore." She pauses. "Looking out for me, I mean."

"So stop doing this," Chase says, sighing.

"I might," she says. "There's always that possibility."

But Michele won't stop because the suite is too nice. The suite will keep the business all under one roof. And the suite comes at a deep discount because Bailey's father is connected like that. In fact, the suite comes at enough of a discount that— if the plan works out—Bailey and Michele are convinced they'll each clear two hundred by summer's end. It's a very rich dream. But Chase isn't concerned about the suite on the twenty-second floor of the Palace and the summer plan: the Web sites and client databases, the mass e-mailings and the training sessions and cash deposits and fifty-fifty splits, the no-shows and the double-bookings, the extra sheets, the candles. Chase isn't concerned with any of that because he will be gone by then.

Chase is looking out the window when Michele starts to pull the T-shirt over her head. He's watching the crisp morning shadows stretch across the pools of clear blue water and the tan bodies already lying prone and baking along the concrete below. He's realizing that today is the nineteenth day of school he's missed this semester. (Chase set a nonmaternity record— according to the principal—with his sixteenth absence.) The window is hot against his forehead and his stomach drops when he gauges just how high up they actually are. Chase doesn't know what he'll do when the teaching gig ends in a few weeks and he's with Julia again—this time in Palo Alto and not New York. And Chase will be twenty-five and not nineteen and he'll be an unemployed—therefore, broke—artist, and not the ambitious student with a future he was when he met Julia. Chase can't wrap his head around it: he is a high school art teacher. And because of this fact Chase still doesn't understand how he is enough for Julia.

*   *   *

"There's a party in the Lakes tonight," Michele says.

Chase won't turn around. "I don't go to parties in the Lakes," he responds.

"It's not like that."

"It's always like that at parties in the Lakes."

"Jesus, Chase."

"Whose house?"

"Some comedian. He's not from here. He's cool."

"I'm meeting Hunter."

"Bring him."

"You can call me later if you want to meet up or something, but not for some party in the Lakes with Bailey because it's always the same kids in houses their parents bought for them and they're always bragging about vacations they took to Maui or Cabo and what celebrity they talked shit to at the Palms and then a fight breaks out. It's tired." Chase pauses. "And I don't like seeing Bailey."

"It's not always like that," Michele sighs.

"Aren't you over all that by now?" Chase says with an edge to his voice that she must pick up on because she doesn't respond.

When Chase turns around Michele is gone and the bathroom door is partially closed and he can hear water filling the tub. Though he can't see her, Chase knows Michele is sitting on the porcelain edge, legs crossed, watching the water.

The prospect of being out with Michele and Bailey tonight triggers something familiar in Chase that he immediately steers away from. It's a feeling instantly recognizable. It's always there

on some level: Chase and Michele and Bailey linked together
in a way that feels unavoidable. They're still bound in a way
Chase thought was over once he realized he was actually leaving Vegas and moving to Palo Alto with Julia. But even now—
with Julia's imminent arrival, his plans to leave—the mention
of Bailey makes it all seem like a dream. The clean white hotel
suite, the rush of hot water filling the tub, talk of meeting up
with Bailey tonight—this is the only reality. It was eight years
ago: the gray early morning, July, Bailey's bedroom, the body
on the lawn. And they never talk about it. They can't. No one
even tried to find the right words to say what it all meant. They
were, as Bailey observed that morning eight years ago, "culpable." That was the word Bailey used. *Culpable*.

Chase pushes the bathroom door open and tells Michele
he's leaving.

She wants him to stay. She offers the couch again for him
to lie down. She bites a fingernail and nods.

"It's all very sudden," she says.

"What is?" Chase realizes she means Julia.

"I mean, what's the rush?"

"I'm sinking like a stone. She wants things settled. It's a criti-
cal time for her. We want this—whatever we are—settled . . ."
Chase trails off.

"Help me," Michele says, hunched over, watching the steam
rise from the water.

"With what? You and Bailey?"

Michele eases her fingers into the water and says nothing.

"I want nothing the fuck to do with this anymore," Chase
says. "Don't you understand that?"

Michele glances over her shoulder at him.

"I need to make some changes," Chase says, exhausted, reconsidering the couch.

"You think so?"

Carly and Michele once ran away together when they were eleven. They used thick blue chalk to write their good-byes on the garage door. They were running away because life was boring and you had to be careful where you went because the world was filled with crazy people and they wrote the names of friends (Tanya, Kelly, Callie, Drew, Mike, Bailey, Little Rick) and scrawled "That's all Ffffolks!" and "Good Luck" and "Have A Nice Life" and "Las Vegas Sucks!" and "Goodbye?" The plan was Chicago but they went west instead of east on I-15 and ended up spending three nights at Whiskey Pete's in Primm before two Clark County police officers brought them back to the house on Starlight Way. Chase's mother never got around to washing the messages off the garage door. Chase was ten and figured that was a good sign because the longer the words stayed the longer they would keep the house even though Chase wanted to leave, maybe go to his dad's in Malibu, someplace green where there was an ocean.

Sometimes during the summer that Carly ran away Chase would walk downstairs in the middle of the night when everything was so still and quiet that he couldn't sleep and he would find his mother standing at the window in the kitchen. All the lights were off and only her silhouette and the orange glow from her cigarette were visible. He would watch silently as his mother stared out the window and into the blackness. Carly told Chase that summer that their mother was in a lot of trouble with money.

Carly told him that they would have to sell the house and move to an apartment or—even worse—go to Indiana and live with their grandparents, whom they barely knew. Carly was positive of this because she had looked through Mom's checkbook and some other papers in her nightstand drawer and swore that Mom was in trouble. The way Carly said that word frightened Chase even more. Chase was scared and asked how much money Mom owed (but to whom? and why?) and Carly said she thought it was like maybe two hundred thousand dollars but Carly was only eleven that summer and not very good with numbers so it could have been much less. But watching his mother—always awake and alone in the kitchen smoking cigarettes in the dark middle of the night—Chase knew that Carly probably wasn't too far off.

Michele scrambles around the suite. They have been there only an hour when Bailey calls. After listening intently to Bailey on her cell, Michele snaps it shut and, cursing, tells Chase to get up. A man is on his way to see her. Michele cancels the room service while frantically lighting candles and then undresses and puts on something sheer and tight and pulls the curtains closed and a chime sounds and the man is at the door and Michele walks Chase in a half-sleep to the closet where he tries to sit among her platform shoes and slinky tops. "Stay still," she says and hands him a pillow. The point of an iron sticks him in the back and his knees scream from bending so low and he realizes he's got to find a more comfortable position because he'll be in the closet for a while. Chase shifts and turns, leans against the ironing board and extends his legs. Finally he's able to slide to the floor.

"I don't want to see this," Chase mutters. "Just let me go."

Michele considers it for a moment. "It's too late." She slides the door closed.

Michele is on her back, naked, her eyes closed. She's been in the same position for fifteen minutes while the man—sunburned, a college ring, fifty-something—tries to make her come. But he's clumsy and drunk and keeps asking her what she likes. "Tell me what makes you feel good," he pleads. He's breathing heavily and says, "I don't want to leave until you come." With his face pressed against her, he says, "I shouldn't be here," and then the man asks her if he can please stay. He asks her if he can lie with her for a while. "I've got more money." The man says that the next time he sees her he will bring things for her to wear.

Inside the closet Chase rests his head against a wall and cycles through a list of things he's going to do when he's not here. After the man goes down on her again and she fakes a fairly authentic-sounding orgasm, Michele is sitting up on the bed, knees to her chest. Chase can't see him, but the man asks her again: why won't she do full service? Michele turns away and glances at the closet. She lies and tells the man it's not negotiable. It would have been negotiable if the man had been someone different. Maybe if the man hadn't been drunk. Maybe if the man had been younger or more attractive. Maybe if he hadn't been the first client in the Sun King suite. Chase spends an hour and fifteen minutes on the closet floor until the door slides open. Michele wears a towel in that way she always does when she's finished.

"Are we still celebrating tonight?" she asks Chase on his way out.

"What's there to celebrate?" Chase asks.

"Don't," Michele warns. "Just don't, Chase."

Hunter's ship lists to the left. Fires rage on deck. Tourists point their camcorders at the show. Flashbulbs pop from disposable cameras. Fanny packs sag from bloated waistlines. Children wriggle from their mothers' grips next to restless babies in strollers. Everyone has his back to the traffic on the Strip. People gasp at a fiery explosion that may have made Chase gasp if he hadn't known it was coming. Every show is the same and the explosions are Hunter's cue. Hunter steps forward and scales a railing at the edge of the ship where he stands and spreads his arms. There's a second explosion. Another pirate no one can see is kneeling behind Hunter, and the hidden pirate lights Hunter's shirt on fire causing Hunter to leap from the stern, a trail of orange flame whooshing behind him. He hits the black water and disappears. Tourists cheer.

Hunter does his goofy dance when he sees Chase. He shakes his head of thick blond hair back and forth to the cheery steeldrum music piped throughout the lobby of the Treasure Island Hotel while people stare at him in his soaked red-and-whitestriped pirate shirt. Hunter slides the bandana and eye patch from his head and asks, "Where's the wife?" Before Chase can remind him that Julia doesn't arrive for another two days, Hunter waves him off and says he has to take a shower.

"That water smells like piss," Hunter says. "You think I need a haircut? I think I should get one for those parties your wife invited us to."

As they approach a bank of elevators, Hunter stays in character and scowls convincingly—he's had a few drinks already with the other pirates before the show—and then lunges at a group of Japanese girls. But without his bandana and eye patch he no longer resembles a pirate: just a tall unshaven dude who needs a haircut. The Japanese girls shriek and Hunter immediately tries to apologize as the elevator doors open. But the girls are frightened and confused. They speak Japanese quickly to one another and refuse to get in the elevator.

"I don't know about the parties," Chase says hesitantly when they're alone in the elevator. "They're not exactly open to the public."

"Dude," Hunter says, offended. "We're not the public."

At a red light half a block from the Palace, Chase signals. This sets Hunter off. He pounds the dashboard. "No more Michele!" he chants. "Adios, Michele!" Without looking at Chase he stops for a moment and asks, "Why are you such an idiot?" Without waiting for an answer Hunter continues beating the dashboard for a little while longer before turning to Chase and saying, "Make me a promise."

"Whatever. Just stop all the noise."

In that brief moment Hunter has already forgotten the promise and says instead that one of the best things about Chase leaving Vegas is that Hunter won't have to see Michele anymore either. "Somehow we always end up with Michele and it's a drag, dude." Hunter pauses. "On both of us."

There are things Chase wants to talk about with Hunter but doesn't: the larger than usual amount of cocaine Chase found in Michele's purse, the fact that Michele hasn't gone to any of her classes at UNLV in over a month, that the party in the Lakes Michele had mentioned probably wasn't a party at all but an appointment she wanted Chase to take her to but then Michele realized (too late) that Julia was going to be in town this weekend and so Michele lied and said it was just a party. Chase has also decided not to mention that he took the day off from Centennial High to move Michele into the suite and that Chase spent an hour in a closet watching a man go down on Michele while the man masturbated himself to a shrieking orgasm. But then he realizes that Hunter likely knows some or all of this. Their group is pretty small.

"I'm sick of talking about Michele," Hunter says. "Thinking about her depresses me. Why is that? I guess because she talks a lot of shit and she's a pain in the ass."

"I find her quite . . . disarming," Chase says, aiming for suave and failing.

"She's a fraud, dude. I can just imagine the shit she's going to talk around Julia in order to impress her. She'll go on about the master's degree she still doesn't have and what she's observed about the people here and how the women and girls have all this pressure on them to conform to certain standards and it'll all be so lame and superficial. The only thing Julia will be impressed by is that Michele is actually trying to impress her."

"You'd fuck her though," Chase says. He can't help himself.

"Fuck yeah, I would," Hunter replies. "But dude, other than being eternally fuckable what does she aspire to? I'll tell you what she aspires to: the house that doesn't even exist yet—that's all she talks about. What does that tell us?" Hunter groans as the Palace comes into view. "She's a fucking idiot."

Michele's spiritualist prescribed both "stability" and "bold decision making" to counteract the turbulence that will accompany her Saturn return—even though Saturn wasn't going to return for another three years. Because of this advice Michele spent a thousand dollars on a two-day real estate seminar at Green Valley Ranch. She drove for hours around the valley looking for homes with limited direct exposure to Saturn. Buying a house was a "bold decision" and nothing provides greater "stability" than owning a home. There were six lots in Green Valley and Summerlin that Michele found acceptable. Three were available and only one hadn't opened for bidding. Though the house was not yet built—was merely a plot of desert in The Hills of Summerlin owned by KB Homes—it would become a three-bedroom mission-style house with a pool for $422,000. Michele had a contact at KB Homes and she bribed him with $5,000 in cash and a $15,000 cashier's check for a deposit so that she'd be in the system and at the top of the list when the bidding opened. What else Michele had bribed the contact at KB Homes with Chase does not want to think about.

"Forty days," Chase says. "The house will be built in forty days and then it's hers."

"But you have to bid," Hunter says.

"She's got it taken care of." Chase veers the Mustang slowly toward a valet. "She's in the system. All they have to do is press a button. That's what she says."

"You're both idiots," Hunter shouts. "But Michele's fucking Queen of the Idiots." And then he calms down and seems to think things through, his brow furrowed. "But wait—if she's the Queen

of the Idiots maybe . . . that makes her almost smart?" He pauses.
"I mean, if she's the *queen,* then maybe—"
  "She's just stuck here."

When Chase and Carly were kids they sometimes used to wait in the Circus Circus parking lot for their mother, who spent a summer next door at Westward Ho working as a croupier. She often stayed an hour or so past her shift to gamble and would emerge from the casino tired and distracted and clutching dinner in a white plastic take-out bag from one of the restaurants inside. During that summer when they were sometimes waiting for their mother, Michele was with them a lot and one afternoon they were going to go to the waterslide but it had closed that morning when a kid fell from the tower and died. So the three of them were drinking banana Slurpees and playing truth or dare in the Circus Circus parking lot when a clown approached them. Carly and Michele were wearing impossibly short denim cutoffs and thin orangey-yellow T-shirts and they flirted with the clown. They were twelve. They told the clown they were playing truth or dare. The clown dared them to get high with him and pointed to a brown van with white stripes in the rear of the parking lot. They got about ten feet from the van when Chase realized he was pissing from fear. He ran after them and grabbed Carly by the arm and lied and said he saw their mother coming out of the casino. They all looked. She wasn't there. Carly pulled away from Chase and kept walking toward the clown's van and so Michele took Chase by the hand until she saw that his pants were wet. Later, sitting by the pool that night with the warm wind washing over his mother's backyard, Chase asked Carly and Michele what happened in the van during the hour they spent with the clown. Carly was short and thin and had huge brown eyes. Freckles that you could barely see fanned across her nose and cheekbones and she wore her hair—like Michele— in a ponytail. Chase asked this as Carly and Michele were taking Polaroids of each other in their bikinis by the lit pool. The girls wanted to share them with Bailey and some other boys and they were ignoring Chase. When he asked it again—this time with an edge in his voice that startled them—they stared at Chase, un- comprehending. And then they looked at each other in mock surprise. Chase got up from where he was sitting by the pool and walked away as they started giggling, rocking back and forth, cov- ering their mouths with their hands.

Michele has stopped her twice-weekly therapist visits. But she still has weekly appointments with the woman who helped her make the decision about the Summerlin house, and who Michele insists is *not* an astrologer per se and who she strongly suggests Chase meet because—like Michele—his Saturn will be in return soon, too, and that may explain a lot. This is what Michele is telling Hunter and Chase after they've entered the suite at the Palace. From the bathroom, Michele's voice thanks Chase again for all his help with the move this morning. Hunter grimaces at Chase and shakes his head and then tips back the rest of a Corona. "What about all my help?" Hunter calls out.

"All what help?" Michele calls back.

"Pointing out all the ways in which you've screwed yourself," Hunter says. "And that includes moving in here for the summer."

"Which reminds me," Michele says, "tonight is special."

Hunter glances at Chase, confused. "Why did what I just say remind her that tonight is special?"

"Why is tonight special, baby?" Chase plays along.

Michele's voice in singsong comes from the bedroom. "Well, to begin with: everyone—with the exception of Hunter—is moving on to better and bigger things, and since it's important to single out transitions and endings and beginnings—"

"Hey, I don't want to hear what your real estate agent's been telling you," Hunter says.

They have been in the suite only ten minutes but both Chase and Hunter are downing second Coronas and then Hunter starts his third because Michele isn't dressed yet. But then suddenly, forgetting why tonight was special, Michele squeals, "Let's get this party started!" and finally comes out of the bedroom only half-dressed in her low tight jeans and black bra. She kisses Chase on the cheek—purposefully ignoring Hunter—and joins them on the massive cream-colored couch and talks about how much she misses her therapist. Michele pulls a thin pink tank top over her head. It is torn from the neck to the lacy edge of her bra. She smells sweet. Multiple bracelets and earrings dangle loudly. Her long black hair is curled tonight and Chase tells her it looks good even though it looks better straight. And then Michele is showing them another letter her mother wrote that came from El Salvador a month ago with a copy of the Lord's Prayer and a wooden crucifix. In the letter her mother asks Michele to hang the crucifix over the front door of the new house that she thinks Michele recently bought. Michele wrote back to her mother and enclosed a photograph of Bailey's house in Summerlin.

"She thinks I already have the house but there is no house."

Michele ponders this lie but only briefly. "In forty days I'll own a house but right now there is no house." Michele lifts her hands, exasperated. "She called me on my cell tonight and was so drunk I almost told her that there wasn't any house."

"What did she want?" Chase asks. "Why would you tell her that?"

"I have no interest in babysitting my mother, Chase." Michele sighs contemptuously. "Because I just found out during that phone call that this is what will happen when I actually buy a house. She wants to come to Vegas. She wants to live with me. In fact, she wants to come *now,* since I supposedly have my own home. Imagine: my mother in my house drinking all day and blaming me for *everything.* Fuck it. Not gonna happen."

Hunter keeps looking at Michele's jeans and it's hard for Chase not to look, too, even though it's nothing he hasn't seen before: they ride so low that you can tell she's not wearing panties.

"Is this the Michele-dumps-all-of-her-shit-on-us-for-an-hour segment of the celebration?" Hunter asks. "Is this the special part of the night?"

"I'm twenty-four years old," Michele says. "I've got the rest of my life to worry about everyone else. Anyway, the next three months this place"—Michele indicates the massive suite with her arms—"is *mine.* And that's what we're celebrating."

"You're only . . . twenty-four?" Hunter asks suspiciously.

"Well, maybe twenty-five." Michele shrugs.

"And then before you know it you're kicking thirty." Hunter lets out a low whistle. "And maybe you're still"—he makes the same arm gesture as Michele, mocking her—"*here!*"

"Why is thirty considered the end of everything?" Michele groans. "I mean, Julia's thirty and she's fine."

Chase plays along. "Julia's not thirty, Michele. Ha ha."

"Bitch, I'm warning you," Hunter says. "If you're still running around with the Baileys of this world when you're thirty it's time for you to get your ass back to that therapist." This is Hunter bored and thinking about his fourth Corona.

"You know what, Hunt? You are so right," Michele says. Then she leans in against Hunter and runs her fingers through his tangled blond hair. "If I find myself sinking like a stone I can always . . . just get married." Michele turns to Chase and bats her eyes.

A palpable silence fills the space.

When her cell rings from the bedroom Michele stands and wiggles her jeans up. As she passes Chase he slaps the soft tan skin around her hips and Michele shrieks playfully. Hunter leans back on the couch sipping another beer, staring at her ass as she walks away.

"She's on something," Hunter says.

"You think?"

"Coke. A lot of coke."

"Yeah. But not a lot."

"More than a little, dude," Hunter says. "Were you listening to that shit or were you off floating around on Planet Chase? Fucking Saturn and crucifixes? A nonexistent house in fucking Summerlin? Jesus, I feel like my brain just fell out of my head and it's hiding in the minibar."

"She says she doesn't use it. She says everyone but her uses it."

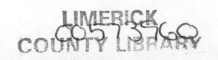

"Whatever, dude." Then Hunter lights up and says in a whiny sarcastic tone, "But she's getting her master's!" Hunter finishes the Corona and keeps looking at Chase to make the point that he's not convinced of anything. "You know you're breaking her heart," Hunter suddenly says, glancing at the bedroom.

Chase doesn't know what to say because he knows it's partially true.

"You can tell," Hunter says. "Look at her when she brings Julia's name up. Her body language, her tone of voice—it all changes. It's like Michele knows how out of Julia's league she is and you're on your way out and it crushes her because, well, where does that leave her? It's not even so much you as it is the absence of the possibility of you. That void is large, dude, and what's left for her once you're outta here?" Hunter just stares at Chase. "Do I need to say it?"

"I think you're right about the coke," Chase says quietly.

"I heard she called you the other night saying she was suicidal."

"She was . . . upset."

"You've got a month left here?" Hunter asks. "So you're not going to watch this thing play itself out? Smart move."

Chase shrugs.

"Maybe you can save her in a month, maybe you can't," Hunter says. "But God, she's still so fucking hot." He says this too loud because Michele hears.

"What's that, Hunt?" Michele calls out.

"You're looking fucking hot, bitch."

"Thank you," she says from the bedroom. "I think it's these jeans."

"How's Bailey?" Hunter asks when Michele flops back on the couch. "I thought it was over-over this time and yet here we are in a very large suite that I'm assuming he must be paying for." Hunter gestures around the suite. "So I guess it's not over-over, huh?"

"Who was calling you?" Chase asks Michele.

"Bailey's come a long way," Michele says to no one in particular, ignoring Chase. "Jesus, his mother drops dead and his father's a Nazi and—"

"—a rich Nazi," Hunter interjects.

"—Bailey's trying to do something constructive and positive with his life and considering what could have happened to him, I think he turned out okay."

"I don't see it." Hunter shakes his head. "Where's all this positivity?" he asks, an arm sweeping across the suite. "He's paying for this and Michele's providing a service. You guys have a plan. Dare to dream. Beautiful. Illegal, by the way, but beautiful."

"Have you noticed I'm ignoring you?"

"Personally, I think that's the definition of positive: putting Michele up here for the summer," Hunter says. "Yet the mystery—the answer she won't give—is . . . why?"

Michele smirks.

"Is he leasing the suite or . . ." Hunter cocks his head and says very quietly, staring at Michele, ". . . is he leasing you? I get confused sometimes."

"In forty short days, Hunter, I will own a house."

"Yes, but—sshhh!—don't tell your mother."

"A four-hundred-thousand-dollar property in my name at twenty-four is a big fucking deal—"

"Co-own," Hunter shouts. "News flash: cosigning is not the same as owning, especially when it's with Bailey and his father's fucking money."

"It's about equity, idiot," Michele says. "And we're not taking any money from the Nazi, so calm down."

"All your immigrant dreams coming true: a pink house with a green lawn and a white man."

"Hunter's just fucking with you, baby," Chase says. "Hunter, chill. Okay?"

"Okay, forget that it doesn't even sound good on paper and you sound like you don't know half of what you're talking about—forget all that." Hunter's getting drunk and sitting up straight. "There's this nagging question: what are you going to do when Bailey dumps your ass?"

"Speaking of Bailey, he has a message for you, Hunter. He said: tell the pirate the girl's real name is Brandi and she's seventeen and a senior at Durango," Michele says. "And yes, she asked for you: she's into older men who drive crappy blue Caravans and live with their parents."

"And I have a message for you," Hunter says.

"What's that, Hunter?" Michele asks.

"For the next three months?" Hunter says. "He *owns* you."

When Bailey was a teenager he had a large head of bleached-blond hair and was tan and his shoulders were covered with acne. He would have been fat if he hadn't lifted weights in his garage every night and drunk Creatine shakes twice a day. He had been diagnosed with severe ADHD and was homeschooled, though his parents were always taking vacations, which meant he had a lot of time to himself. "T-t-t-too, too, too much sugar," Bailey would say, imitating his cousin Mike's stutter, twitching, his thumbs tapping the table as his head bobbed. "D-d-d-d-don't think I'll m-m-make m-m-much of myself." Bailey would laugh but Mike wouldn't care since he hadn't stuttered for years, and nothing seemed to register with him anyway since he returned from juvenile detention in Reno. Bailey spent more time with Mike, and Chase spent less time with Bailey for that reason.

Toward the end of August the summer they were thirteen, Bailey had been at Chase's house all weekend and on Sunday afternoon, when Bailey was supposed to go home, he closed Chase's bedroom door, leaned against it, slid to the floor, and cried. Chase didn't need to ask why. He knew Bailey didn't want to go home because he was scared of his father, especially on Sundays when his father would drink all day, and by the time dinner came he'd be a wreck. That's when he would force Bailey and his brother to wrestle in the garage on cardboard mats he'd laid down. Bailey's father had wrestled in high school and wanted both Bailey and his brother to wrestle in order to win scholarships at UNLV, so the two brothers would wrestle for hours, shirtless and sweaty, the bare white fluorescent lights that lined the ceiling of the garage buzzing as they pummeled each other. Their father would try to focus but sometimes his eyes glazed over and he would be in some other place. Then he would suddenly explode, cursing at them, disgusted with their effort, prodding them with a golf club. Once, when Chase was there, Bailey's father told Chase he wanted him to take his shirt off and wrestle, too, and Chase lied and said he had a knee injury. When Bailey's

father insisted, Chase lied again and told him he had asthma.
Bailey's dad called Chase a faggot and sent him home.

Another weekend from that summer they were thirteen:
Bailey spends the night at Chase's house and Mike comes over and
after they all go to sleep Chase wakes up to the sound of voices
coming from Carly's room. In his half-sleep Chase walks to her
door and puts his ear against it and hears the same sounds he hears
Bailey making when he wrestles in his father's garage. Chase also
realizes that Mike hadn't been in the sleeping bag next to Chase's
bed when Chase stumbled up out of sleep. Chase turns the door-
knob to his sister's room slowly but it's locked and so Chase stands
in the hallway unsure of what to do, gripping the doorknob, until
the noises stop and everything is quiet.

Michele loves hotels: clean white sheets twice a day, goose-down
pillows, air-conditioned rooms. (Because of Bailey, Michele will
never spend another night in her grandmother's old house in
North Las Vegas where her cousins now live. Because of Bailey
she will never again fall asleep breathing in the scent of stale cat
urine.) Michele loves the way room service waiters remove the
steel cover from her heirloom tomato and Burrata salad dotted
with green olives. She loves requesting turndown service at three
in the afternoon. She loves leaving twenties for her Latina "sisters" under the pillows of the unmade bed. Michele loves hitting the floor with eight hundred in chips, drinking comped
Cosmos, and playing roulette until she's down too much or up
just enough. She loves returning to her room to find chocolate
mints scattered across her pillows. She loves sliding the window

open as far as it will go and leaning outside, listening to the hum of the Strip. "Imagine all of that power," she once told Chase. "You can hear it, actually feel it surging upward." It made the fine hairs on her arm stand up straight. (She showed him—it was true.) She says the currents help her sleep but Chase knows Michele never really sleeps. Bailey will spend the money it takes to keep a suite at the Palace for the summer where Michele can be served fresh melon and strawberries in the executive lounge each morning and wear a bathrobe all day and receive complimentary massages from the Brazilian girl with the soothing voice who tells her stories in Portuguese that Michele pretends to understand. Bailey will keep the suite because it will keep Michele satisfied. Bailey knows that if Michele isn't totally comfortable there will be no business. And Michele knows that if Bailey is convinced that she loves him (and she might), getting what she wants this summer will be easier and safer than she thought. Also: hotels, nice ones with white and gold walls, can make her forget about Chase.

They don't make it to Rain or the Double Down, or anywhere for that matter. Their celebration ends abruptly when Michele's cell rings while they're waiting for the valet at the Palace to bring the Mustang. It's Bailey calling. Michele walks away from Chase and Hunter and enters some info into a Black-Berry and when she returns she tells them again about this party in the Lakes and then the Mustang appears, idling. While Hunter tips the valet Chase turns to Michele. She glances at Hunter and then looks back at Chase and shrugs and something inside Chase sighs.

"I'll drive you," he says.

* * *

There are only two cars parked in front of the house in the Lakes.

"Doesn't look like much of a party," Hunter says.

"You guys don't have to stay," Michele tells them and Hunter sighs and gets out of the Mustang and pulls the passenger seat forward so she can get out of the car. Michele steps away very slowly and just stands there, the wind tangling her hair, blowing it across her face. "I'm taking a cab back."

"You okay?" Chase asks.

"Oh God," Michele laughs. "You know I never know the answer to that question."

Hunter rolls his eyes and mutters something under his breath and gets back in the car. When Chase puts the Mustang in drive Michele calls out, "Wait!" and runs around to the driver's side and leans in. Chase thinks she's about to whisper something in his ear when she suddenly kisses him hard on the mouth.

"What's that?" he asks.

Michele shakes her head, her lips tight, and says, "Nothing." She gives an awkward wave before walking up to the house.

"What was that all about?" Hunter asks.

"I don't know."

"Yes. You do."

Chase used to drive Michele around town just to look out for her. Twelve hours after his plane touched down at McCarran, when he returned from his sophomore year at NYU—Chase would never go back to Manhattan and received his BA at

UNLV—he was letting the engine of his sister's Mustang idle outside Mandalay Bay while Michele sat in the passenger seat checking her lips in a compact, then searching for the client's room number on her cell phone. Michele thanked Chase for doing this favor (the driver they had been using "flaked") and she repeated what she had told him when Chase called her, panicked and furious after reading the casually alarming e-mail Bailey sent Chase to his dorm room on Fourteenth Street in New York. "I'm fine."

Sometimes Chase would meet her clients and let them know he'd be outside or downstairs, waiting, or that he would be back in an hour or—depending on what they paid for—two. Sometimes Chase would wait inside the room without the guy knowing he was there but only if that was what Michele wanted. (Sometimes it was what the guy wanted as well.) It had been only recently—the last couple of months really, since January—that Chase started leaving Michele at the door and then it was at the elevator and then it was in the lobby, and finally outside at the Mustang where Michele would wink or purse her lips and kiss Chase quickly and not say anything because she understood what he was trying to do and that it wasn't easy for him.

2

Chase is hustling—he's late. It's a Wednesday morning and on Wednesday mornings at Centennial first-period study hall for nongraduating seniors is his responsibility. The phone rang at four a.m. and again at five and once more at six-fifteen. After taking a shower and getting dressed he checks his caller ID. All of the calls were from Michele but she didn't leave any messages and she doesn't answer when he calls back. He assumes the "party" at the Lakes went fine but he's irritated when his call goes to her voice mail. Outside, in the overcast light of another hot morning, Chase rushes to the Mustang. He's already sweating and hungry and needs coffee but has no cash (or time) to stop at Starbucks. On Boulder Highway the city looks dirty in the gray light and the heat won't break. Last night the eleven o'clock news on KLAS insisted the heat wave wasn't going to end, that it would stay right through the summer, which gives Chase a little jolt of satisfaction, since he'll be in Palo Alto, and then hopefully San Francisco, with Julia.

Two blocks from his apartment and nearing the Strip, Chase notices a huge billboard that recently went up: a black-and-white image of a male model in red boxer briefs, his long blond hair falling over his eyes. There's a question hanging over the model: "What Kind of Man Are *You*?" Chase's nose starts to bleed—a summer heat-related ritual—and he twists the corner of a napkin and slides it up a nostril. It's now 8:05. He has ten minutes to get to school but he passes a flower shop off the Strip. What would he miss at Centennial if he stopped? (Twenty minutes of class, kids copying homework under the flicker and hum of fluorescent lights, Chase sinking into his chair a little farther with the recirculated air flowing through the teeth of the vent over his desk muffling the sound of someone's ring tone, Chase slipping into a trance while gazing at Gabrielle's miniskirt, which will have risen as high as it can go.) So Chase parks and finds the large yellow French tulips that Julia likes: soft, cool, fragrant. His presence in the flower shop seems to annoy the heavy, tired woman working there and she reluctantly asks if Chase wants the tulips wrapped. He says, "Sure, thanks," and grins and the tired woman doesn't respond and wraps the tulips while Chase's American Express card is processing. When the card is declined Chase tells the woman there's no need to call. He checks his wallet even though he knows he has only one dollar in it. But then he remembers the jar of coins in the trunk of the Mustang.

Chase grabs the coins and jogs to the Vons on the other side of the parking lot. He dumps the coins into a change machine next to a bank of video poker slots. When he finally pushes the last of the coins through the mouth of the change machine he's now twenty-one minutes late for school. But the machine chokes and rattles and then stops working completely and the panel goes blank and the red numbers that had reached an impressive $212 vanish. Chase shakes the machine and then calls for the manager, who ignores him when Chase explains that he's late for work and that the machine broke and that the panel had read $212. When Chase asks if they can just give him that amount the manager says he needs to call someone else. Chase begs him (he'll just take $200 to make things easier) but the manager doesn't care and it's another eight minutes to get the machine back on. The ticket prints out and reads $214.33, which the manager counts for Chase, slowly, as if on purpose, and then winks at him when he finishes. Chase leaves Vons, rushes to the flower shop to pay for the tulips and is now forty minutes late for school.

Last night Chase sat on the edge of his futon in his one-bedroom apartment on Boulder Highway. He had just read a story in a magazine about a twenty-four-year-old artist in New York whose new murals sold for $100,000 apiece. The twenty-four-year-old artist had sold three in the first two hours of his second solo show in Chelsea. The twenty-four-year-old artist was pictured with a smiling actress sitting on his lap. The twenty-four-year-old artist was unshaven and thin and wore corduroys and had a smug-little-genius expression on his face. While staring at that face Chase understood where the anxiety was coming from: he had not painted anything worthwhile in months.

And Chase was twenty-five, and a year had passed since he landed the teaching job at Centennial. It had been over a year since he convinced Julia to choose California over Philadelphia for her MBA and move to Palo Alto instead of staying back east because they had tried back east at NYU and Chase never liked it. But Julia would remind him that it wasn't so bad. Her proof: the seventeen works Chase completed, getting an entire wall at Spring Jamboree sophomore year, selling three paintings in one day, flying his mother out, taking her to *The Phantom of the Opera,* sleeping in on Thursdays when neither of them had class and sharing a plate of scrambled eggs and sipping coffee in the empty cafeteria, the two of them alone in her dorm room, Chase adjusting the white sheets against Julia's brown skin so he could sketch her while she slept.

Last night Chase stared at a Kandinsky print Julia had sent him until he had to look away: the Kandinsky print was a question she was asking. Chase gazed at the piles of failed sketches— incomplete with ideas he had been sure would lead to something. Three blank canvases he needs to fill for a local group show he is in (now only a month away) hung on the walls in a lame attempt to help motivate himself. He made a list of galleries in San Francisco and e-mailed them to Julia in order to prove that he'd done his research and was making an effort to plan for the life they both wanted, somewhere that wasn't back east or Vegas. He would stare at Web sites and read reviews of other artists. He let himself imagine his first opening, selling it out, the profiles that would appear in magazines he's never read. The same way he had imagined an NYU dorm room with his work on the walls and meeting a funky East Coast girl and never going back to Vegas. He let himself imagine living anywhere Julia wanted and with enough money to paint full-time. He knew he was nowhere close to that. Taped to the stucco wall over his drafting table, on glossy black paper in silver script, was the flyer for the upcoming group show, his first since college: *White Trash Paradise*. After he sent the e-mail, Julia called.

Chase still could never say anything that made Julia feel better when she asked him why he hadn't yet moved to Palo Alto to be with her. He didn't know how to answer Julia when she asked him why he was still living alone in a place that made him miserable. Chase was supposed to teach for a year and that was supposed to be it. He was supposed to earn enough in one year to finance the move (and he lived so cheaply that this was possible on a teacher's salary). In Palo Alto he would find a job and support himself so he could continue painting and then the two of them could begin the next phase of their life together. Chase would tell her that he was, in fact, getting ready for the move to Palo Alto, and that he had to do it like this, and to please stop asking him when he was coming. Chase resented that Julia knew the answer: he was coming when he had something worth bringing. Because if he didn't show up with something worth bringing where did that leave them?

Last night, after their phone call, Chase tried to sleep but ended up thinking about his mother getting old alone and who else was in his life and what kind of life was it anyway when he was cashing in four hundred dollars in Bally's chips that his grandmother had left him instead of borrowing the money that Michele was always begging him to take? He still hadn't paid AOL or DirecTV or his student loans. Chase hadn't even paid for the groceries his mother bought him the week before. And so Chase got out of bed and called Julia back. He told her that maybe there was something significant about the fact that the National Black MBA Conference was being held in Las Vegas this year. Maybe this was a sign. Chase leaned back on the stool at his drafting table after finishing a bottle of Yellow Tail merlot, a cocky grin on his face, and said, "Maybe when you're here we can stop by a chapel."

On bad mornings, when Chase was sure he couldn't walk into Centennial one more time, he would call Julia in Palo Alto. He would be on Summerlin Parkway heading west past the Stratosphere toward the high school and Julia would say things to Chase that he knew weren't true anymore, but it made him feel better to hear them. Some mornings were worse than others and it really wasn't the school or the teaching gig or the desert rats that made up the student body that bothered him—it was something deeper, messier. He couldn't express it directly— he needed help—so he would call Palo Alto and just sit on the phone, silent, waiting for her to say anything. And on the bad mornings when he called and she wasn't there—or didn't pick up—he wouldn't leave a message. He would just slide lower in the seat, driving faster, struggling to remember why he was pissing away twenty-five.

Nearing the school, Chase is relieved that Julia picks up the phone and that she doesn't mention visiting a chapel. Instead she mentions California because she's interning this summer with Accenture in San Francisco and has a weekend orientation and wants Chase to meet her there. She'll be at the Argent, in a suite. "You can order room service and swim in the pool. We can look for apartments."

Something clenches inside him. Chase tells her he's late.

"When are you ever on time?" And then she sighs when he doesn't say anything. "Listen, my flight gets in at two tomorrow. Can you pick me up?"

Chase passes the lime-green sign for Centennial High and tells Julia, "Don't I always? When haven't I?" but also that he has to go.

Last semester some kids in Chase's class wanted to nominate Chase for Teacher of the Year. It was Chase's first year at Centennial and he was full of steam and driven from the talks he had with Julia about their future. Chase was never going to stay at Centennial long (that had never been part of the plan) but he was good at what he did: he brought in xeroxed articles from *Artforum* and took the kids to galleries and had models come in to pose. (Michele modeled once and Chase made the class pledge secrecy if he allowed nude figure drawings. So the shades were drawn and the door was locked and Michele dropped her robe.) And there were faculty who said some supportive things and the principal called Chase in and asked if he'd address the school board about the importance of funding the arts or something like that. The principal mentioned the newspaper articles written about Chase and the murals he had painted on walls around the city when he was in high school. The principal said that Chase was an example Centennial needed to promote. So the kids nominated him and Chase was supposed to present a statement before a panel about why what he taught mattered. But a week before the panel presentation a girl committed suicide. Her body sat slumped against a wall in a bathroom stall for an entire day, and kids came and went, saw her feet and legs under the door and either figured she was sleeping or passed out, and if anyone had gone over to ask if she was okay, they would have seen the pools of blood all over the floor from the gaping wounds in her wrists. A custodian eventually found her. A week later a kid named Rush threw a party (complete with a bonfire) out in the desert and circulated invitations through-out the school: "This event is in honor of the strong only: criers, whiners, bitches, and bleeders stay home!"

Chase told Julia about the suicide the night it happened. He told her about Rush and the plague of desert rats that haunted Centennial. He told her he wasn't sure he could take it anymore. "What does that mean?" Julia asked him. And he closed his eyes—jaw tight, teeth clenched—and tried to pic-ture something precise that he could no longer accept and all that came was color: a throbbing white rage. When he opened his eyes and exhaled he said that he would quit Centennial. When Julia asked what he was going to do about an income Chase didn't mention that Michele had offered him money again. And he didn't tell Julia that he was considering taking it. Michele had said "thousands" though Chase wasn't sure how or why it would be so much. Michele said the money would come his way "over time" in irregular installments based on nothing more than Chase saying "fine." The only thing Chase told Julia was that he was finished with teaching and ready to go and he made up some shit about this Mormon girl who got freaked out and told her parents about the nude fig-ure drawing (in this scenario it was Hunter and not Michele who was the model) and that Chase was called into an end-less meeting with her parents and the principal and they wanted to fire him but since he was popular with the kids they didn't.

After a long silence, Julia said, "You've been there a long time."

Chase never wrote the statement. He skipped the panel and a middle-aged phys-ed coach—whom none of the students gave a crap about—became Centennial High's Teacher of the Year.

Chase pulls the Mustang into his parking space and walks quickly toward the massive beige building that seems to effortlessly blend in with the sand and mountains surrounding it. Centennial opened two years ago on Annie Oakley Drive and had originally been built as a prison. After construction began, the overwhelmingly white population in northwest Vegas threatened a lawsuit against the county, arguing that property values would plummet and so instead of a prison the massive beige building became the largest high school in the valley. But there are no windows at Centennial High and the center of it is a hollow courtyard: a place where the inmates would have spent their recreation time.

After he declined Teacher of the Year, Chase gave up trying to teach anything. So now Chase works on his sketches during class and tells his students that they can sit quietly and finish their homework for other classes or sleep if they aren't too obvious about it. His students are all seniors and the ones who graduate will go to UNLV or CCSN or nowhere in the fall. They're mostly white, mostly tan, and drive their own cars. They smell like coconut oil and sour candy and cigarette smoke and weed. They're like every other high school class: a few have potential and two or three offer something intelligent to say, but

most of them have no ambition and no opinions about anything
and they're there only because they have to be. Chase hates
them all. The only thing that gets him through the day is the
thought that he's leaving Centennial in six weeks. Not one of
these kids, he has finally decided, will go on to do anything
worthwhile in this world. That every teacher Chase had when
he was in high school thought the same thing about him occurs to Chase for some reason this morning when he finally gets
to class, twenty minutes late for second period.

Leaning against his desk Chase takes a deep breath and
exhales as he tries to think of something to say.

"You look like shit," someone calls out from the back of the
room.

"I feel like shit," Chase says.

"Look a little loco, actually, *dawg*."

"What's that mess on your shirt?" someone else says.

Chase looks down at the droplets of tomato sauce and the
white paint.

"You're not going to shoot us, are you?" someone asks and
people laugh.

"Would it make a difference?"

"You should shoot yourself." Another voice he doesn't
recognize.

Chase glances at the clock. Someone notices and calls out,
"Yeah, that's right: twenty-one more minutes of this shit."

Laughter.

Chase takes another deep breath and closes his eyes.
When he opens them he looks out over the fluorescent-lit room
filled with tan eighteen-year-olds and says, "You're not *going*
anywhere." He pauses as he scans the room. "Maybe you, Isabel,

if you focus and stop hiding, and Anthony, yeah, you could do something. But the rest of you . . ." Chase stops. There's an uncomfortable silence. "Look, you can sleep or do whatever it is you want to do the rest of the period. I've got a headache, so please keep it down."

"Teacher of the Year!" someone calls out and the room laughs.

"Thank you. Stay the course. Keep hope alive. Shoot for the moon. Even if you miss you'll be among the stars. Now please leave me alone for the next . . ." Chase looks back up at the clock and someone calls out, "Eighteen minutes."

There is a long silence before someone in the back row says, "Thanks for not shooting us."

In celebration of their one-month anniversary, Bailey suggested that they skip summer school and head to the shooting range. It had only been thirty days but Carly and Bailey were now inseparable. In that one month Bailey convinced Carly to bleach her hair blond. He convinced her to double-pierce her ears. He convinced her to go down on him in the parking lot of Wet 'n Wild. He convinced her to fight a girl he swore had come on to him repeatedly, just to see if she'd actually do it (Carly did). The new clothes that Bailey made Carly wear were trendy, and sexier than what she usually wore. Most of the clothes that Bailey bought Carly in that one month were designed primarily to show off her prematurely large breasts. On that Tuesday when Bailey decided to celebrate their one-month anniversary by skipping school, he talked his father into driving him and Carly and Chase (Michele was sick; she was bleeding; it wouldn't stop) in his Suburban to the

Line of Fire shooting range on East Flamingo. Before they were picked up at the house on Starlight Way, Chase got worried watching Carly apply too much eyeliner. Chase told her she was lucky Mom wasn't home because Mom would never let Carly go anywhere dressed like that: a short-short denim skirt, a tight V-neck T-shirt, the black bra that showed through—none of it would have been acceptable. "If you're going to be a fag the whole time," Carly said, inspecting her face in a mirror, "stay at home." Bailey rode shotgun with Carly in between him and his father. Chase rode in back, alone, and watched Bailey's father occasionally glance at Carly's tan legs and then at the breasts squeezed into the T-shirt that his son had bought for her. Chase had to look away each time this happened. He wondered why he had even come along. It was a hot clear day and the city was all black asphalt and dirty brown and gray concrete. School would have been the better option.

The four of them spent two hours at Line of Fire, outside in the sun. For some reason there weren't enough earplugs, so when Chase wasn't shooting he had to cover his ears and watch as Bailey shot cutout targets of faceless black silhouettes, his eyes burning from the dust and the outrageous heat. Bailey's father wrapped his arms around Carly and pressed against her, holding her hands steady and pulling the trigger over and over again. Carly would bite her lower lip and close one eye tightly. She was determined. They spent half an hour in the gun shop where Bailey's father bought Bailey, Carly, and Chase black T-shirts that read FROM MY COLD, DEAD HAND. *For himself: a new $750 Bushmaster AR-15 assault rifle. (Chase was amazed at the purchase.) They stopped at Del Taco, where Bailey's father told a story about the heroic actions of the eighteen-year-old son of the proprietor of the Line of Fire shooting range. The proprietor's son was in a Circle K*

*when it was held up by a couple of Mexicans. The proprietor's son
had a brand-new Glock .22 "standard issue," Bailey's father said, as
though this should have impressed them. "The same kind they give
to DEA agents." The proprietor's son shot and killed the men. It
took only two bullets: both to the back of the head. The son had
just come from the shooting range his father owned. The son said
he felt like God put him there for a reason. The boy said that God
had sent him for that can of Red Bull at that Circle K on that particular Friday afternoon. The story made Chase queasy: there was
no point to it, there was no lesson, it was meaningless. The only
thing he took from it was the mental image of two men's heads ex-
ploding. But Bailey seemed to interpret the story as a challenge. For
him it was something that needed to be sorted out and he seemed to
have located the story's point. Bailey kept nodding. And because
Bailey was convinced of something by this story, so was Carly.*

Between second and third period the wide bright hallway is
crowded and the din of conversation and laughter is amplified
as it always is this time of semester: late spring, the end of a
school year, summer close. As Chase leaves the classroom to
find coffee he realizes that he forgot to put on deodorant. This
happens when he notices the sweet smell of a familiar girl's
perfume passing too closely and her soft arm brushes against
his and then she pinches his waist. This girl who touches him
is Rachel. She's sixteen and passes Chase with a pack of girls
in low-cut jeans and tight T-shirts revealing tan hips smeared
with body glitter. Rachel wears a short checkered skirt and pink
sandals. The crimson streaks in her straight black hair are new
and something Michele recommended. Rachel looks over her

shoulder at Chase, who mindlessly watches her long enough to notice her bare legs and for an instant wonders what it would feel like to slide his hand between them.

Suddenly a fist hits his chest, hard, and Chase flinches out of the fantasy. He hears the voice and laughter. It's Rush, with his cocky half-smile, roaming the halls, and his crew of white boys—in pressed collared shirts worn purposefully too long and silver rope chains around their tan necks—stand in a posse behind their leader. Rush has the same smirk he had two weeks ago when he stumbled out of his white Escalade in the Double Down parking lot, high on sticky weed. This was the night one of the blonde girls Rush was with vomited at Hunter's feet, splattering his pant leg, when Chase and Hunter were on their way out of the Double Down. Rush told the girl to make it up to them ("Hey, that dude is one of my teachers, bitch") and unzipped the top of her Abercrombie tracksuit and clumsily pulled one of her breasts out, squeezing until it bulged grotesquely, and Rush told Chase and Hunter that she would blow each of them if they had any meth. Chase hung back. Hunter actually paused and seemed to contemplate the offer. When Rush saw that Hunter was taking this seriously, he grabbed the girl and walked away laughing. Now, this morning in the hallway, grinning, Rush points at Chase and then says something to the crew, who all laugh as Rush brings a ringing silver cell to his ear and answers, "Yo."

Chase shakes his head and grins back. Rush's high-pitched laugh and manic green eyes compel Chase to take three quick steps forward. Chase gets close enough to smell Rush's hair gel. Chase tells Rush to put the goddamn phone away. Rush just laughs and says something Chase can't hear because the hallway seems more crowded than usual. Suddenly someone pushes someone else into

Chase from behind and he stumbles into Rush and Rush raises
his hand to strike out—or Chase thinks he does—and as Chase
regains his balance he instinctively lunges forward, slamming Rush
into a locker, sending them both flailing to the ground. Things
escalate quickly. Chase has a handful of Rush's shirt in his fist while
Rush grabs Chase's throat and squeezes. For this one moment
everything is frozen. Chase can hear himself telling Rush to "Let
it go, just let it go, it's okay, let it go" while pinning Rush's head to
the floor. The only sound coming from Rush are rapid short breaths
interspersed with whining.

"This is what you fucking want, isn't it, bitch?" Chase is so
lost in the moment he will not recall ever saying this. "You like
being a little bitch, don't you? Fucking little bitch."

"Hey man, you're really hurting him," one of the crew calls
out.

Chase immediately starts to apologize. He eases the pressure against the boy's head. Rush turns to stare up into Chase's
eyes. Their faces are inches from each other. Someone calls out
for them to kiss. Rush starts to grin. Chase exhales, relaxing.
Chase closes his eyes and hears a hocking sound. A thick glob of
warm saliva hits the bridge of Chase's nose and slides quickly
toward his mouth.

This activates something in Chase and he slams Rush's head
against the ground three times in quick succession. Kids start to
cry out and there are high-pitched shrieks coming from the girls.
Someone yells, "Let him go!" Chase shouts, "I'm not the one!"
Chase is surprised at how little resistance he's getting and it makes
him feel powerful knowing how much stronger he is than Rush.
But then Chase realizes something.

Rush is bluffing. Rush is waiting Chase out. This is an act.

Shrill whistles sound somewhere down the hall. Chase whips his head around, looking left and right, but there's too much fear and rage and adrenaline to let go of Rush. To get up and walk away is impossible. The sickness and disgust Chase has managed to keep just beneath the surface are why he's still on the ground with Rush under him, pinned to the floor.

Chase doesn't want to be the one to let go. He's waiting for another teacher to pull them apart. Chase wants this to end, but one of Rush's boys starts kicking Chase hard in the ribs, which prompts Chase to grind Rush's head harder into the floor as if this would act as a warning to the boy to stop kicking Chase.

Chase growls at Rush through his clenched teeth, "Tell him to stop."

But Rush, crimson-faced, just stares up at Chase, and the boy backs away as the whistles become louder and start closing in, until finally Chase hears authoritative voices commanding them to break it up. Chase's eyes burn from pepper spray.

One of the security guards pulls Chase to his feet but it's too fast and they twist his arm behind his back, thrusting it upward until he feels a ligament tear. Chase screams. He spins around and throws an elbow at the security guard's jaw and watches the guy fall before Chase is thrown back to the floor and hit twice with a baton by the other security guard. Through the tears in his eyes everything suddenly looks calm again and voices seem to be telling Chase to *fucking chill out, chill out, dude* while everyone's asking Rush if he's okay. From where Chase lies he sees the tan thighs and pink sandals of Rachel, who had passed him what now feels like days ago, watching the scene from a safe distance.

*   *   *

Chase has been sitting in the small administrative office since eleven o'clock answering questions and filling out incident reports.

He nodded after each question was asked.

Did he strike a student?

Did he initiate the confrontation?

Did he feel his actions were inappropriate and/or would be deemed criminal in nature if they occurred outside of a school setting?

He was fired.

He leaned back in his chair. His heart raced and his throat tightened.

"I need this job," he finally managed. "I think I can stay and be okay."

He was hardly convincing.

They couldn't imagine why he would want to stay.

"I fucked up." He corrected himself. "I messed up. There's a month left. Let me just . . ." And then the words spilled out. "Look, that kid's a fucking monster."

This sentence was met with silence.

"If you knew him you'd have wanted to do the same thing every fucking day."

They speculated openly about the reasons.

Maybe it was Chase's age. He was Centennial's youngest teacher.

Maybe there was something else he'd be better suited for.

They mentioned words like "patience" and "maturity" and "perspective."

Chase laughed.

This was deemed an "inappropriate" response.

Chase repeated the word "inappropriate" as a statement, then a question.

But their definition of the term was somehow fixed and universally accepted.

Their definition of the term was not open to interpretation.

Chase was still smiling as they stood and left him alone in the room.

They returned in an hour when the call came from the superintendent.

All of them were in the small room again but this time they stood.

Chase didn't notice that all the eyes in the room were on his right hand as he tried to keep it from trembling while signing his termination papers.

A hot wind stings his face when Chase walks outside. Squinting in the harsh sunlight, eyes still puffy and red from the pepper spray, he moves gingerly across the soft asphalt of the parking lot toward his Mustang, shielding his ribs, taking only shallow breaths because it's too painful to breathe normally. Three girls are smoking cigarettes in a white Jeep next to the Mustang, Ashlee Simpson blaring from the radio. The girls shriek with laughter when they see Chase because they recognize him and the pretty one in the backseat blows Chase a kiss and sings a verse of the song to him while waving a large yellow French tulip.

*   *   *

Chase turns off Annie Oakley and onto Centennial Parkway, which leads to the Outer Band—an asphalt ring rounding the city—which he stays on until it becomes I-215 and then he simply drives through the sudden hole that has opened up on this bright Wednesday afternoon in late May. What Chase is feeling right now—the wrenching of his body—seems similar to what he felt yesterday when the gold elevator seemed to free-fall twenty-two floors and jolt to a stop as the doors opened and Chase stepped out into the cool marble lobby, having moved Michele into her suite at the Palace and listened as a naked man pleaded with her to stay with him a little bit longer.

Chase swerves across two wide lanes into the far left one. His neck burns. He keeps pace with kids in a shiny blue Cabrio for a while until his mind drifts and the kids pull away and 215 becomes 93 and then he's past Boulder City and nearing Hoover Dam so he turns around because he doesn't want to slow down. He imagines lying awake tonight—the air conditioner off so he can hear everything—waiting with a butcher knife under his bed for the sounds of pounding on the door or the window that cracks then shatters. And then Rush and his crew clamber in. But what are the options? Head back to Centennial? Look for a white Escalade? Rehearse his lines? Stage his approach? Locate the mother? Simply get out of the Mustang and say "Excuse me?" Get their attention and talk fast? "I'm sorry. Okay. This was out of control and it shouldn't have happened." But the mother will shake her head and threaten Chase, mentioning the police and lawyers. And Rush, lean, handsome, blank-faced, will make a throat-slashing gesture. Rush will tell Chase he's a dead man. And soon it's almost four and the sun is swollen and orange and starting to drop.

Chase's eyes are raw and dry and his ribs feel like they might be cracked and he briefly considers driving to the hospital. This thought triggers an intense wave of sadness when he imagines waiting alone for hours in the emergency room at UNLV. So he skips it and ends up in Green Valley where his mother's old house is, because he likes driving there, away from the city, past the bronze statues of families painted in bright outfits that line Paseo Verde. Cruising the wide thoroughfare where he used to race shopping carts, he continues until he reaches the homes nestled in the rim around the valley, the city a blanket of lights below when the sun goes down. On this Wednesday afternoon, his last day at Centennial, Chase takes Black Mountain Drive, passing the wooden skeletons of unfinished homes. This causes him to accelerate because there aren't any cars around this far out and no one lives up here yet and soon the skeleton houses stop and all there is are empty concrete plots, just long stretches of desert waiting to be filled. Even with the orange streetlights overhead it's still pretty dark and when he comes to a traffic signal he stops even though it's green because the road stops, too. The asphalt ends and only gravel and desert lie beyond it.

Julia is coming tomorrow and Chase knows how he'll look to her: eyes bloodshot from the dry air and the insomnia, his head recently shaved, his face sunburned from too many afternoons by the pool at the Venetian or the Mandalay or the Mirage, waiting for Michele, the lacerations across his neck still fresh from a fight with a seventeen-year-old student. He wonders whether he'll lose Julia if he tells the truth about what happened. On

the drive back to his apartment on Boulder Highway he turns
onto Starlight Way. The house he grew up in seems as generic
as every other house: Mediterranean, seashell pink, Spanish tile
roof, a plot of thick green grass in front. Looking at the bedroom windows he remembers sneaking out of Carly's room, each
of them hanging from the roof, dropping to the lawn, running
in the black summer heat all the way to the abandoned golf
course, where they would smoke clove cigarettes and drink the
peach wine coolers that Michele would bring.

3

Thursday morning, one a.m., two days after moving Michele into the suite, Chase is on his way back to the Palace because she called. And though Chase was finally drifting off—a steak knife on the beige carpet next to his bed when the call came— he picked up. At first Michele didn't say anything other than "hey"—but after a long silence during which he could hear the low moan of the power surge coming through the open window in the suite on the twenty-second floor, Chase asked her what she needed and after a pause Michele said, "I'm high."

Chase asked Michele, "How high?"

She said too high for her own good.

"Why are you whispering?"

At the Circle K Mobil on Maryland, Chase debates about filling up the Mustang's tank because the two hundred dollars in his wallet is for this weekend with Julia and it's all he's got and his last paycheck won't direct-deposit into his empty checking account for a couple of weeks. Chase stands next to the Mustang and watches two pretty girls argue by a green Dumpster while a third is on her hands and knees vomiting onto the asphalt. He finally buys ten dollars' worth of regular.

After Chase gets back into the Mustang he makes his way back to the Strip. At a red light on Sahara, teenagers ride their bikes in lazy circles. A dazed and overweight mother sucks on a straw from a Jack in the Box cup and pushes a child too big for its stroller past Circus Circus. A black SUV swerves up next to him and he hears laughter over bass so heavy it makes his steering wheel vibrate. Chase pulls his blue bandana low on his forehead like a white Crip and waits for something to happen. He tenses up and runs his tongue over the swollen part of his lower lip from where his face hit the floor yesterday.

The thought that Rush is next to him—right now, in the SUV filled with his boys—forces Chase to swallow. He's suddenly aware of the stiffness in his neck and the scratches that tingle and burn when he starts perspiring. He is positive that whoever is next to him in the SUV is staring. The light won't turn and he's convinced that they will, at some point, try something. He has convinced himself that they want him to look. The feeling that they're pointing at Chase—poised to fire something into the open car—becomes overwhelming and he has to give in and turn cautiously: tan teenagers in striped Polo shirts and spiky hair blasting 50 Cent; kids who probably go to Durango or the Meadows School where Bailey went and where Chase's mother couldn't afford to send him. The SUV is in the left lane and the kid driving gestures: can they cut in front of Chase when the light changes? Chase nods and the kid gives a thumbs-up. When Chase reaches the Palace and sits in the car waiting for the valet he realizes his hands won't stop shaking, not even after he grips them into a knot. It's almost three a.m. by the time Chase knocks on the door that leads into the Sun King suite.

Not much happened during summers in Las Vegas. No one could stand the heat so most people who could afford it left for Tahoe or Aspen or L.A. The summer Chase turned thirteen, Michele stayed in the city even though her mother was in El Salvador because it was too expensive going back and forth. Carly and Chase stayed in town as well. One vacation consisted of a three-night weekend at Treasure Island where their mother received employee discounts on room rates. Michele stayed with Carly and him at Treasure Island for those three days and when there were no more movies to watch on cable and they were tired of swimming and bored with the arcade and had seen all of the magic acts and pirate shows in Buccaneer Bay, they called the number on a flyer that was handed to Chase by a heavyset Mexican man in a baseball cap on the Strip. The flyer promised a girl in twenty minutes or less.

The girl showed up in an hour.

She was thin and beautiful and smelled sweet. She wasn't much taller than Carly or Michele, though she seemed to take up all the space in the hotel room. Her long brown hair looked soft and she was tan and wore a tight pink T-shirt, jeans, and black boots. Her fingernails were painted silver. When she sat on the edge of the bed to light a cigarette she crossed her legs and the lacy edge of her bra crept above the low neck of the T-shirt.

The girl wasn't as angry about the situation as Chase thought she might have been. She just told them they should all be careful

*and that they were lucky they got her because someone else would
have kicked their asses. The girl noticed Michele staring at her and
told Michele she had beautiful skin and then the girl cocked her
head and, after sizing Michele up, asked her how old she was.
Michele swallowed and said nothing even though she didn't seem
embarrassed. And Michele didn't turn away; she was unable to stop
staring at the girl. The girl touched the place on Michele's chin
where she had broken out. "That'll clear up," the girl told her.
Chase had a hard-on the entire time the girl was in the room at
Treasure Island.*

    *After the girl left Carly and Michele gave each other mani-
cures and Carly talked about a girl she knew at school who did it
around the holidays so she could buy people really good presents.
Carly said that she could do it only if she knew it would be safe
and if it was with someone really hot and nice because then it
wouldn't matter so much that they were giving you money for letting them fuck you. All that mattered, Carly said, was that they
liked you enough to spend hundreds of dollars on you. "And that's
got to feel pretty great." Chase breathed in deeply and held it. The
girl's perfume still filled the room. What Chase remembers most
is that Michele said nothing.*

Bailey stands in the doorway wearing unzipped Diesel jeans and
no shirt, revealing a tan, muscular abdomen and chest. He wears
a coral necklace and has a tattoo of a blazing sun covering his
right shoulder. Chase can smell the gel in his spiky bleached-
blond hair mixed with faded marijuana smoke. Bailey's eyes are
barely open and standing this close to him in a hotel room late
at night Chase's heart suddenly starts racing.

"Is Hunter with you?" Bailey asks.

"I'm alone," Chase says and inches back slightly while Bailey processes this and nods.

"Well, when you talk to Hunter could you please tell the dude to return my calls?"

Bailey stares at the scratches that stretch from Chase's earlobe across his neck to his collarbone, to where they disappear beneath his T-shirt. The antibiotic Chase put on when he finally got home makes them glisten, but they look worse than they feel.

"That's disgusting, dude." Bailey reaches out and brushes the wound. Chase flinches. Bailey grins and wipes his hand on his jeans. "Relax."

The suite is dark and cool and the only light comes from the television, which is muted. The massage table is set up, sheets and used towels bunched on the floor around it. The scent of massage oil is stuck to the walls.

"Got six tickets to the Killers Sunday night," Bailey says. "You should come. Bring your girl. Michele says she's going to be in town."

From where they're standing in the suite, Chase can see into the master bedroom where Michele is asleep on the bed facedown over the covers. She wears black underwear and a white T-shirt that is pulled halfway up her back.

"Michele says your girl's a star," Bailey says. "Is that true, dude? Is your girl a star?"

Chase is too busy assessing the situation before him to locate an answer for Bailey. Chase stares at a sliver of light beneath the closed bathroom door. Does this mean someone else is in the bathroom? Why does it look as if somebody other than Michele hurriedly pulled on Michele's underwear and white T-shirt?

"It's a good move for you, dude, getting out of here," Bailey says. "You don't want to waste away for another summer."

"What do you mean?" Chase asks, slowly turning back to Bailey. "Waste away another summer with you guys?"

"No, dude. Waste away another summer in Vegas. Doing what you've always done."

"And what's that, Bailey?"

Bailey has had a sleepy grin on his face ever since he opened the door—almost as if this mask is painted on.

"We're all adjusting our plans, aren't we?" Chase looks around the suite. "Heard you got a great deal on this place."

"The best," Bailey says. "Yeah. My dad. He said as long as he doesn't know anything he's cool with it."

"So this is really working out?" Chase asks. "Very big move."

"It's keeping her happy." Bailey stretches. "Plus it's all very contained. We're protected. Classy, too. There are fucking four thousand rooms in this place. No one's gonna notice."

"And it's really making you money?"

"The overhead is very low," Bailey says. "Dad knows people."

"Yeah," Chase murmurs. "I guess that's how you're making the big bucks."

"Us, dude. We're in it together. Me and her. And yes, it's really making us money." Bailey's voice suddenly changes. "Speaking of which—now that you've got time to kill before the big move to Cali, do you feel like getting paid?"

"Won't be here," Chase answers quickly.

"But you're here now." Bailey inspects his image in a mirror. "She seems to think you have a calming effect on things."

Bailey shrugs and motions to Michele on the bed. "And I need— well, *we* need—some help, and as long as you're around you could do some things for us and I'll stick some cash in your pocket."

Chase stares at Michele's motionless body. "She called me and said you guys were having people over tonight. She sounded a little freaked." Chase looks around the suite. "I guess they've left."

"She smoked. You know how Michele gets when she's on it."

"No, how does she get?"

"She calls people and says there's a party."

Bailey grins and Chase keeps looking back at the bathroom and the sliver of light under the door. Bailey pulls a black T-shirt over his head and resumes studying himself in the mirror over the couch. "Does this shirt make me look like a fag?" Bailey seems to be asking the mirror. "I hate this fucking thing," he says and changes shirts. "I hate looking like a fag." He studies himself again and shrugs, giving up. "Shit, everyone looks like a fag now—what can you do about it?"

"So you're working out of here, but why the party in the Lakes?"

Michele curls up into a fetal position on the bed when Bailey says, "A very lucrative out call."

"Did you pick her up?" Chase asks quickly.

Bailey shakes his head and reaches into his pockets and pulls them inside out before he checks the top of a dresser. "Wasn't that supposed to be your job?" Bailey laughs. "Really, Chase, I'll put you on the payroll. Just until you go to Palo Alto.

Shit, dude, we've been tight for like, as long as anyone I know. Let me help you out a little while we're all still together."

The bathroom door swings open and light floods the room. It's a friend of Bailey's whose name Chase can't remember. He's nude. The guy moved here from Chicago and worked for two weeks at Olympic Gardens as a stripper and then as a sales representative for KB Homes and now valets at Aladdin. He's also Bailey's dealer. He comes out of the bathroom with his hands over his crotch. Chase tries to remember his name.

"She broke the skin, dude," the guy says. As he passes Michele he reaches out and squeezes her ass, one hand still cupped over his crotch.

Ted. Chase remembers his name is Ted. Chase leans in to Bailey. "Bailey. What the fuck?"

"She's a grown woman," Bailey says calmly. "I totally appreciate your . . . issues around her but"—and now he places an open hand on Chase's chest, urging him to step back—"she's not your responsibility. This is *my* girlfriend we're talking about here." He turns to Ted. "Hey, Teddy, look who just showed up." Bailey snaps his fingers and tilts his head in Chase's direction.

There's an awkward silence when Ted notices Chase. Nothing registers.

Bailey counts out five hundred-dollar bills and folds them. He reaches over and eases them inside the waistband of Chase's underwear, inside his jeans, and leaves his hand there. The bills feel crisp and dry against Chase's skin. "Listen," Bailey says, standing too close. "I know you're going to need this." He gives Chase's jeans a tug then removes his hand. "And Michele wants you on board and you can even pick up a decent shirt or something."

Bailey makes a face. "Who the hell dresses you? You could be a little more stylin', bro."

"I don't really care, Bailey."

"And I'm trying to figure something out . . ."

The two of them stare at each other for a while, before Chase again looks over at Michele and the naked guy getting dressed by the bed.

"What are you trying to figure out, Bailey?"

"What the fuck you're doing here."

When Chase wakes up in the suite at the Palace Michele is still sleeping facedown on the king-size bed. It hurts to open his eyes because they're so dry. The black digits on the glowing blue screen of his cell phone read 5:11. It occurs to him that he no longer has to go to Centennial. He could lie back down on the couch and sleep and when he wakes up he could order room service and hang with Michele. Or he could do some of the coke in her purse and slide under the covers and pretend they're seventeen again. In the bathroom Chase looks at himself in the mirror: the scratches aren't so bad; his left eyelid twitches from lack of sleep; the sunburn is fading. Michele mutters something in Spanish and rolls over as Chase leaves. When Chase leans against the gold wall of the elevator he closes his eyes and thinks about Julia—a girl who is convinced things only get better. And even though Chase doesn't believe her most of the time, he now wonders how much that matters because he would like to think that Julia's optimism about their life and everything waiting in front of them is justified. As the elevator stops at the lobby with a jolt, Chase tells himself that as long as Julia believes it then maybe that's enough.

The main floor in the Palace is quiet and cold and Chase moves through it unnoticed by the bored croupiers lounging at the empty tables. A group of young Asians in Prada suits are laughing and bet in quick little bursts as the roulette wheel spins. As he walks out of the hotel, Chase forms a plan: shower, sleep, read *The New York Times,* get dressed, Starbucks, call Centennial and try to work something out, paint, meet Julia at McCarran and talk about Palo Alto and San Francisco and the summer and the rest of their life together. By the time Chase is pushing open the heavy gold doors and the warm wind hits his face he's not even thinking about Michele in the suite last night with Bailey and his friend. (Bailey and Ted both split for an after-hours club, leaving Chase alone in the suite with Michele.) Waiting for the valet to bring the Mustang, Chase realizes that last night is inconsequential next to two facts: Julia's flight gets in at three, and Chase is leaving Vegas.

Chase doesn't mind the Strip this early because it's peaceful: the gray morning sky softens the glare of the marquees and there's no traffic and the wide boulevards are empty except for the occasional street sweeper with its spinning orange lights and swirling brushes inching past maids waiting at bus stops. A pickup truck pulls up beside the Mustang at a red light. The driver is white and wears a baseball cap. In back, construction workers of various ages with brown skin stare at nothing in

particular. They sit perfectly still and no one speaks to anyone
else. The driver looks straight ahead and Tim McGraw singing
"Live Like You Were Dying" soars from the radio. The wind
blows one of the worker's hats off his head and a few of the
men turn and watch it tumble to the asphalt. The one who lost
the hat stares at it and worriedly looks back at the driver and
then at the hat again. The light is still red. Someone next to the
man urges him to jump out and grab the hat but the man decides it's not worth it. They have houses to build.

*When their father was in town for business ten years ago he drove
Carly and Chase up to Black Mountain Drive in the hills. Their
father had wanted an ice-cream cone and so he took them to Baskin-
Robbins. Looking down at the valley, sucking on a frozen gumball,
their father pointed out the patches of light that he had a hand in
creating: a strip mall in Summerlin, a housing development called
Sunrise Manor, another strip mall off Boulder Highway. It was
easy money and their existence didn't seem to bring him any real
satisfaction. It was matter-of-fact, business as usual. An idiot could
make money here. Take it and run. That's what he did. Carly and
Chase stood there and listened as he told them about the limitless
possibilities for growth and how Carly and Chase would prosper
here if they stayed. He said this without asking them if that's what
they wanted.*

*Carly pointed out how the border kept changing. She pointed
out how the amoebae now expanded in every direction. Carly
pointed out how the entire desert was being enveloped with lights.
She said it looked like someone spilled a gigantic glass of sparkling
lemonade on the desert and no one was willing to mop it up.*

"It's a toxic spill," Chase said.

"Liquid gold is more like it," their father laughed.

"It only looks this way at night," Carly said. *"Tomorrow the sky will be brown and the lights won't shine and all you'll see are pink roofs and black asphalt."*

Chase felt a quiet satisfaction in the way his older sister saw through the bullshit and the way she challenged their father. His pulse quickened at moments when Carly punched through the façade of a pleasant family outing with the dad who had run away. Sometimes Chase would team up with her in moments like this and he'd add something not quite as biting, without the same edge, but he'd feel emboldened knowing she was next to him.

"It's pretty ugly during the day," Chase said.

"It's called growth." Their father laughed a little less as he said this. *"And it's paying for the pool you swim in every night and your sister's Mustang."*

Before he left the next day for the new house and the girlfriend in Malibu, their father gave them each three crisp hundred-dollar bills in his suite at the MGM Grand after the bellhop took his bags to the lobby.

That night Carly and Chase went to a party feeling flush. Carly offered to share the crystal meth she had bought from a dealer she met upstairs—a dealer Bailey introduced her to—but only if Chase would take her to another, better party that Bailey mentioned. Chase refused the meth but took Carly anyway. Bailey had left Carly behind. The one-month anniversary seemed like it happened in a distant era. Chase didn't know what was happening between the two of them. They were breaking up. They were getting back together. Chase couldn't keep track. Bailey had started doing things, like leaving Carly behind at parties, with a frequency that suggested the idea of that one-month anniversary had vaporized. But really, no, it was just to fuck with her, he explained to Chase. And it always worked: after a week of complaints Carly would follow Bailey anywhere. Now Carly was drunk but not enough to cut through the meth and her paranoia intensified as Chase drove, positive that he didn't know the way, that she wouldn't make it in time. "In time for what?" Chase asked. "For that asshole?" Carly was seriously wired and couldn't say anything because she didn't know. She snorted two more bumps from a small plastic Baggie and then asked Chase to stop the car so she could throw up. The sky was purple and Chase couldn't see the stars and when he heard the car door slam he realized Carly was ready so they kept going.

 He was still tired even after doing a couple bumps, and then they had an argument when Carly insisted she knew people at the party who would drive her home—"Michele is here!" she whined, which almost made Chase stay—and so he gave up and left Carly and she blew him a kiss before disappearing inside the house. Chase got lost driving home—every street looked the same and they all seemed to turn back into one another. He finally made it to Starlight Way and as he lay awake in bed, his heart still pounding from the meth, the call came from Michele. At the second, better party, Bailey acted like "a total dick." Carly caught Bailey making out with another girl in the kitchen. Carly pretended this didn't bother her by getting completely "shitfaced." And there were some college kids who thought that Carly and Michele were older and even though Carly was "a mess" the boys took them out drinking and then—

 Chase couldn't listen to the story anymore. He told Michele to get to the point.

 "The point?" Michele paused. "I suppose the point is that we're at the emergency room at UNLV."

"Why?" Chase asked, gripping the phone.

Carly fell off a jungle gym.

Carly split her head open.

Her scalp was sewn together with thirty-three stitches.

Five days after Carly's accident Chase called their father in Malibu.

"Carly's a mess," Chase said. "Her stitches come down to her forehead. She looks like a monster."

"She'll be okay. She's tough."

Chase heard a woman's laughter in the background and then his father was laughing, too, and salsa music was turned up suddenly.

"She's fucked, Dad."

"Shit, Chase, then why didn't you stay with her?" his father was yelling over the music. "She's your sister."

Thursday afternoon. Michele has spent ninety minutes inside a terra-cotta mansion in Green Valley Ranch for a one-hour appointment and won't answer her cell. When she finally answers Chase has to remind her that he doesn't want to be late meeting Julia's flight from San Francisco, and was she pulling this shit on purpose? Julia's flight gets in at three and it's now 2:45. Finally, driving fast to the Palace, Chase tightens his grip on the steering wheel as Michele apologizes and thanks Chase in the same breath. Chase nods. He's actually made a decision. He's actually leaving. Michele has appointments the rest of the day in the suite. The terra-cotta mansion in Green Valley Ranch was five hundred dollars for an hour. "You're more reliable than a cab," she says sweetly, and then her expression changes and she touches the scratches along Chase's neck for the fifth time that day. "Oh, poor baby—how are you going to explain those?" When Chase doesn't respond Michele starts scrolling through her BlackBerry and notes the appointment she just came from, with the date and duration next to the man's name. Day two in the suite with the new Web site and they are already getting bookings. Traffic slows on Tropicana. It is now three o'clock and Michele is oblivious. She mentions a girl Bailey hired to help build the Palace business and then explains why they decided to fire her anorexic butt. Chase doesn't hear the reason. The white sun beats down, bleeding the color from the sky. A bumper sticker on the pickup truck in front of him reads HELL WAS FULL: SO I CAME BACK. Chase checks the clock on his cell. "I am *fucked!*" he shouts over the wind and the chop of a low-flying Channel 3 News helicopter. He pulls onto the shoulder and accelerates.

"I'll walk," she says. "Stop the car. I'll walk."

4

Chase sits on a stool next to a bank of slot machines in McCarran, sweating through the expensive blue Prada button-down Julia bought him because she thought it brought out the color in his eyes. Julia called from the plane and the flight was late and it still hasn't arrived. At a newsstand Chase picked up a copy of *The Wall Street Journal,* a *Barron's,* and a *Financial Times* for her but decided buying all three was overdoing it. He put the *Barron's* back and added a tin of Altoids and a bottle of Evian because his mouth was so dry. In Chase's wallet is most of the cash from Vons—about $175. His last paycheck from the Clark County School District should be about $500. He'll owe $820 for rent by June 5th. Utilities, Internet, cable, food, gas. Chase has no idea how he will pay for any of it. He could leave Vegas with Julia next week. If he did that he could even get back his rental deposit of $450. The idea is no longer just an idea: this summer he'll live with Julia and look for work in San Francisco. He'll be a waiter. He'll paint.

When people start pouring into baggage claim Chase folds the papers together, wedging them under his left arm to avoid getting ink on his hands. His torn black Diesel jeans are too big (purposely) and he scuffed his Timberlands with sandpaper when he bought them. With the scented lotion on his freshly shaven face and the crisp blue shirt Chase feels okay about the way he looks and he imagines how Julia will see him when she gets off the plane. Then he remembers the scratches and loses the confidence he'd felt a moment before.

Julia doesn't see him. He's standing between two banks of slot machines, watching her as she glances around and lowers her Persols. She wears her hair in a ponytail. A tight white tank top stops above her pierced navel. A leather bag is slung over her shoulder. A suitcase on wheels rolls behind her. A tall young black man smiles and says something to Julia as she passes by. Julia is small but her full breasts, smooth brown skin, and perfectly symmetrical features always attract attention. Her forehead and almond-shaped eyes confuse Ethiopian women, who inevitably speak Amharic to her. Chase swallows, amazed that Julia is actually his girlfriend.

In college Chase used to play Tom Petty's *Greatest Hits* in his dorm room while Julia studied—she didn't mind. When "American Girl" would come on Chase always sang the opening lines to her and he even started calling her "my all-American girl" until she became irritated and asked him to stop. Chase now plays the song in the Mustang as he pulls out of McCarran but realizes right away that it's too sentimental. Julia says "hey" like she remembers the song and then touches his hand. It's too late—he's already self-conscious and changes CDs, turning up the volume on Etta James, one of Julia's favorites. Julia runs her hand over his shaved head. Chase had a short bleached-blond crew cut the last time she saw him.

"I liked your hair. What happened?"

"It'll grow back."

"You look tough," she says. And then she comments on the scratches.

"It's nothing."

"Did you see a doctor?" she asks.

"They're just scratches."

"From what?"

"Basketball."

"Did you get into a fight?"

"No. A guy just grabbed me. He was going for the ball. It happens all the time."

She leans in for a closer look. "Shouldn't you at least cover them up?"

"I'm supposed to let them air out."

"You're falling apart."

"See what happens when you're not around?"

The Hard Rock is where Julia and the other National Black MBA members are staying but the lobby is also crowded with porn stars when Chase and Julia walk in. Two tan women in cowboy hats and half-shirts stuffed with huge implants strut past them. And then Chase remembers that the Adult Video Awards are this weekend and a lot of the performers (the "nominees") are staying at the hotel. There was a story on the news last night about an overdose in one of the rooms and when Julia gets her key Chase wonders if they'll be on the same floor and before he can ask the guy at the front desk, Julia says, "Is your prostitute friend going to be here?"

Unlike the other casinos in town the interior of the Hard Rock is bright and accented with polished wood and has a circular bar at the center of the casino. Chase likes it because it's not a difficult place to find your way out of. Julia looks around for someone she might know from Stanford but doesn't see anyone.

Alone in the elevator Chase tells her he hopes she doesn't feel like she made a monumental mistake coming to Vegas.

"I don't make monumental mistakes, Chase," she says.

"I know," Chase says. "I know you don't, gorgeous."

"I like that we did it this way," Julia says. "Being apart and living separate lives for a while. I think it was a good thing."

"Yeah. Sure. For a while."

"I just think we have to see it like everything else we do that matters. We know certain things, and if we value them like we say we do, then we should act, and I want to be with you."

"You're sure?"

"Of course."

"If you need more time—"

"What's the point? There's nothing else I need to learn about you that's going to change the way I feel."

There's a purple Warhol print on the wall and the balcony overlooks the hotel's fake beach. They stand outside and study the porn stars lying under the sun, glistening and motionless. Chase

can't shake off the anxiety even though he knows it's just because they haven't seen each other in a while and he badly wants
to get beyond this moment and have sex. The water below them
is green and still and palm fronds sway in the unsteady wind.
"I love hotels," Julia says and slides her hands around his waist
until they meet at the small of his back. She undoes the top
two buttons of the shirt she bought him and rests her head
against his chest. Chase breathes in melon-scented shampoo.
She asks him what's wrong.

"Nothing."

"Are you scared?"

"I just wish we could be there now."

"Where?"

"In Palo Alto. In your apartment."

"After your show?" she asks, and hearing her say it (*his*
show) makes him feel like everything's wrong. Julia doesn't know
that the *White Trash Paradise* show next month is not his alone.
Julia doesn't know that the show involves four other artists. Julia
doesn't know that the show will occur in a room smaller than
the one they are in now.

"Yeah," he says. "After my show."

They stand there holding each other for a while until Julia
kisses him and Chase relaxes.

"I'm this close to leaving with you," he says.

"Just keep kissing me."

After a shower Chase stands in front of the closet mirror getting dressed while Julia is in the bathroom filling the large
sunken tub with water.

"Can I bring Hunter?" he asks.

"Where?"

"To the parties this weekend. He wants to come. He's even getting a haircut."

Julia pauses and then says, "Sure."

"He really needs to meet someone."

"Hunter really needs to meet someone?" Julia pauses again. "Hunter really needs to meet someone . . . at the National Black MBA Conference?"

"Exactly. This is a rare opportunity for Hunter."

"Is he still . . . a pirate?"

"He just wants someone who has her shit together."

"I asked you if he was still a pirate—not who he was looking to hook up with."

"He fell off a ship the other night. He tripped over some ropes on deck."

Julia laughs. "Will he be in costume?"

"He's not so bad. He actually wants to teach."

"Maybe he can take your job."

For a moment Chase considers telling Julia the truth: about the fight with Rush and getting fired from Centennial. But right on cue Hunter calls Chase's cell and says his last show at Treasure Island was canceled because one of the girls (the "wenches") got her hair caught in some kind of machine on the deck of the *Buccaneer,* which managed to tear most of the scalp from her skull, so everything pretty much closed down for the night. "You can imagine. Come get me."

"But there's nothing tonight."

"Oh, dude." Hunter overdoes the disappointment.

"Tomorrow are the parties."

"So what the hell am I supposed to do tonight?"

"Call Michele."

Julia makes a face when Michele's name is mentioned. She walks out of the bathroom.

After Chase clicks off and tells Julia about what happened with Hunter and why he has the rest of the night off, he hesitates before mentioning that at some point this weekend they might bring Michele along even though he already slipped and mentioned the name in front of Julia.

"That's not a problem," she sighs.

"Really?"

"No. I'm glad you feel secure enough with me to maintain your friendship with a prostitute."

Chase sighs and collapses on the bed next to her.

"I'm sincerely impressed that you don't even bother trying to hide it," she says.

Chase considers telling Julia that Michele is not a prostitute and that she's intelligent and ambitious and is only two or three or four semesters away from completing her master's in women's sexuality at UNLV but in the end he doesn't because he is so tired of lying to her.

"What if I went back with you?" he asks. "Really. What if we drove back together?"

"You have a job."

"I'll quit."

It's Friday and still hot and after a day spent inside, eating room service and Julia going to receptions and Chase ignoring repeated calls from Michele and one from Bailey (who left no message) he is alone in Julia's room again because she left for an Accenture cocktail party that they both agreed he should not attend, considering the condition of his neck. They make plans to meet later and Chase suggests maybe they could do some gambling. ("With what money?" Julia asked sarcastically.) When Chase mentioned a party at a club called Light in the Bellagio (Michele invited them but there was no way he would tell Julia that) Julia said she didn't feel like going out tonight but reassured Chase that tomorrow night they would.

Chase walks out onto the balcony and returns Michele's call. He tells her he's on his own for a while but can't go back to the suite because he has to pick up Hunter and Hunter's not a big fan of the suite.

"Well, he seems okay with it." And then Michele calls out, "Hunter, are you comfortable, hon? Grab another Corona because Brandi's coming over in about twenty, so you know, if you want to hit the ATM, now would be a good time."

Chase sticks a finger in his ear when the winds pick up and he hears Hunter yelling something in the background about the "real parties" and then Michele says, "I have to be somewhere in maybe an hour, maybe two—but I can meet up later."

Chase asks her, "Why tonight?" and then, "Who is it?"

Michele sighs. "I don't know who *it* is, Chase."

"Does Bailey?"

"Does it matter?" she asks. "Wait a minute. What are you trying to say?"

There's a long pause and then Michele delicately asks, "Are you taking Bailey's offer or not?"

"Why do you fuck with me on this?"

"Because you need the money."

And for a moment Chase tries to take offense but the anger is manufactured. He does need the money. If he does this, he won't have to ask his mother for cash she doesn't have. Another leap forward: he won't have to sell the Mustang. What else? He won't have to wear a puffy shirt and eye patch and leap from a ship. He won't have to squat down at crowded tables at Rum-jungle and recite the plantain and swordfish specials to fat-assed tourists from Minnesota for the next month. He won't be forced to pitch gated living to wealthy retirees. He won't have to park Navigators and Escalades for assholes he graduated with at UNLV. During this pause Chase makes a decision. He will combine two things he likes: driving his Mustang with the top down around the valley on warm summer nights with Michele riding shotgun, and taking as much of Bailey's money as he can before fleeing to California.

"Look, we're going either way," Michele says. "You're just driving us."

"How much?" Chase asks. "For tonight? Michele? How much?"

"Two." After she registers Chase's pause she fumbles. "Wait, three because it's short notice and it's your first official job and it could be a long one and—"

"Fine, Michele. Tonight. For three I'll take you anywhere you want to go."

Chase stands perfectly still on the balcony overlooking the fake Hard Rock beach. A cluster of people stand around sipping drinks. He wonders if the gathering is the Accenture reception Julia went to. He looks but can't find her. The din of energetic conversations drifts up to him. They're all young and well dressed and seem to glow in the soft yellow light that spills out from the casino. Chase envies them. They will be in Vegas for four days. Then they'll go back to Los Angeles or New York or London or San Francisco. And where has Chase been? In the past four days Chase has moved Michele into a hotel suite. Chase has squatted in a closet for over an hour listening to Michele fake an orgasm. Chase has lost a teaching job for beating the shit out of a student. Chase has agreed to accept money for driving Michele and anyone else she hires to out-call appointments that she's probably not telling Bailey about. He scans the crowd again for Julia while insisting to himself that his plans haven't changed: he's still leaving Vegas for California to be with Julia. The only alteration: he's just not sure when.

They sat in the new Olive Garden at Town Center that had just opened and was nearly empty at four o'clock. It was June and their mother took Carly and Chase there early because she had to work and wanted them to have a decent meal. She was worried that they never ate. Carly smoked at the table and their mother didn't care.

Their mother drank three glasses of white wine before the food came and then had the courage to ask if they'd heard from their father. They hadn't except for a postcard from Japan a month ago. No one spoke for a long time and the food came and Carly and Chase ate in silence and their mother didn't touch her meal. She just smoked and stared out the window, the bright sunlight hitting her face as she gazed at the long shadows stretching across the parking lot.

"The reason," she finally said, squinting, still looking outside, "we never got a dog is because it's just not fair to leave an

*animal alone in the house all day." She glanced at her children.
"And the summer comes and it's burning up and if it's not the
coyotes, it's the snakes or the scorpions, so you can't just leave it
outside."*

*Then their mother put her cigarette out and told them they
were moving. She tried to smile when she said this and added that
they could get a dog if they wanted. She was now officially drunk.*

Carly muttered something under her breath.

"What was that?" their mother snapped.

"You need help," Carly said. "I said you need help, Mom."

"The dog will help," Chase said sarcastically.

"I don't need this from either one of you," their mother said.

*They sat very still until their mother motioned for the wait-
ress to bring the check.*

"Are we leaving Las Vegas?" Chase finally asked.

*"No." His mother smiled tightly at the approaching waitress.
"We're not."*

5

Along with Wendy (the anorexic), Michele and Bailey had hired Rachel: the girl who took Chase's class at Centennial for the second time this year after earning an incomplete last year. Rachel, the girl who watched Chase wrestle Rush to the hallway floor three days ago; the coked-out skinny bitch who pinched his waist when she brushed past him that day. Rachel's first appointment is tonight and she needs to be picked up. Michele is going with her. Chase is driving. Tropicana Gardens, the four-story building where Rachel lives, is all beige stucco and Chase remembers that Carly used to see a guy who lived here. He follows Michele up the stairs to the third floor. She is looking for 317. Inside the darkened apartment teenage boys sit around drinking beer and passing bottles of Jack. The sweet smell of marijuana permeates the air. The boys, shirtless and tattooed, wearing baggy jeans and Timberlands, play video games on a plasma screen in which they pretend to be criminals turned loose on the streets of Miami.

*   *   *

Rachel says that Chase looks familiar and winks at him while Michele smokes a cigarette. He can't figure out if she's serious. The three of them stand in an upstairs hallway in 317 of the Tropicana Gardens. Rachel is as small as Michele and smells like bubble gum—that's it, that's all she's got. On their way out, one of the shirtless boys tries to keep them from leaving by blocking the path to the front door.

"Ronnie," Rachel protests. "I told you it's cool, okay?"

But the shirtless, muscled boy grins—he was just putting on a show—and stares at Michele while aiming his comment at Chase.

"Aren't you a little old to be hanging around my sister, dude?" the boy asks. "What's up with that?" The boy laughs. "Dude, if my sister turns into a skanky ho I'm gonna kill her."

"Fuck off, Ronnie," Rachel says.

As the three of them leave apartment 317, Ronnie calls out, "And don't give her any coke no matter how many times she promises to blow you because she never shuts up when she's high."

When Rachel gets in the Mustang she sits in the back and pulls a seat belt across her waist. In that movement Chase notices that Rachel looks even smaller and younger than she really is and realizes that this must have been what Bailey responded to when he first approached her.

"So what are you?" Rachel asks. "Like her manager?"

Chase ignores her.

"I guess it's better money than teaching art to high school kids," Rachel says. "Probably more fun, too, right?"

Their eyes meet in the rearview mirror.

"Your brother's a pain in the ass by the way," Michele says, clicking off her cell.

"My brother's been shooting cats from his bedroom window." Rachel sighs. "And ever since he started taking all that shit to get big all he wants to do is start shit."

"He's obnoxious," Michele murmurs, clicking open the cell as it rings again. She takes the call.

"I heard you got fired and arrested," Rachel says. "Though not in that order."

Chase tries concentrating on the road but keeps failing. "No one got arrested." Though he spoke with the police and charges may still be filed by Rush or the school or both, probation and some community service look like the worst-case scenario.

"You totally won that fight," Rachel says.

Michele clicks off the phone after muttering something into it that Chase could not hear.

Rachel tells her, "You should have seen him. He was all *fucking chill, dude, fucking chill* and he has Rush's head pinned to the floor and he's like that dude in *American History X*, you know with his shaved head and kicking ass? And I'm all *Rush is just a fucking dickless punk and he so deserved to be getting his ass handed to him.*"

"Why are you so thrilled?" Chase asks.

"Because that was rad, dude! Thank you for kicking his ass, Mr. Chase."

"It's not something I particularly wanted to do, Rachel," Chase says evenly, his eyes on the road.

"Rush is all *You know you can't live without me. You can't deny who we are Rachel!*" Rachel does a lame impression of Rush and then returns to her normal voice. "And I'm all: *you're a teen-age boy with a four-inch penis.*"

Michele smiles at this. Chase looks at Rachel in the rear-view mirror again. Her arms are crossed and she stares out the window and says, "I cannot *believe* I ever went out with him."

Chase tries to meet her eyes in the rearview but the bright lights of the Strip and the hot wind blowing her dark hair across her face make it impossible.

"What?" Chase asks casually. "You guys dated?"

"We were like, *the* item in school for like, all of first se-mester." Rachel says this in a way that suggests Chase should have known. "We have a MySpace page." A longer pause. "Wait, why do you think he went after you?"

Chase is silent. He thinks it was all attitude. Two angry guys. A teacher reprimanding a student. The student ignoring the reprimand. It was just simple. Animal. Basic.

"I don't know why he went after me," Chase says.

"He doesn't like that I'm working," she says casually. "I told him that you were driving girls around and shit."

Chase glances over at Michele. "But I wasn't then."

"He used to be rad," Rachel says. "He used to take his meds." Rachel leans forward and fills the space between Chase and Michele. "Ronnie says they're plotting something." Rachel says this with a nonchalance that Chase can't help but find threatening. "Rush and his posse of faggy little gangsters who jumped you."

"What exactly did they say, Rachel?" Chase asks.

"Exactly?"

"Yeah. Exactly."

"*We should shoot that motherfucker.*" Rachel pauses. "I guess that means you."

The valet reached for Chase's keys but neither he nor Chase paid attention to the exchange because both watched—the valet with amusement, Chase with dread—as Rachel, without opening the door, tried to swing her legs over the side of the convertible, like she was hopping a fence. But the tip of her platform shoe clipped the top of the door, sent her to the ground, to her hands and knees, skirt flipped up over her ass. Rachel shrieked with laughter, hopped to her feet, checked her knees, fixed her skirt, and skipped toward the entrance of the Palace. Chase and Michele traded a look then followed her inside.

Rachel paces the Sun King suite on the twenty-second floor and she's touching things—a faux-marble statue, a vase—and commenting on how nice it all is. Michele is setting up the massage table in the main room of the suite and Chase wonders where Hunter is and starts to ask Michele if she has heard from him lately but Rachel interrupts the question.

"Taste this," Rachel says.

Michele leans in and presses her lips to Rachel's skin just above the right breast.

"I like it," Michele says. "What is it?"

"I stole it from my mom before she split for Utah. She had tons of this shit."

When Rachel notices the condoms stacked next to the bottle of Astroglide, she suddenly loses whatever confidence she had built up on the ride to the hotel. Michele notices and tells Rachel they probably won't even need those things.

"Oh." Rachel tries to act disappointed. "Cool."

But it turns out that the guy who scheduled the two-girl session for 8:00 doesn't show and there are no other appointments for the rest of the night. This was confirmed after a phone call to Bailey. Michele says it's probably better this way because Rachel still isn't ready. "She laughs too much," Michele tells Chase.

Chase is sitting on the cream-colored couch while Michele smiles at him from a white leather chair.

"Why would Rush attack me when I wasn't even driving her?" Chase asks.

"Because Rachel's crazy and she doesn't know what she's talking about," Michele says. "That's the answer and I'm sticking to it."

Her eyes shift to Rachel when she walks out of the bathroom and then back to Chase.

"Chase looks hot," Michele says teasingly. "Doesn't he look hot?" she asks Rachel.

Rachel shrugs and says, "I guess you could turn on the air-conditioning or something."

She removes a Tasmanian Devil bong from her purse. Michele grabs a couple of tiny Jack Daniel's bottles from the minibar and makes everyone a drink, and after a few monster hits Rachel says she's starving so Michele orders room service—pancakes, shrimp cocktail. When Michele hangs up she asks Chase where Julia is and he tells her that Julia has "events" this evening and not to worry about her.

"Who said I was worried about Julia?" Michele mutters. "I'm not worried about Julia."

Michele says she's going to take a bath while waiting for the food. She undresses completely and Rachel giggles. Michele walks over to Rachel and kisses her on the mouth. Rachel blushes and watches as Michele, totally nude, walks to the bathroom and closes the door behind her.

"Are you okay?" Chase finally has to ask.

Rachel nods, and when she turns she registers the expression on his face.

It causes her to ask back, "Are you?"

Rachel squeals when she figures out how to order porn from the pay-per-view menu. On the TV screen two men are ejaculating very loudly all over a woman's face.

"No one really wants to see that," Rachel says.

"Someone must," Chase says after taking a call from Hunter.

Chase tries to open the bathroom door but Michele has locked it.

"Hunter's on his way up," Chase tells her through the door.

Rachel switches to *Rugrats in Paris* and says, "This is better than cum shots." She changes the channel and finds E! Rachel says she saw her friend on a reality show about the Palms on E! The friend was wasted and some dude had his hands clutched around her breasts and the friend was completely oblivious. When Rachel confronted the friend with how gross she had been on the reality show, the friend insisted Rachel was jealous.

Without looking at Chase, Rachel lowers the volume and says, "Michele told me I could make so much more, like tons, if I actually, you know, did it with them, so I think I'm gonna try it."

Chase glances away from the TV and over to the closed bathroom door.

"Which is making Rush fucking insane with jealousy. But fuck that. He's *so* juvenile. He said if I did this I don't respect my body and all that shit but first of all that's not true and anyway that's what they want, so it's like, what are your choices?" Rachel pauses thoughtfully, considering something. "I'll be eighteen in less than two years and that's like still pretty young, you know? I've heard what you can earn in two or even one year. It's fucking limitless." She nibbles her fingernails. "As long as they're hot, you know?" (Chase chuckles grimly at this.) But Rachel is only sixteen and she doesn't need *tons* of money right now: all she wants is that silver Audi convertible with the cool seats and to never have to work in her dad's office again and to move to South Beach and she wouldn't mind bigger boobs but only because Bailey thinks she should and she doesn't give a shit about Rush's opinion, though he wanted her to get breast implants, too, but he's history and again, to make it perfectly clear: what Rush wants doesn't fucking matter.

"This doesn't look like the National Black MBA" is the first thing Hunter says when he enters the Sun King suite. Searching the room, squinting, he adds, "Nope, this doesn't look very impressive at all."

"And yet you're here," Chase says.

"So did the wife call?" Hunter asks. "Are we going to the parties that matter or will we spend the rest of the weekend nursing stray kittens?"

"It's early, dude."

"Your fly's open," Michele says.

"I like it that way." Hunter grins and zips it up. "Wait, we're not staying here all fucking night, are we?"

Michele looks up at Hunter and, barely suppressing a grin, asks, "Chase is taking you to the parties for the *Black* MBA Conference?"

"We may gamble later," Chase says, noting and ignoring Michele's sarcasm. "Julia and a friend or two." And then to Hunter: "If you have any money left."

"Why wouldn't I have any money left?" Hunter asks.

"Did Brandi ever call you?" Michele asks, propping her feet on the glass coffee table, her chin between her knees. She's giving herself a pedicure.

Hunter nods and looks for somewhere to sit down and does a double take when he notices Rachel silently watching Michele.

Surveying the suite, Hunter finally says, "It's official: we're all going to hell."

"Did Brandi leave me anything?" Michele asks. "She's not calling me back."

Hunter reaches into the pocket of his jeans. "Yeah, a wad of sweaty cash and an I.O.U." Hunter hands Michele the bills.

"I don't get this," Michele says. "Why didn't Brandi give this to me?"

"She actually told me to give it to Bailey."

As she counts the cash Michele blows on her toes because the brown polish is still wet. "That's it? This isn't the rate. Where is she?"

"She said she'll explain it to you when she calls you back," Hunter says.

Michele looks at Hunter then loses herself in her Black-Berry and jots something down in a notebook. She repeats the process: sending a two-way and writing down names. Michele does this multiple times until she calls Bailey. Chase hears her say, "We're set." Then she says that she will see him later. Michele adds, "About forty or so." She says, glancing over at Chase. "Yes, he's here." Pause. "He's with Hunter." Pause. "And they're leaving." Pause. "I don't think so but I'll ask." Michele ends the call abruptly and tosses her cell on the table.

"Bailey wants to know if you're coming back later," Michele says to Chase.

"No."

"No?"

Chase realizes something. "I mean, am I?"

"Are you?" Michele grins.

"Is there a particular reason why I should come back later?"

"I think so. Yes."

"Then call me."

"But you're not leaving now."

"Hunt?" Chase asks.

"I'm cool," Hunter says, holding up a drink, staring at Rachel. "I'm getting trashed. I'm getting my jollies." He gestures at the room service cart. "And I even had a pancake."

But Rachel is staring at Michele: her thin legs held slightly apart, her faded cutoff shorts, the backs of her tan thighs—they all demand attention. Everything in the room is quiet as Rachel's gaze shifts from Michele's calves up to her chest and then her face. Michele either doesn't notice that Rachel is staring or she knows and likes it. Rachel sighs and leans back in her chair, studying Michele's feet again. Hunter has been watching Rachel watch Michele and he nudges Chase.

"Someone's in love," Hunter says in singsong. "I think Rachel has a crush on someone in this suite."

Rachel's face is flushed. Michele smiles and keeps blowing on her toenails.

"She's so digging you," Hunter says. "I don't know who she is or where she came from but I know she's craving your Salvadoran ass."

"And I'm digging her," Michele says airily.

"I think she wants to *be* you," Hunter says.

"Whatever," Rachel groans, embarrassed.

"Are you still hungry?" Michele asks Rachel.

Rachel nods and Michele tells her to order something else from room service.

"Should I get some more pancakes?" Rachel asks.

"Perfect."

"Where's your momma, little girl?" Hunter asks delicately.

Rachel flashes her middle finger and says, "I'm emaciated, bitch."

Hunter puzzles over this and cocks his head. He glances over at Chase and then back at Rachel.

"Emancipated," Michele corrects.

"My mom moved to Salt Lake with her latest boyfriend and I'm all, *as if*?" She repositions herself on the couch. "So Ronnie and—"

"Who's Ronnie?" Hunter asks, concerned.

"Her brother," Chase says.

"Oh. Whew." Hunter wipes fake sweat from his brow.

"Yeah, so Ronnie and I get the apartment because Linda is all about compromise." Rachel stares at Hunter's black T-shirt and then reaches over and plucks something off it.

Hunter purrs like a very large cat.

"You've got dandruff," Rachel says. "It's all over your shirt."

"Why don't you lick it off?" Hunter asks.

Michele tells Rachel in a soft voice, "Come here a sec," and Rachel moves toward Michele and Michele puts her nail polish down and turns to Rachel and takes her face in her hands and says, "You're wonderful," and they kiss, softly at first, but then with an intensity that's just part of the show.

Hunter yawns loudly. "How original."

"It's not for you," Michele says.

She kisses Rachel again and then Michele's cell rings. Michele grabs the remote control and mutes the television.

Michele gets up from the couch and tells whoever has called that they can be there in half an hour. Michele waits, listens, and turns away when she says, "Yes, she really is that young." Michele pauses. "Can she look even younger? I guess." Chase realizes that he will take them. Michele guides Rachel to the bathroom where Michele tells Rachel that she's going to make Rachel look even hotter than she already is.

Chase and Hunter chill in front of the giant plasma TV, the sound off, the voices of the girls carrying into the main room of the suite.

After an innocent back-and-forth there's a silence and then Rachel's protest: "I look like I'm in junior high." Chase closes his eyes when he hears Michele say "Good," and after another longer silence Rachel apologizes and Michele tells her that she's

so beautiful and Rachel asks, "Honestly? Do you really mean
that?" and Michele assures her she does and tells Rachel that
she's going to be great and the guys are so totally going to dig
her. When Rachel comes out of the bathroom she has her hair
in pigtails and wears a checkered skirt and a thin yellow T-shirt
with a cheerleader's megaphone over the chest.

Michele asks Hunter if he thinks Rachel looks hot.

"I think you should kiss again," Hunter says.

"I thought you said it was boring."

"I lied."

"We should go," Chase says.

"You're free to go, dude," Hunter says. "I think I want to
stay."

Michele turns to Rachel and asks softly, "Are you ready?"

"Yeah," Rachel says and bites her lower lip. "I am *so* ready."
She giggles.

Chase has heard this sound before: giggling disconnected
from humor.

"I thought I'd be scared, you know?"

"You're wonderful," Michele tells her.

"But I'm really not."

"You look so hot."

"Do I?"

"Yeah. Definitely."

"And Cabo next Thursday?" Rachel asks.

"You know it, baby."

Rachel bobs her head up and down, dancing to a song only
she can hear.

*   *   *

The house is in the Lakes.

When Michele tells Rachel this she nods and says, "My stepdad lives in the Lakes."

"Well, I hope that's not where we're going," Michele sighs.

"As if!" Rachel snaps. But then she frowns worriedly.

The Mustang passes through a security station and a name ("Olivia Rose + two") is on the clipboard held by the guard. The house is enormous and made of stone with a Spanish tile roof. It lies on top of a mesa at the end of a winding driveway. Sprinklers water the sprawling lawn. Only a porch light glows over a blood-red front door. A shiny pickup truck and a black Navigator are parked in the driveway. When the three of them get out of the Mustang Michele turns to Chase but then changes her mind. Walking to the house Chase notices that Michele has Rachel by the arm. She whispers into her ear as if giving instructions or a warning. Rachel looks at her wonderingly. It takes a moment. But finally Rachel spits her gum into Michele's open hand.

The man who opens the door is in his late thirties and tan and wears a sheer lime Versace shirt and DSquared[2] jeans and too much cologne. Another man stands beyond him, watching. The first thing that occurs to Chase is that these men are past the age of pretending—these guys know precisely what they want. Chase's presence doesn't seem to bother them. They smile, holding tumblers of Scotch, and ask them all to come in. They introduce themselves and offer martinis. The house is cool and softly lit and generic jazz pipes in through speakers in the ceiling and drifts through the vast room.

"Can I have an apple one, please?" Rachel sings from the white leather couch where she sits with her legs crossed.

"Of course," a deep voice says.

The slit in Rachel's checkered skirt reaches her upper thigh and her leg is smooth and dark and Chase can see the edge of her white panties.

Rachel notices a Ms. Pac-Man machine sitting in the corner of the enormous living room. She gets up and starts fiddling with the joystick and the guy in the lime shirt hands her something neon green in a martini glass and Rachel sips it as he presses the Play button. Chase notices the Ruscha on the wall over the fireplace.

The guys turn their attention to Chase.

"He was my art teacher!" Rachel blurts out.

Her game ends with a theatrical groan of disappointment and Michele says that's enough for now.

The guy in the lime shirt is named Tanner. The other man is Luke and they recently moved from Sherman Oaks. Chase asks what they do.

"Development," Tanner says, stretching out the syllables.

"Were you really her teacher?" Luke asks.

They laugh when Chase nods. "Did you keep her after school a lot?"

"He's an incredible artist," Michele interjects and then points at the Ruscha, and yes, it's an original. "Chase's are better," Michele says. "He's really good. Whoever that is." Michele motions to the Ruscha again. "You're better," she says.

Chase sighs, "Thank you."

"Have you sold anything?" Tanner asks.

Chase hesitates. He hates this part. "I've got a show coming up. Hopefully. But no. Not yet."

"In Vegas?"

Chase nods and feels flushed. He mentions the name of the gallery and loses the guy.

The guy examines the wet-looking scratches on Chase's neck and winces and says they look infected. But then everyone turns their attention to Rachel, who is now transfixed by a wave-shaped copper waterfall mounted on the wall as she downs the apple martini. The only sound is the continuous cascade of water until, unaware that everyone is watching, Rachel sticks both hands under the wall of water and sprays herself and jumps back and the guys laugh and Rachel glares at them.

"Are you guys gay?" Rachel asks.

"No, we're not gay." Tanner says. "It's just a very faggy house."

"Have another martini," Luke says.

"I need to pee."

"Down the hall and to the right."

Rachel struts past the men and flips her skirt and bobs her head side to side then disappears into the darkness of the hall. Michele starts to apologize ("I told you—it's her first night") but the guys wave her off (they're thrilled) and turn their attention back to Chase.

"So where do you go?" Tanner asks.

"Outside."

"In the car?" Tanner asks. "That's got to get old. Just sitting around."

"It's not a problem."

"You can always stay." Tanner grins.

"We've got a home theater downstairs," Luke says. "You can watch a movie."

"Or us," Tanner suggests, shrugging.

"I'll be fine outside," Chase says.

Tanner seems disappointed. He nods. His smile disappears.

"Then maybe it's time for you to go sit in the car," he says.

Chase turns the radio on when he gets tired of listening to the sound of the sprinklers above the wind. Pink Floyd's "Wish You Were Here" is on KKLZ and Chase turns it up, loud. Michele left a bag in the car filled with underwear and bras and other things and inside he finds a pack of cigarettes. He lights one and puts the seat back as far as it will go and watches the sky. He knows he will be on this canvas in Rachel's mind forever: her first time, Michele and two dudes with teeth that are too white in a rad house in the Lakes and a Ms. Pac-Man machine and a waterfall and Rachel getting drunk on apple martinis and Chase—her old art teacher—playing sentinel. Whatever cash Michele hands Chase is now his only income. His relationship with Julia keeps what Chase is doing now from defining him. Soon they'll be somewhere else entirely and here won't matter anymore. The sudden irrelevance of this place is a revelation. He takes a long drag off the cigarette and slowly exhales, watching the gray smoke dissipate in the moonlight.

"Let's go to Dad's," Chase said to Carly on a hot gray morning in July after he picked her up at an apartment complex near UNLV.

Michele had called Chase early that Saturday morning and told him where his sister was. Michele apologized for not being there but she had to leave the party early. (Alone? Chase thought, but didn't ask.) Michele said Carly was "probably" fine, that she was with the guy she was seeing from the UNLV baseball team. Michele gave Chase the address and apartment number. When Chase got there he found the door to the apartment open. Carly was lying in a fetal position on a black leather couch next to a guy passed out in boxer shorts and a mirror misted with coke residue. Chase carried her down four flights of stairs to the Mustang.

"Will Dad be there?" Carly asked, mumbling.

"I don't know. I don't think so. Let's go. Let's get out of here."

"I don't want to go if he's there."

"Don't you miss the beach?" Chase asked her.

She was crumpled in the backseat. Their eyes met in the rearview mirror.

"Why do you want to go?" Carly asked. "It's nice here."

"No, it isn't," Chase said.

"You go," Carly said. "I have things to do."

"Just come with me," Chase said.

There was a long pause. Chase looked at Carly in the rearview mirror again. She had turned away.

"I have plans," Carly said. "I have things to do."

"Change them."

"I can't," she said.

"You're sixteen. You don't have plans you can't change."

Carly finally looked at Chase. "I can't."

"Tell me why."

"Because I made plans," she screamed. "I have plans."

"And you can't change them?" Chase was yelling.

"No, Chase. I can't. I have plans I can't change," she said.
Chase put something together and asked, "To fuck who?"

While waiting in the Mustang in front of the house in the Lakes, Chase calls Julia. She tells him she's playing roulette with her friend Monique and that there's an adult film star sitting next to them and they were invited to a party at the Bellagio.

Julia asks Chase where he is.

"Male or female?" he asks, ignoring her question.

"Does it matter?"

"Do you want to go?"

"Definitely," she says teasingly, the casino roaring behind her. "But I want you to be there, too."

Chase has been sitting in the Mustang for close to two hours. Neither girl says anything when they get in, which isn't unusual for Michele (who never says anything afterward), but Rachel seems like she has been stunned by something. Chase starts the car and begins the drive back to Summerlin Parkway and the city. Michele is staring out at the darkness. In the rearview Chase notices that Rachel looks pale.

"You just should never say something like that." Michele is shaking her head.

Rachel runs the back of her hand across her mouth as if trying to clean it.

Michele turns around in her seat. "What possessed you to say that?"

"It was the truth."

"You spent an hour in their bathroom because you drank too much."

"You told me to."

"No, I told you to have one drink if you were nervous," Michele says. "I did not tell you to drink enough apple martinis to make you throw up half the night."

"It doesn't always," Rachel protests meekly.

"What happened?" Chase asks.

Michele points at Rachel. "You owe me big-time. I don't ever do that. It's just not safe. But that's the position you put me in tonight. You're lucky they're into that."

In the Tropicana Gardens parking lot it takes close to a minute before Rachel realizes she's home. She finally kicks the back door open and when it slams into a giant potted plant Chase whips his head around and says, "What the fuck?" Rachel stumbles out of the car and falls to the ground. On her hands and knees Rachel heaves but doesn't vomit. Michele stares straight ahead. Rachel turns and looks at Michele, who is now lighting a cigarette. Rachel seems to wait for Michele to help her up or at least acknowledge her. When Michele doesn't, Rachel pulls herself to her feet and trudges away. Rachel is halfway up the staircase when Michele sighs bitterly and calls out her name. Michele motions her back to the car where she hands Rachel a wad of folded bills.

Rachel says, "I'm really, really sorry."

And then Rachel looks at Chase for some reason. Chase thinks she's about to apologize for the car door but she says nothing and continues to stare sadly at him. Chase wonders if she's dazed from what happened earlier at the house in the Lakes or if he's simply an invisible thing in her line of sight. But when Chase meets her eyes it's clear that she's aware of him and it seems as though she's processing something.

"What?" Chase asks. "What are you looking at?"

"Nothing," Rachel says and finally walks away. "Thanks for the ride."

Chase drives fast alongside shimmering black pools and the bright white geysers stretching from the Strip to the entrance of the Palace. He slows to a stop behind an idling white Hummer limousine. He leaves the engine running. The rush of splashing water from the fountains seems louder tonight and he tells Michele that he's not coming up to the suite after she asks him to. Chase tells her he needs to lie down for a while before seeing Julia. Michele starts to insist but he cuts her off.

"Not now. Don't do this now."

A wave of nausea forces his eyes closed. The last time Chase ate something—an orange and a cup of coffee—it was morning.

Michele asks him when he wants his money. He tells her it doesn't matter. She starts to hand him some of the cash from tonight. But when she sees Chase's gaze stuck to the crisp bills in her hand she reconsiders and puts the cash away.

"You look awful," she says.

Chase is shivering in the warm wind. "I don't know what's wrong. I feel sick."

"Come on," Michele says and touches his leg as she gets out of the car. "I have something upstairs that'll help."

The rush of cool air flowing through the gleaming gold hallway on the twenty-second floor relieves Chase's dizziness, but Michele says he looks green and when she asks him if he's going to be sick he can't answer. Hip-hop blares inside the suite. The air reeks of marijuana. The room is filled with girls rapping along to Ludacris, mock-taunting each other and rolling their necks. "Stay the fuck up out my biznass!" they keep shouting along with the heavy beats of the chorus. All the BlackBerry messages Michele sent out were obviously received. Michele moves easily through the girls and Chase follows closely behind—he just wants to make it to the bathroom. Then it occurs to him: the girls are here to be recruited.

Chase catches a glimpse of Hunter slumped on the edge of a bed gazing blankly at the television, a white sheet draped loosely over his shoulder. They exchange a glance as Chase pushes past Michele to the bathroom. He manages to get the door closed and the toilet seat raised before vomiting so violently that it feels as if something has torn loose from the lining of his stomach. When Chase can finally stand up the harsh vanity lights make the lacerations on his neck look brighter, irritated, infected. He turns away appalled and slowly moves out of the bathroom. Hunter stands up still wrapped in the sheet. He leans in to Chase. "Are you okay?" Chase closes his eyes and nods.

"Bailey was looking for you," Hunter yells over the music. "He says to keep your phone on." Then Hunter grabs Chase's shoulder. "Look," Hunter says. "I'm ready for an upgrade, if you don't mind. I'll get dressed and we'll move on to the adult world." Hunter grabs a pile of clothes off the floor and staggers into the bathroom.

Two girls share a joint on the couch across from the bed where Chase has taken Hunter's spot. He stares past them and loses himself in the swaying mass of bodies. He finally looks away when he feels a cool hand on his neck. Michele says something into his ear but Chase can make out only one word: Bailey. This night has taken forever, Chase thinks.

"Pay me," he says. "Just pay me and I'll leave."

"Bailey said later." Michele moves her forehead against his until it's resting there.

Chase pulls his head away from hers and wraps his hands around her wrists.

"Now, Michele." Chase squeezes them and she smiles but stops when he doesn't.

6

Julia is not in her room at the Hard Rock and Chase is relieved. He didn't call her after he left the Palace because he still felt sick and needed time to pull himself together. He splashes cold water on his face and gently touches the red gashes on his neck. Sitting on the edge of the unmade bed, he eats half of a cold Snickers from the minibar and downs a bottle of Evian and considers skipping the parties. It's midnight. Chase just wants to get undressed and hide under the covers. He'll lie down. He'll turn off his cell. He'll eventually fall asleep. Tomorrow he'll feel better. He'll explain that he wanted to meet her but simply didn't have the energy. Tomorrow his mind will be clear. Tomorrow there will be a space between tonight—picking up and delivering Rachel to that house in the Lakes, getting sick in the suite filled with all those girls, taking Michele's money—and the morning. But his cell rings and it's Julia and without thinking he takes the call and tells her he's on his way.

* * *

Julia's choking on a cigar. It looks huge in her small hands and at one point almost slips from her fingers. "I got it," she keeps insisting, "I got it." She squints when a breeze sends gray smoke back into her eyes. The guy who offered Julia the cigar is tall and dark-skinned and has an immaculately shaven head that's so clean-looking it almost glows. He's wearing a black Hugo Boss suit and an expensive Tank watch and seems to enjoy watching Julia struggle. The guy yells something over the loud hip-hop beats into the ear of a light-skinned girl in a halter top who is Monique, Julia's friend. There are, according to Julia, two crowds at the National Black MBA Conference: the Anxious and the Arrived. And they have both convened on the fake beach at the Hard Rock Hotel and Casino on a warm and windy Friday night in May.

Those still in school are the Anxious: wide-eyed and spreading rumors about fielding offers and twenty-thousand-dollar signing bonuses and 100 percent annual salary increases, New York "I-banks," Goldman, Morgan Stanley, a quarter million in three years. Compared to the Arrived, the Anxious see everything unfolding in front of them in ways they never dreamed. An example: Accenture will offer Julia one hundred thirty a year with a twenty-thousand-dollar signing bonus upon successful completion of an internship this summer. Julia's parents taught in an elementary school in Philadelphia for twenty-five years and only recently earned forty thousand annually—a fact Julia finds instructive but that just bothers Chase.

The Arrived is a smaller and mostly male group. They offer fifty-dollar cigars to the Anxious, laying the foundation for inviting the girls to an after-party party in their suites, a reward for all that hard work. The Arrived are deserving of a little extra, the wife and infant child at home notwithstanding. They savor the moment with the knowledge that the ninety thousand for Harvard or Chicago or Stanford was totally worth it. They talk matter-of-factly about imported luxury cars that idle in subterranean parking lots for weeks on end in Manhattan and complain that they *never get to drive that thing* and then it's the Hamptons and the outrageous monthly American Express Platinum bill and the golf club in Bermuda and the Brazilian masseuse at the W on Union Square.

"It's not weed," Chase tells Julia when she takes a long drag off the cigar and holds her breath. She nods, cheeks expanded, a pained expression on her face. Slowly, unevenly, Julia exhales, sputtering a stream of acrid smoke. She looks relieved— and then confident—as the smoke evens out and the last of it leaves her mouth. She manages to make a crude but discernible smoke ring that impresses everyone.

"It's a 1999 one-off Julieta, one of the better non-Cubans," the guy tells Hunter, who asked.

"I love one-offs," Hunter says as if he knows the difference, nodding to the hip-hop, grabbing another beer from one of the pretty Coors Light Girls wearing tight silver minis and clear plastic six-inch heels who move through the crowd handing out complimentary beer. Hunter tries to talk to the Coors Light Girl and tells some lame joke that she either doesn't hear or doesn't get because she stares blankly, fixes her hair in the wind, thanks him for the small tip, and walks away.

"I've got some Cohiba Esplendidos upstairs," the guy grins. "Cubans," he tells Hunter.

"Aren't those illegal?" Julia asks. Chase glances at her wondering: when did she learn that shit?

Hunter mentions something to Monique about his year as an apprentice to a muralist in Rome, which was actually four months in an exchange program paid for by his father, where Hunter met a gay painter who let him attend a private workshop that he led especially—and exclusively—for Hunter (Hunter, like always, took it in stride).

The guy says something to Monique that makes her laugh and they both look at the scratches on Chase's neck. The guy asks Chase what he did.

"I teach."

The guy shakes his head. "No, I meant what *did* you do?" The guy points to Chase's neck.

"One of the inmates showed a little too much courage."

The guy raises his eyebrows.

Julia turns to Chase. "Yeah, I'd like to know, too. What really happened?" she asks.

"Nothing." Chase shrugs.

"I thought it was from basketball," Julia says, remembering the lie he told when he met her at McCarran.

Chase looks back at the guy. "What can I say? The kids are wild here."

"What do you really want to do?" the guy, suddenly and inexplicably interested, asks.

Chase hesitates. It's been a very long day and he realizes he's a little drunk.

Julia speaks up. "He's a painter. An artist. A really good one."

The guy nods, considering this.

"You hear about that dude? What's his name in New York? Arular? Arulo? Some one-name motherfucker? I know someone

who paid three hundred fifty thousand dollars at auction for
that painting of those three naked girls."

Hunter nods. "Yeah, I heard about that dude."

"Three hundred fifty thousand." The guy whistles. "I saw
his show at the Whitney."

"Yeah, so did I," Hunter says, glancing nervously at
Monique.

"The money can be so fucking sick," the guy says. "And
Arulo's really good. I mean, enough of this postmodern shit.
Reward something real. Something people can fucking relate
to. You know what I'm talking about?"

Julia grabs Chase's hand.

For some reason Chase looks to Hunter for a way out of
this but Hunter's staring at Monique, who starts sharing whispers with Julia.

The guy takes the opportunity to lean forward and smile,
offering a sudden unwanted intimacy and a set of gleaming
veneers, and says, grabbing Chase by the wrist, "You realize
what she's giving up for you?"

Shocked, Chase tries to pull away but the guy tightens his
grip.

"You know that staying with you just might be a half-million-
dollar decision when she could have any guy here? Are you going
to make it worth her while? Giving up a two-income household
worth over a mil?"

Chase shoves the guy's arm away but the guy keeps leaning closer.

He whispers into Chase's ear with the same horrible grin.

"That's a lot of pressure on a brother."

*   *   *

The suite they move to—where a Stanford alumni party is in full swing—is about the same size as Michele's suite at the Palace but feels smaller because the room is overcrowded with people dancing in small clusters to a loud OutKast CD. All the men are trying to convince the women to come to their rooms for the night and they seem to be succeeding. Chase is now officially drunk and he just watches Hunter talking to Monique, gesturing with his arms, crouching, and then Hunter hops a few inches from the ground, explaining the concept of pylometrics: jumping exercises that have increased Hunter's vertical leap so that he can dunk a basketball with two hands instead of one. Monique looks over her shoulder for help.

And then Chase catches Julia staring at him. She is standing with a group near the balcony, a serious expression creasing her face. She used to do this in college when they got separated at parties or sat at different tables in the dining hall. She would study Chase as though trying to figure him out: a white boy from Las Vegas who ended up at NYU, a guy who took a work-study job as a "Safe Walker" for students uncomfortable walking around the city alone at night. When she used to stare at him he felt reassured. Julia knew what it took for Chase to get all the way to Greenwich Village from that hotel room in Bally's, in Vegas, after that terrible week of the body on the lawn.

Julia was the first person Chase had ever met who seemed to have an innate understanding that everything could always be worked out. There were always solutions. For example: if Chase couldn't handle flying home then Julia would go with him. If Chase stayed in New York for Thanksgiving his freshman year—this was his first Thanksgiving away from Vegas and his mother was going to Tahoe with her boyfriend and Chase never heard from his father—then Julia didn't go to Philadelphia and stayed with him. They ordered Chinese take-out and watched a DVD of *Honeymoon in Vegas* in his dorm room. When Nicholas Cage and Sarah Jessica Parker checked in to their hotel, Julia asked if that was the Bally's Chase stayed in after what Chase referred to as "the incident." There was only one in Vegas, he said, so yes. Julia even understood when Chase explained why he was leaving New York. Everything was too fast and crowded and everyone except him seemed so comfortable and confident. He couldn't keep up. He hated the kids who wore designer scarves and expensive boots and sat on hallway floors eating apples they had bought at the farmers' market in Union Square and talked about foreign movies Chase had never heard of. Julia pointed out that she'd never been to the farmers' market and never sat on the floor and saw none of the same movies and yet she was staying. But in the end she reassured him about his decision. She always insisted, gently, that everything would be okay. Chase could never tell Julia the real reason he left NYU. The real reason was that everyone was better than him.

Her understanding used to comfort him—it used to make Chase feel grounded. But now it only makes him uneasy, as if the longer she stares the more she will figure out about him and the greater the chances are that she will change her mind about everything. Chase raises his glass and she does nothing. She just continues to stare and as Chase lowers the glass (he doesn't even know what's in it) he wonders for the first time since Julia arrived if he's ready for this. The hot crowded suite is filled with men and women more like her than like Chase:

better-educated, more accomplished. The Anxious and the Arrived fill the room, dancing and flirting, giddy with the knowledge that the party is just getting started. They divide Chase and Julia, causing a large and impossible rift. Getting to Julia from where Chase stands will take real work and he's just not up to the task of pushing through all these bodies so he stays on the other side of the suite, where it occurs to him that it might always feel this way.

"She looked a little scared," Julia tells Hunter as they weave down the hushed cool hallway to the elevator. "I think the fall from the couch kind of threw her off."

"I thought the thing was longer," Hunter mutters. "I don't know. It was dark and that leather was slippery."

"Did you happen to tell her you were a pirate?" Julia asks on the ride down in the elevator.

"She wasn't too impressed with that either," Hunter says glumly. But then he lights up and says, "I feel optimistic anyway."

"*What do you do?*" Chase asks himself.

Julia looks at Chase quizzically.

"*What do I do?* That fucking guy's in my face about what do I do. You know what I do? I beat the shit out of punks who get out of line. That's what I do." Chase slaps Hunter's chest. "He's the pirate. I'm the teacher." Chase wraps his arms around Julia, clasping his hands over her breasts. "And Julia—my all-American girl—is a Master of the Universe." He kisses her flushed cheek. "Yes, she is. A little Master of the Universe. Aren't you, baby?"

"You're drunk," Julia mutters.

"No, I'm unemployed," Chase says quietly. "That's what I am."

Julia looks at him. "I'm not sure what you mean by unemployed."

"And once I leave here and get to Palo Alto, I'll be unemployed again," Chase tells her. "Because the teacher is also the fuckup!"

After a long silence Hunter says, "Dude, you can always temp."

And then suddenly they're in Julia's room and Michele calls and Chase doesn't answer and Michele leaves a message telling them to meet her at Curve. "I want to see this girl," Julia says, staring at Chase. He smiles nervously. "I want to see who I beat out." Hunter says that if this is where the night is heading then he is either going home or getting shitfaced with the chubby Goth chick at the Double Down or calling Brandi again. Chase ignores this and is relieved when Monique calls Julia's cell and wants to know why they left her at that awful Stanford party and Monique's hungry and wonders where everyone's going tonight and if they want to get something to eat. Chase knows a place. "Monique!" Hunter bellows and leads them from the room. And after a late meal at Aqua (that Julia pays for), Julia, Monique, Hunter, and Chase play roulette at the Mandalay casino and drink Cuba Libres (Monique insists) and Hunter leans over to Chase and tells him that Monique's brushing her leg against his again and it's driving him crazy. "That's me, dude," Chase tells him. Getting in the Mustang Julia kisses Chase and Hunter lets Monique get into the backseat first and she smiles slyly at him and Chase wonders for a moment if it's possible that they'll hook up—he hopes so. The four of them leave the Hard Rock—the top down, the warm wind strong tonight—and Julia holds Chase's hand and when Monique laughs at something Hunter says Chase sobers up and thinks: maybe it's all possible.

The four of them are waiting in line outside Curve when Michele comes outside and they all introduce themselves and Michele kisses Julia on the check as she takes her hand and leads them to the bouncer and says, "They're okay—they're mine." The bouncer nods and unfastens the velvet rope. Michele knows everyone working at Curve and tells a built Asian bartender in a leather vest with blond spiky hair to send someone over to table seven and the group dutifully follows Michele to a large semicircular booth in the corner of the room.

As predicted, Michele focuses on Julia, explaining her graduate work and what she wants to do for the immigrant women who can't speak the language but need health care and child care and help with all sorts of bureaucratic bullshit. The music is loud so she's talking over it and Chase can barely hear her but he's sure Michele mentions a PhD and Chase thinks he hears something about an MBA and definitely hears "UNLV" and "scholarship" and "completely paid for." Julia seems impressed enough to ask Michele questions about El Salvador and Michele tells Julia that she came to Vegas when she was nine and that she walked across a desert. At this point Michele throws her leg onto the table and slides her jeans up over her calf to show everyone the scars from the sidewinder that bit her.

"And some man I didn't even know sucked the venom out of my leg. I was this close to being dead. I was nine." She shakes her head, running her thumb over the condensation clinging to her glass.

The conversation hits a lull after that and no one says anything. Michele stares at Julia for an unusually long time but Julia doesn't notice and sips her frozen drink through a straw as Michele's eyes glaze over and then shift to Chase and she's still not focusing but Chase grins at her anyway and Michele smiles back weakly and then stops when she realizes Julia is watching this exchange. Michele doesn't know that Julia is holding Chase's hand under the table.

"So, Chase tells me you're a prostitute."

Julia says this in a normal tone and Chase can't ascertain if Michele heard Julia but he studies her face for a reaction. Michele's expression doesn't change and she casually shakes her head and leans forward and asks innocently, "What did you say, sweetie?"

Julia looks at Chase and he squeezes her hand—a small warning—and Julia relents and says to Michele, "So, Chase tells me you're in a movie?"

Relieved, Michele rolls her eyes and leans back. "I agreed to let a guy I kind of see follow me around and record what I do. His name is Bailey. Honestly, I don't really get it. I think he's kind of obsessed and uses it as an excuse to be near me. There are clearly a lot more interesting things to film than me doing laundry or calling my mother but, hey, it's his movie."

"Does this guy, Bailey, film you while you work?" Julia asks.

"Work?" Michele asks. "What do you mean?"

"When you're . . . giving massages?"

Michele glances at Chase and then turns to Julia and forces a grin. "No, sweetie."

"Why not?" Julia asks. "I would think that would be pretty entertaining."

"Well, not a lot of men are willing to be filmed in that setting." Michele's eyes move to Chase and before he can respond her eyes shift back to Julia.

"But are *you*?" Julia asks. "Willing to be filmed, I mean?"

Michele laughs and her hand lands on Julia's knee. "I'm not a hooker or a porn star so the answer is probably not."

"Chase seemed to think you'd get upset if I brought it up," Julia says.

"Do I seem upset?" Michele asks, lifting her arms up. "This girl is having a blast tonight."

"That's because she's high," Hunter says. "The girl isn't upset because the girl is high."

Monique watches Hunter while sipping her drink, suddenly conflicted about the night's prospects.

Chase stands up, glaring at Hunter, who simply shakes his head at him. Chase asks Hunter to go to the men's room with him, and Hunter—recognizing the tension he has caused at the table—nods, slides out of the booth, and follows Chase.

Standing next to Hunter at the urinal Chase tells him, "I'm a little freaked out and you're not helping."

"Your past and future side by side—is that it?" Hunter asks.

Chase realizes he can't urinate standing next to Hunter.

"Look," Hunter says, "you're fine. Julia's just cutting her down. If you'd relax a little bit it's actually kind of fun to watch."

"What exactly is fun to watch?" Chase asks.

"Michele squirming around these women who are actually out in the world doing something." Hunter spits into the urinal and shakes his dick off before zipping up.

"Why do I feel the same way?" Chase asks.

"Because you're drunk and you're scared because you're about to leave Vegas, dude."

"How drunk do you think I am right now?"

"I think you're pretty drunk—at least as drunk as I am." Hunter smiles. "But Monique smells nice. Monique keeps rubbing her leg up against me."

"That was me, dude. "

"Monique sobers me up." His voice trails off. "I want to dance with Monique, the freak, so unique, so chic . . ."

Ice is on East Harmon between Paradise and the Strip and Michele knows all the right people so they don't have to wait in line.

"It's very impressive that you can get everyone in to all of these places," Julia says.

Michele accepts this as a compliment. "Vegas is really small if you live here. It just seems bigger when you visit."

Staring at girls dancing inside elevated cages, the five of them are pressed together at the bar and can't hear one another over the music and Julia gently pulls Chase's head down and yells into his ear that she and Monique are going to the restroom. Hunter stares sadly at Monique as she leaves and seems to realize that somehow he's blown it (she has been frozen since the remark Hunter made at Curve about Michele being high) and Chase suddenly looks around and realizes that Michele isn't

with them anymore. Chase asks Hunter where Michele went and
Hunter grimaces and shakes his head and when somebody bumps
into Chase he's surprised—and saddened—that it's not her.

It's after three and Chase is seriously buzzed. They all are. He
can barely hear Hunter mumbling something in his ear over the
din of conversations in Hookah Lounge. No one wanted to go
back to the Hard Rock after leaving Ice and they had been standing around in the parking lot when Monique got a call from the
dark-skinned guy who had grabbed Chase's wrist at the party
on the fake beach. The guy and some of Julia's business school
friends wanted to meet up with Monique and when Monique
mentioned this after clicking off, Hunter yelled out "Conflict
of interest!" and started making this crude siren sound over and
over yelling "Conflict of interest!" Chase was surprised to see
Monique laughing and when she asked if anyone knew a good
place to just chill, Chase hesitated and then from behind him
he heard someone say, "I know a place." It was Michele.

But Hookah Lounge is too dark and Chase doesn't know
any of the guys sitting with them grouped around a series of low
tables. Michele is across from Chase and whenever they make
eye contact Chase keeps looking away, focusing on Hunter who
is sitting slightly apart from the group, glaring at the two guys
from Wharton at whom he mumbled "cockblockers" when they
claimed the hassocks on either side of Monique. Michele has
sunk deep into a couch, looking small and sipping a Moroccan
beer. Julia leans tiredly in to Chase.

The ambient music drifting through Hookah Lounge
means Chase can hear voices though he wishes he couldn't

because somehow Michele is in the center of things. She inches forward, out from the darkness into the blurred orange glow of recessed light directly overhead. Looking around the circle Chase notices that everyone is staring at Michele. She's the only one any of them can see clearly: her face shiny with traces of body glitter on her cheeks and forehead, the crucifix stuck to her chest with sweat. She's talking about real estate even though Michele knows nothing about real estate. But she's saying she does because one of the guys—short, brown-skinned, from New York, works at Goldman—had asked her with lascivious interest what she did and Michele's answer was: "I wear a lot of hats."

"What does that mean?" he asks, leaning closer, actually breathing heavily. "Are you, like, a hat model?"

The urge to leave overwhelms Chase when he hears Michele mention "investment properties" and at that point the other conversations wind down and Chase wants to tell Michele to shut the fuck up. She keeps going but the vibe is off now and Michele seems somehow unaware of this. Goldman understands that this girl is a poseur: he sits perfectly still, considering Michele, plotting his next move. He still wants to fuck her (that vibe isn't off) but he also knows she's probably full of crap and he's wondering just how far he'll go tonight.

"Like Ghost Bar at the Palms, only a little more sophisticated," Michele says.

"What is?" Goldman asks, still staring.

"The development," Michele says blithely.

"*Your* development?" Goldman can't mask his incredulity. He looks around at the group to make sure people are watching this.

"It's not my development *per se*. I'm just in on a lot of aspects. You have to be. There are a lot of opportunities here. If you lived here you'd know."

"Right."

"It's a total sellers market here."

"Is it?" Goldman asks.

Monique looks quickly at the guy next to her, a faint smile on her face.

"Hey, what are you getting your PhD in again?" Monique asks Michele, trying to move the conversation in a different direction.

"Women's health."

"And . . . real estate?" Goldman asks.

"And . . . cage dancing," Hunter says.

"I think that's really impressive," Monique says, sounding like she means it.

Michele shrugs. "I like to have lots of iron in the fire, so to speak."

There's silence. Michele meant to say "irons." But it's past that now.

"Who's financing your . . . property?" Goldman asks, then adds, *"per se?"*

"Wells Fargo," Michele says. "They're putting a lot of it up. We're still working on some things."

"Wells *Fargo?*" Goldman asks. "Wells Fargo is putting a lot of it up? It's investing in this property? Here? In Vegas?"

Michele nods, her face completely flushed. Nervously she tucks some hair behind her ear and crosses her legs, a foot twitching wildly. Chase stares at her pedicure—white tips, French-style—and the Jimmy Choos with thin leather straps that wrap around her smooth, toned calves. Michele loves being the center of attention but right now she's only the entertainment—a cartoon.

"Okay, what do you *really* do?" Goldman asks, again leaning forward in his chair, only inches from her, "because now I'm actually curious. I think we all are."

"What do *you* really do?" Michele counters.

Goldman sits perfectly still with his eyes locked on Michele. "The funny thing is," he says, head tilted, "Wells is a client of ours." He wraps a thick hand around Michele's knee. "And as of two years ago, they don't do real estate in Nevada." He pats her knee and removes his hand. "So why don't you try again."

Chase is barely aware of Julia squeezing his hand.

Michele: weak smile, eyes locked on Goldman's.

"You know—" Michele starts and stops. "Maybe it was another bank, we've got so many people it's impossible keeping track . . ." Michele trails off, mutters something about Saturn.

Chase cringes, closes his eyes, and hopes no one heard, and just as he's about to say something to change the subject it's too late.

"Your *what?*" Goldman grins.

"It may be Bank of America and not Wells and there are other investors and all sorts of zoning issues and specs to work out and nothing about it is easy—and it's not supposed to be. It's a completely transitional time and a structural change and it wears on you but it's all about growth."

"What is?" Goldman asks. "What in the fuck are you talking about, girl?"

"Tell me," Michele leans toward Goldman for the first time. "What year were you born?"

He tells her 1977.

She considers this. "You're okay. I'm '81 and I'm *not* okay. My Saturn is in return, which can mean drudgery. Which means it takes time and it's a growth period—only it's drawn out so you feel fatigued and exhausted and depressed a lot of the time . . . unless you manage it. And most people don't. I do. You have to plan and adjust and work through it. Everything is about change and going through the process of living in an entirely different way."

Goldman nods with a mock-serious expression. There is nothing Chase can do now. No one says anything. Everyone watches Michele.

After a long silence Goldman rests his hand on Michele's knee.

"If you're going to make up some shit about what you do—all your 'business' and 'development plans'—don't be doing it with this group," he says. "I don't give a damn where your Saturn is. Just don't fuck with this group." Goldman is now glaring at her. After an icy silence the guy grins and squeezes Michele's knee. "But you could definitely be selling something." He removes his hand and slides his Centurion card across the table, then falls back in his chair, laughing and giving the pound to the other guys around the table. Michele starts to ask Goldman a question but catches herself and glances at Chase, who can't mask the sadness in his expression. She winks at him and reaches for her drink and brings it to her lips and only when she tips it back does she realize the glass is empty.

* * *

And then the five of them are standing in a parking lot. Julia and Monique try to keep their hair in place but the hot wind is too strong and won't allow it. Michele doesn't care about her hair and stands apart from them checking her cell and Chase catches her glancing up at Julia and then averting her eyes.

"Ready?" Julia has his hand.

"Can I borrow him for a second?" Michele asks Julia.

Julia nods but Michele has already pulled Chase's hand from Julia's and is walking Chase back to the entrance of Hookah Lounge.

"I've got to go to this guy's house tonight," Michele says.

"Another party in the Lakes? You need me to drive? Are you kidding?"

Michele closes her eyes for a long time and then remembers to open them. "Come by later and I'll give you the rest of your money."

Chase is too tired to respond.

"You're leaving, Chase." Michele sighs. "I can't believe you're doing this to me."

Chase laughs but wants to touch the side of her face. He wants to brush the hair from her eyes. And he would if Julia weren't watching. Chase realizes he also wants to walk Michele to the Mustang and drive her wherever she needs to go. He wants to sit outside the house in the Lakes and turn the music up and smoke a cigarette and wait for her—which is what it has always been about: waiting for her. Chase wants to go with Michele back to the suite on the twenty-second floor of the Palace and take off his shoes and stand at the window overlooking the Strip while she showers, the television on, room service on the way, Hunter showing up drunk and making them all laugh. Chase realizes that he should want to go back to the Hard Rock with Julia and not with Michele. So he doesn't stand with Michele too long and he doesn't touch her hair. Instead, he shoves his hands in his pockets and cuts the conversation short.

"I realized two things tonight," Michele says.

"What?"

"The first thing is that your girlfriend is fucking beautiful."

"Don't do this tonight."

But Michele isn't listening. "The second thing I realized"—Michele looks away and her lips are trembling and then she looks back at him—"is that I'm not loved . . ." Chase knows what she's going to say next. Michele grabs his face and turns it toward her and squeezes it. ". . . by anyone."

It takes a minute before Chase realizes that Julia is watching them.

It was summer again. The girls, Carly and Michele, had summer school then one more year before they graduated. Chase, Hunter, and Bailey had two years left and summer school as well. They were all relieved that it was vacation but three weeks lay ahead with nothing to do before summer classes started. The heat was insane and for that stretch they would go outside only at the end of the day and lie around Bailey's pool or drive out to Red Rock Canyon and sit on the edge of the striped rocks drinking Coronas, smoking marijuana, letting the drug wash over them. They were all bored and dared each other to do various things. For instance, they would play the Pain Game. They watched as Bailey held a lighter under his hand, the flame licking his palm as he counted out loud until his face was red and everyone could smell his skin burning and he screamed when he got to twenty-seven. Bailey and Hunter and Chase were good at this game because Hunter did construction work for his father and Bailey lifted weights all the time and Chase's hands were callused from stretching canvases and painting all day. The girls felt shut out of the Pain Game so suggestions for other games were made: the Lust Game or the Rage Game or the Fear Game, which finally convinced Michele and Carly to play. They decided to start with Fear.

"This game rocks," Carly said as she hung from the edge of the waterslide tower at Wet 'n Wild, drunk, her thin body swinging three stories up in the hot wind that rolled across the desert while the kids in line gawked and cheered her on and the boy working there stood frozen, with no idea what to do. No one could believe what Carly was doing and Chase got pissed at her later and threatened to tell their mom and that's when Carly got scared and apologized and since no one wanted to try and top Carly's stunt (she'd won!) the Fear Game ended and the Lust Game was about to begin. But Carly and Michele had friends who wanted to play the Lust Game (friends who had things for Hunter and Bailey and Chase) and with others involved the interest in the game—for the girls—stopped abruptly. And so everyone—Chase and Carly and Michele and Hunter and Bailey—agreed that whatever game they played should include only the five of them and no outsiders. When that decision was made Chase had a sense that things were getting out of control.

So Lust was skipped (the boys were disappointed) and they moved directly to the Insult Game. Anonymous notes were written to one another with the goal of insulting the recipient so harshly *that he or she had no choice but to quit the game—it would be proof that some boundaries could be crossed. The winner would be the one who cared the least about what was said about him or her.*

Chase was the first victim.

According to Hunter or Bailey or Carly or Michele: Chase was too skinny and his nose was too small for his face and his neck was too long—almost swanlike, almost effeminate—and he was unable to do anything about his hair and he should just shave it but his head was too large and he'd look even worse if he did so he was fucked either way. He was too serious. He was too intense. He was hard up and never got laid and would likely end up paying for it, though—according to one of the anonymous notes relaying the insults—Carly might give it up to him if she were drunk enough because that's what Carly did: she got fucking wasted and turned into a ghetto-ho slutbag who once sucked three guys off at a party and they were all black and members of the West Side Crips and none of them wore condoms and she begged them to finish her off in the ass and they laughed at her as they threw her out of their Cadillac convertible naked and crying onto her front lawn—did anyone remember that night? Yeah, if that's your sister, dude, how do you think you add up?

According to the group Chase was a freak and a loser. He was someone whose so-called art sucked ass. Everyone thought his wigger ways were bullshit. And it was abnormal that he spent all that time on the west side playing basketball with the black guys who thought he was as much of a geek as everyone else did. And all the tacky murals he painted in the ghetto and that got written about in the local papers were fruity and full of shit. And the truth remained: he was self-absorbed and delusional if he thought he'd get to New York and sell a single painting, much less make it as an artist. Instead, Chase would end up teaching high school at forty and luring little sluts like his sister back to his apartment by offering to paint them but he would just end up getting them drunk and stoned, anything to get them nude.

Chase never cracked. He sat with Bailey late one night at Del Taco and they looked at each other for a long time without speaking. They had decided to meet because things were getting pretty intense. Bailey was convinced that Chase would be the one most affected by the game. But Chase wasn't.

"Nothing, dude. I swear."

Bailey had a stupid grin on his face. He didn't believe Chase. "Nothing?"

"Not a thing. Nada. You're all losers anyway, so what's going to be said that'll affect me?"

"Look me in the eye and tell me you're not bothered."

Chase did so without hesitation.

"Want to know who wrote what?" Bailey asked.

"Doesn't matter," Chase said.

"It might."

"I don't care."

"It would matter to me."

"It's all a game," Chase said. "Isn't that the point? That once I start caring who said what then I'm affected and then I lose? But honestly I don't care."

"This is for real," Bailey argued. "This isn't a game anymore." He paused. "You know who thinks your art sucks?"

Chase thought about it for a moment. "You?"

Bailey shook his head. *"I love your shit. I'm trying stuff and then I look at yours and I stop because what's the point? I'll never be that good."*

Chase suddenly wanted the conversation to stop. *"I don't care, Bailey. I really don't."*

"Michele."

"Please."

"She thinks you're a fraud. She says you copy shit from books and magazines and what you don't steal and claim as your own is shit and the whole black and Mexican and white unity theme you've got going on is weak and no one's feeling it and the one you did at Doolittle that was in the paper is like comic book art that doesn't move anyone. She was the one who went off on you the most." Bailey paused.

Chase shrugged and Bailey grinned.

"Wow." Bailey was really impressed.

"Nada. Unaffected."

"Even the part about your work being totally lame?" Bailey asked. "That didn't get you even a little?"

Later that night Chase wrote an anonymous note to Michele because she was the next victim. It was brief and vicious and the words came with a certainty and clarity that was so strong Chase almost couldn't type them. What Chase wrote about Michele he would regret telling her as long as he knew her and she would most likely never forgive any of them. The game had overtaken him— it was too powerful. Chase wrote: You are not loved by anyone. Not by your drunk mother who sent you here to Vegas to live with your clinically depressed grandmother or by anyone who thinks they know you and calls you a friend or by Bailey who thinks you give lousy head (but at least you swallow) or by Carly who thinks you're pathetic and doesn't have the heart to tell you to just GO AWAY or by Chase who thinks you're a slut and a bad influence on his sister. No matter how many hours you spend at Chase and Carly's house asking their mother if there's anything else she wants done—doing anything that will keep you near them in their home with their lawn and their view and their pool and trying desperately to BE like them—it will NEVER happen. That's the trick here that you don't see. The whole thing is set up to keep you wanting what you can't have and what you can't become until it drives you away or makes you kill yourself. You're lucky you're beautiful, Michele, because without that you'd be nothing. You wouldn't exist. And beauty always fades. So you're fucked either way.

7

Everyone is dreading summer. It's still only June and no one can believe that for eight days in a row the temperature has topped a hundred degrees. The heat wave is the lead story on the news every night because the heat has driven the coyotes down from the hills looking for water and food. The news carries warnings about the coyotes and people are told not to leave garbage out and to keep an eye on their children and pets. But no one seems to listen to the warnings. Dogs and cats vanish in epidemic numbers. A three-year-old Mexican boy playing with his sister on his second day in Vegas (after being sent from Camarillo by his stepfather to live with his mother) was attacked in the backyard of his mother's Summerlin home. He was found by his sister near a wall surrounding their backyard, devoured: a mound of bones, shredded clothing, a tiny pair of blood-soaked Nikes.

"Is she still here?"
       "Yes."

Michele smells like apples, which means she has appointments this morning. She runs her fingers through her damp hair,
checking her image in the rearview. Traffic is clogged on East
Charleston. It's seven-thirty and it's Thursday. Julia was going
to leave with everyone else from the National Black MBA Conference but decided to stay. She had money saved from her work
at JPMorgan and since Chase and she both loved the Hard Rock
they spent their extra days in the hotel and on the fake beach
and playing roulette and watching pay-per-view porn. But this
morning Chase left Julia in the room at the Hard Rock to meet
Michele, who has errands to run and two appointments before
noon.

Chase and Michele are at a Public Storage on East Charleston, walking the hot and narrow concrete hallway to locker
number 3114. Every few days since Michele and Bailey started
hiring girls to work out of the Sun King suite at the Palace,
they store their cash in one Public Storage location and then
move it to another: from Industrial Road to Henderson to East
Charleston. Today is one of those days. Bailey is in Cabo and
there is too much money, already, for Michele to feel safe moving it alone. It's all cash because it's "the best way" now, especially this summer, with the huge spike in earnings. When it was
just Bailey and Michele—when they started "it" four years ago
(when Michele started accepting money for massages with "extras")—it was easier to keep the money in shared bank accounts
because deposits and balances were never high enough to "alert"
the IRS. The "plan" is: until they can figure out the "smartest way"
to pour the money into "other ventures," they will store the cash

in red canvas bags and bury them beneath piles of clothes like
the one Michele is now kneeling over on the concrete floor. The
cash is wrapped in cellophane bags and held together with thick
rubber bands. Michele peels one stack of bills open and counts
out five thousand and then puts the cash in her purse. She re-
wraps the money and places it back in the red canvas bag.

"What are you doing with that?" Chase asks.

"I'm depositing this into my account because this is mine,"
Michele says.

"But isn't it also Bailey's?" Chase asks. "What are you doing, Michele?"

They drive to the Strip.

Michele will open a savings account tomorrow. This will
be her second account. The other account is in San Diego.
Bailey doesn't know about either account. Bailey knows only
about the account the two of them have always shared—the
one from the very beginning—along with a mutual fund in his
father's name that they contribute to and occasionally draw
from. Bailey doesn't know that Michele is keeping more from
each appointment. Bailey doesn't know that Michele books
more appointments than she acknowledges. Bailey does not
know about all of this extra money. But what does it matter?
Bailey's not going anywhere. Bailey wants to direct movies yet
won't apply to film school. Bailey wants to open a chill cocktail
lounge but doesn't want to bother managing it.

They pass Treasure Island and Hunter's ship is idling and
dark and Chase glances at it as if it means something. Michele
is saying she sees a window and it's fluid but closing fast. Chase
tries not to picture the watery dark hole that's sucking in everything around them even while Michele keeps insisting this

summer is *it*. Chase can't ask what "it" means because Michele's talking too fast and he's feeling queasy and Chase simply nods. "You look so scared, Chase," Michele says. She touches his thigh and stops talking. But then she says, "They want forty-two down for the Hills house and now I've got twice that."

His mother's house—the one they had to move to when Chase was fifteen—is small and down the rim and out of sight from the Green Valley house he grew up in. Beverly Way: one floor instead of two, two bedrooms instead of three, no pool. It lies hidden in the late-afternoon shadows of the Strip. It was the kind of street where couples fought violently and at night you heard loud thumping hip-hop and sirens wailing across the desert and the echoes of helicopters whirling in the dark sky above, their searchlights aimed at kids drag-racing, tearing through the smooth wide boulevards. It was the kind of place where Chase always felt he needed to be prepared. And he still feels that way as he turns onto the gray street lined with pick-up trucks and motorcycles, the occasional used Oldsmobile, the ancient Cadillacs. Cheap boats sit on trailers their owners take to Lake Mead on weekends. Trash cans are knocked over and garbage is strewn across dirty yellow lawns. Rusted car parts and porcelain toilets have been left discarded in the brown weeds of an empty lot. Someone spray-painted a white swastika on a palm tree across the street from his mother's house a year ago and it's still there.

Julia tells Chase to relax and lets out a huge sigh when she says it again. She massages his hands, which are gripping the steering wheel too tightly.

"Where is it?" Julia asks, looking over the row of ranch-style houses.

Chase points out the latest version of the Sahara Hotel & Casino marquee, with its vaguely Arabic lettering and the two neon camels facing away from each other under the words. The marquee displays a kaleidoscope of red, white, and blue bulbs listing concert dates and the names of performers, and the colors actually spill onto the edge of his mother's lawn. Gigantic orange numbers tell the time and temperature (5:34; 97) and a booming garbled voice invites people to visit the NASCAR café inside.

"Listen." Chase holds up a hand.

"What is that?" Julia asks.

"Electrical currents."

The asphalt feels soft from baking in the sun all day and as he shields his eyes from the wind Chase looks up at the giant marquee.

"With all the other noise it's not so bad, but when it's quiet you really notice."

Julia nods when he asks her if she's feeling it. She extends her hand toward the marquee and closes one eye and Chase can tell from the shadow stretching across Julia's face that the sign blocks out the sun completely.

His mother's house is minimally nicer than the rest of the generic boxes that line Beverly: the grass is green and wet and a cobblestone walkway stretches from the sidewalk to the front door. In the driveway sits the red Subaru station wagon that his mother has had since Chase was a kid. It's missing a hubcap and duct tape keeps a sheet of plastic in place where a window used to be before a neighborhood kid shot it out with a paintball gun, remnants of the blue paint still visible on the door. On the porch overlooking the street, two white wicker chairs sit beneath wind chimes, a small table between them. During the summer his mother and Carly used to share Marlboro Lights and give each other manicures on the porch and watch the numbers on the Sahara sign change, and when midnight came Carly would sing along to the Pink Floyd record that she always played until their mother finished her gin and went to bed.

The man lounging on the couch sits up quickly and grabs a T-shirt, pulling it over his head when he hears Chase and Julia walk in.

"Your mother's getting cigarettes. She'll be back." Edward seems more at ease in the house on Beverly than he did the last time Chase saw him here.

"Why aren't you getting them?" Chase asks.

"I quit." Edward grins.

Edward is in his late forties and has tan muscular arms covered with murky tattoos. He lives down the street in a yellow house that is the same color as his thinning hair. He wears a black T-shirt with the words WELCOME TO AMERICA: NOW SPEAK ENGLISH written in fat white letters across his chest. Chase introduces Edward to Julia but he doesn't want to spend too much time in the house after Edward glances quickly at Julia's breasts and lowers his eyes to the silver stud in her navel and then glances back to Chase. Edward's a mechanic who does odd jobs around the neighborhood and talks a lot about leaving Vegas for Idaho or Montana where he can fish and hunt (he actually tells people this), and since Edward's shirt had been off when they came in it occurs to Chase that he might still be sleeping with his mother.

"You should come up for the Fourth," Edward says as Chase and Julia leave the room. "It'd mean a lot to your mom."

"So you've met the boyfriend," Chase tells Julia when he closes the door to his bedroom. His mother has cleaned it recently because mail addressed to Chase sits on his desk along with an article she clipped from the *Review Journal* about First Fridays, a monthly art fair downtown. And piled on his drafting table is a stack of old notebooks from high school. His mother left a cardboard box and a Hefty bag next to the table because she wants Chase to decide which ones to keep and which ones to throw out. Julia sits on the bed and starts to flip through one of the notebooks and Chase briefly considers asking her not to. Casino chips—the reason Chase is at the house on Beverly Way today—are lined up along Chase's dresser. The chips confirm his fears: they're worthless. Five $100 chips from the Dunes, three $50 chips from the Hacienda, and a $500 chip from the Sands. He can recall the demolition of each casino—having watched the Hacienda and the Sands with his sister and Michele and the Dunes with his father, who had been extremely drunk that afternoon. Only the Stardust chip is worth anything: burnt orange and white around a gold center with the Stardust logo and its value: $500. Chase's grandmother told him that Tony Bennett sat at the blackjack table with her when she won that chip. Chase decides to leave it for now.

*   *   *

Chase's grandmother—his father's mother—followed her son and his wife to Vegas from Illinois and lived alone in a small house near Nellis Air Force Base and stayed in Vegas even after her son left his family behind for California twenty years ago. She liked to drink martinis and play bingo at Sam's Town. She would catch the shuttle in the morning, spend the day there. Chase's mother would get a call from one of his grandmother's friends to come pick her up because she'd had too much to drink and passed out on the couch in the lobby. Chase's grandmother would hand over to her daughter-in-law the casino chips she'd won, with instructions to give the chips to Chase and Carly for birthdays and Christmas, for high school and college graduations. "Security," his grandmother would tell Chase. "Whenever you come home you'll always have a little security." She would joke that it was his inheritance, since her worthless son was blowing all of the money he made on bimbos in a beachfront house in Malibu. Chase's mom has been dispensing the chips since his grandmother died. When Chase still lived in the house on Beverly Way he would sometimes wake up to find a small stack of chips on his dresser or next to the bathroom sink or in an empty cereal bowl in the kitchen. Next to the chips there would always be a note with a smiley face and nothing else.

Julia skims through a box of old notebooks and sketch pads and finds a Polaroid of Chase at sixteen wearing jeans and no shirt and flexing West Side Vegas Crips gang signs, a black skullcap on his head. "It's a pretty convincing pose," Julia says before reading a passage from one of his poetry journals: "*SMACK-crack! motherfucker break your back, wannabe a star, far, is not where you're going—*"

"Let's not do this now," Chase interrupts.

Julia solemnly turns the page.

Chase peers out the window at the wilted palm tree across the street and the swastika wrapped around its trunk.

"She just doesn't look like a hooker," Julia says, staring at a Polaroid of Michele. "Did you take these?" She's holding a small stack of pictures that Chase shot of Michele when they were in high school. In most of them Michele is wearing only a bra and panties.

"I drew from them."

"I'm sure."

"She liked to show off."

"Did you sleep with her?"

"What?"

"Did you have sex with her? When you were in high school?"

Chase doesn't say anything.

"Well that answers that," Julia says. "Have you had sex with her since high school?"

"No."

"And you never loved her?"

Chase hesitates. "No."

"So you just fucked her?" Julia flinches.

"Yes."

"And it meant nothing?"

"Maybe it meant something to her."

"But not to you, though."

"I don't know what it meant, Julia."

"Why not, Chase?"

"Look, we just slept together for like a month and we did a lot of shit we probably shouldn't have and then it stopped when I went to college and met you."

"And you didn't want her to be your girlfriend?"

Chase shrugs.

Julia stares at another Polaroid. "She's beautiful. She's funny. Why wouldn't you want her to be your girlfriend?"

"Because there was nothing there, Julia."

"But I think there was," Julia says.

When Chase flicks the light switch in his mother's room the television comes on, too. Something about that makes him sad, as does the wooden crucifix hanging over her bed. In the top drawer of a filing cabinet in his mother's closet is a small black box. In it is a white gold diamond engagement ring that his mother said was appraised at $11,000 and was left to Chase by his grandmother when she died. He examines it and decides that it might be something Julia would like. It would be the kind of ring that she would choose. The top of his mother's dresser is mostly lined with framed pictures of Carly and Chase, though there's a small black-and-white photograph of his mother with her parents when she was a little girl in Indiana. The photo that he hates the most is of the three of them—Carly, their mother, and Chase—standing in the backyard of the Green Valley house. Chase never knew what his mother liked about the photo or why she bothered to frame it (expensively) and keep it on her dresser because all of them are wearing sunglasses and Chase holds a basketball while his mother drinks from a can of Diet Coke and Carly, hungover, turns away from the camera. Chase realizes the reason he hates the picture is that he can't remember who took it. Outside his mother's window, next door, the neighbor's son stands in the front yard spraying two pit bulls with a hose as the dogs bark wildly and try to catch the water with their snapping jaws.

His mother meets them on the sidewalk in front of the yard holding a bag of groceries. She kisses his cheek. Chase smiles as his mother and Julia hug. His mother removes her sunglasses and offers them each a Snapple. Chase goes through the motions: he tells her the house looks great because he knows that's what she wants to hear. But his mother wants a lot of things. She wants the kids to stop drag-racing down Beverly. She wants the neighbors to remove the discarded sinks and the couch cushions from their yellow lawns. She wants the helicopters to stop flying low over the neighborhood. She wants the wrinkles and the dark circles under her eyes to disappear. She wants the blond dye in her hair to last longer and look more natural than it does. She wants the large sloping lawn she had back in Green Valley. She wants to tear down the Sahara marquee. She wants her husband to come back from Malibu. She wants Chase to help her.

"Edward's sitting on his ass again," Chase says.

"Eddie just bought the time-share in Idaho."

It makes Chase sad that he's supposed to be impressed. "I thought he was aiming for Montana."

His mother suddenly looks confused. "Wait—it might have been Montana."

"Are you gonna go with him?"

"Is there any way you two would come up for the Fourth?"

"We'll see," Chase says, thinking automatically: no way. "So are you moving up there with him?"

His mother avoids the question again and asks if they want to come inside and get something to drink but Chase feels anxious and is ready to leave—he feels trapped. It's the stale cigarette smoke clinging to the walls and the illegally watered lawn and all the memories of the two years before he left the house on Beverly. He tells his mother that they just stopped by so Julia could say hi. When they're getting in the Mustang, the pale sun swollen and the air heavy, his mother wheels around and calls out to him.

"Some boys came by the other day looking for you."

Julia's getting a massage when Michele calls Chase's cell. She says she needs to see him. Chase is lying on the bed in the room at the Hard Rock trying to sleep. He tells her he can't. He vaguely mentions something about dinner plans.

"I'm bleeding," Michele says.

Chase used to sit with Michele at her grandmother's house when Michele was in bed because she was too weak to get up. She would get terrible migraines. Nosebleeds spurted out of her. Menstrual cycles wouldn't end. Chase changed the sheets and then he'd wash and bleach them. Chase would walk Michele to the bathroom and hold her as she sat on the toilet. He would tell her some lame joke or recent gossip about celebrities to make her laugh. These memories harden him.

"I'm sure the coke helps."

"I gave that shit up," Michele says.

"Did you give up going to school, too?" Chase asks. He can't control it. "Don't you have some kind of comprehensive exam this week?"

"It's tomorrow."

When Chase starts laughing, Michele screams, "I postponed it, fucker."

"You can do that?" Chase asks. "You can postpone—"

"I mean I will."

"When are you going to do it, Michele?" Chase yells. "The test is tomorrow."

"I'm taking a leave of absence," she finally admits in a small voice.

"A leave of absence," Chase shouts. "A leave of absence from what?"

"I'll go back in the fall or maybe winter."

"That's fucking great," Chase mutters. "You're fucking miserable."

"You treat me like shit," she says.

"How did it go last night?" Chase asks because when he left her last night, outside of Hookah Lounge, Michele was a mess. And despite Chase's protests, Michele was on her way to a man's house. "Did you actually go?" Chase asks.

"Suddenly this matters to you?" She's sobbing.

"Shouldn't it?"

She laughs harshly through the sobs and then says, "I don't remember, Chase."

Chase feels his chest clench and he closes his eyes. He might cry; he might not.

"Seriously Chase, please grow the fuck up," she says, after the crying subsides, and then in a sarcastic tone, "Well, supposedly I was just so coked to the gills, right? How could I remember anything? According to Hunter I was doing so much coke—supposedly because I was so quote-unquote upset about your little girlfriend—that, of course, I probably just passed out, so who knows what he did to me."

"Jesus, Michele."

"You want to know the truth, Chase?"

"You don't know what the truth is anymore, Michele."

"The nice bald man with the twin daughters in Colorado laid out three thousand dollars and begged poor little coked-up Michele—who was so upset about Chase's girlfriend being in town—to let him go down on her because he loved her shaved little pussy because that really does it for him and that's about as far as it went." She pauses. "And you know it, Chase, so why do you make me tell you the same damn story every time?"

A wind and dust advisory is issued that night. Part of the Strip—from Spring Mountain to Flamingo Road—is closed when pieces of the Venetian sign tear loose just before midnight. Palm fronds scratch against the window of Julia's room. In the morning there's a message on Chase's cell. Michele called at three: the wind out at Bailey's house up in the hills would not fucking stop and it was such a completely bad sign and there were positive and negative ions in the atmosphere and when the wind was like this the ratios were distorted and the fragile balance in the atmosphere was thrown off and it made everyone insane and she couldn't help it she was completely wired and just so stressed these days and she was actually a little scared for Chase because she loved him and didn't he think there were more sirens and police helicopters than usual? She was wide awake and had just scrubbed Bailey's bathtub and done three loads of laundry and driven to the Hills in Summerlin where they had broken ground on the house already. And there were suddenly all of these new girls with appointments at the suite all night and she wanted Chase to know that she had tons of money for him and that he could come and get whatever he wanted whenever he wanted it and to sleep tight and not panic even if there were demons scratching at the door because sleeping makes them go away.

Julia is sleeping. Chase stands outside on the balcony under a gray morning sky. He comes out onto the balcony the first time the cell vibrates. The Hard Rock beach: brief stretches of sand punctuated with palms and green umbrellas and purple chaises around a jigsaw-shaped pool. It looks dirty when it's empty. He turns away. Only Julia's head is visible under the covers because the air-conditioning Chase likes makes the room too cold for her. Clothes from bebe and Ann Taylor—pastel work shirts and several different pairs of black slacks she tried on and decided against—are slung over chairs everywhere. Chase checks the airline's Web site to see if Julia's flight is on time, hunched over Julia's laptop, which sits on the table near the window,

surrounded by name tags and a Hermès leather-bound notebook and her Palm Pilot and a half-empty wineglass and the
copy of *The Wall Street Journal* Chase bought for her in the
shop downstairs that morning and a stack of her résumés. She
used thick paper with bold print. He runs a finger over the raised
black lettering: her name, NYU, Stanford.

What no one who reads the résumé will see is the row house
in the North Philadelphia neighborhood where kids walk pit bulls
off leashes and empty vials are wedged between sidewalk cracks
and a burned-out television sits for a month on the strip of high
grass in front of the neighbors' house and transvestite prostitutes
rummage through her mother's garden to steal strawberries and
bell peppers and men with lazy eyes and nappy hair show up
unannounced at the front door asking for money because the
word spread that Julia's house was where they gave out food.

His eyes scan the table again: her business card; Stanford;
her résumé, thick paper, bold print, NYU; bebe tops; Hermès
bag; Palm Pilot; the *Journal*. His cell keeps vibrating and he
gazes at the number and it's local and he steps back onto the
balcony and writes the directions on an ATM receipt. It's just
after six in the morning and even though Chase knows he's
pushing it he agrees to do the drive. He slips out of the room
and slides the DO NOT DISTURB sign on the doorknob, and manages to get back to Julia's room before she's awake.

Julia's flight is leaving on time so Chase is driving too fast. He'd
like to slow down, take his time. He feels the same way every
time Julia leaves him, every time she's come to Vegas in the past
five years, every ride he's given her to McCarran. He wants Julia

to stay. He'd like to leave with her or skip the flight and drive her all the way to California.

"Remember when I used to fly home and you'd come with me to La Guardia?"

He's thinking of New York. He's thinking about when they were in college. His voice is shaky. He's suddenly nineteen and in New York and their first summer apart lies ahead and that same panic grips him now and he's so sure that he'll lose her. Tears well up in his eyes, as they did then, and he looks away. She touches his cheek, which makes it worse.

"It's June," she says. "You'll be there in less than a month."

Chase takes Maryland Parkway until it hits Boulder Highway and when he passes the Hard Rock he gets caught gazing at the giant electric guitar after reading the third of four two-way messages from girls he's never met who need rides at three and seven. He runs a red light at the intersection. Horns blare and a car swerves. He checks the rearview. No one hit anyone so he keeps going. He turns at Sahara, which takes him to Paradise and then to the Strip, and he pulls in to the Palace and slows down and watches the blond kid, the valet, start toward the Mustang. The radio is on and the Rolling Stones are singing "Gimme Shelter" and Chase leaves the volume turned up and sits in the car. The valet doesn't know what to do and finally opts for knocking on the window and asking, "Sir?"

His cell rings and he squints to see the display.

"Hey."

"Hey."

"Where are you?"

"Driving."

"It's a busy day," Bailey says, a tense energy in his voice.

Bailey texts Chase the information. Bailey says the girls will meet Chase at the suite. Bailey tells Chase to just go from there.

"Where?" Chase asks and suddenly realizes it doesn't make a difference. "Oh, yeah."

"We owe you some money," Bailey says. "For Rachel."

"Michele got me."

A beat of silence. "Right." Bailey can't mask his uncertainty. "How much again?"

"I don't know. Didn't count it."

"Whatever, dude. Right. You didn't count it. Jesus, Chase."

"Bailey—"

"I'll just ask Michele. I'm sure *she* counted it."

Chase ignores the DO NOT DISTURB sign and pounds on the door of the Sun King suite on the twenty-second floor. A girl— eighteen or nineteen—finally opens it, wearing a tight pair of gray cotton short-shorts and a tank top that reads STAY HIGH. *Pimp My Ride* is on the TV in the background. The room is a mess of clothes and champagne bottles and glasses and room service trays piled all over the place. From where Chase is standing in the hallway he can hear male laughter and someone else telling the guy to shut the fuck up. When Chase turns back to the girl he figures something out and waits for her to do the same.

"Yeah?" she finally asks, annoyed.

Chase introduces himself. "I'm the driver. Are you ready?"

"For what?"

Pause. "You don't need a ride?"

"Where to?"

Chase grins. "Do you recognize me?"

"Should I?"

"Your hair," Chase says. "It was dark before."

"Yeah?" she says as she backs away from him. "And?"

"Centennial."

"What are you talking about?"

"Your name's not Gabrielle? You don't go to Centennial?"

She blinks a few times and slowly shakes her head, clearly lying. "What do you want?" She keeps backing away.

"Look, I don't care if it's you or not, okay?" Chase says. "I'm supposed to be driving someone at three and I really don't care who it is or who you are."

"Hang on."

The girl swings the door closed and leaves Chase standing in the cool hallway.

When the girl returns Chase asks her: "Do you know where Michele is?"

The girl shakes her head again. "Either San Diego or L.A. I'm not sure." The girl bites her lower lip. "She'll be back Thursday or Friday." Someone calls out to the girl but she doesn't turn around.

"So no one here needs a ride?" Scowling, Chase pulls out his cell to call Bailey.

The girl leans in conspiratorially. "Honestly, dude? Michele's a complete bitch now and she does all this coke and she's almost thirty. She's *totally* not worth it."

"What does that have to do with anything?" he asks before he realizes that the girl meant something else entirely.

She looks Chase over—eyes scan the scratches on his neck—and thinks: no way.

"You should always call first, sweetie."

"And you're not"—he checks the text Bailey sent him— "Gabrielle?"

"No."

"And you don't need a ride."

The girl shakes her head.

"And Michele isn't here and *no one* here needs a ride today?"

The girl rolls her eyes. "She's back on Tuesday or Wednesday, dude, okay? Call and make an appointment if you want."

"What the fuck, dude?"

"Sorry, she bailed," Bailey says as if this is enough of an explanation. "Tonight though is for real. Can you still do it? At seven?"

"Call me when you know for sure."

"Keep your phone on."

8

Chase can hear the contestants on a reality show screaming from the television in the apartment next to his. He's sitting at the kitchen table listening to the wind. He leans back in his chair taking deep breaths as he stares out the window at a bright blue sky. He needs to finish three paintings for the *White Trash Paradise* show. Devon, who owns the gallery, went to Durango and UC Davis and laughed when he told Chase he came back to Vegas two years ago to "do something moderately constructive." Devon's is Chase's first show in the five years he's been back in Vegas. In response to Devon's question—it was vague and about why any artist would *leave* New York—Chase offered something hollow about New York being "too commercial." But to Chase, New York was NYU and Julia, which bled together until it became nothing more than a debilitating blur of impossible expectations. Of course he doesn't tell Devon that, though in retrospect he probably should have. Chase's paintings were oils on linen canvas done with the expensive Winsor & Newton sable brushes Julia bought him: his mother's house on Beverly, neighborhood panoramas and the blood-red skies, a hot Salvadoran babe. There was enough that Devon liked in Chase's portfolio to offer him space. The painting Devon liked the most—the one Devon told Chase he thought should "anchor your wall"—was the one that Chase was the most reluctant about: a girl sits on a bed and stares blankly out a window. Early-morning sunlight fills the room, bathing her in yellow. The girl wears her hair in a ponytail and her tan skin seems smooth until you move in closer and then you see the sores around her mouth and the white scar on her forehead. Outside the window is a sea of pink tile roofs that bleed together so that it's impossible to distinguish one from the next. The painting's title: *Carly*.

Chase sleeps past noon. He wakes up with a headache and the vague sense of guilt he always feels when he sleeps this late. The soreness from his workout yesterday—his first in weeks—alleviates some of the shame but it also makes him feel older and that leads to loneliness. The midday silence of the apartment would depress him even further if he weren't staring at the pencil outlines he managed late last night on one of the three canvases. Plus there's the cash in his wallet from Michele, which means he'll be able to write a check (that won't bounce) for the rent—without taxes the three thousand dollars is more than he was earning at Centennial. A long, hot shower and the thought of coffee picks him up. At a Starbucks on Maryland he reads the *Weekly* because there's supposed to be a listing for the show and Devon told him he'd try to mention Chase, but leafing through the newspaper he finds nothing and figures next week he'll be in there because the show is still two weeks away. Chase thinks about today. There is a plan. Chase will give at least two rides and then he'll work on the canvas a little more and then go to the gym again if he has time. He'll also go to the party Bailey's throwing because Michele suggested he should. The caffeine starts kicking in and he's okay again and the prospect of a full day and being productive and moving forward energizes him. It feels right, all of it. He calls Julia and gets voice mail and leaves a rambling message about the summer ahead: looking for apartments in San Francisco neighborhoods, North Beach and South of Market, the Marina (but that's too white), and he goes on until the tone sounds and cuts him off. Chase calls back and says he misses her and maybe she can come to his show but his cell beeps and when he sees that it's a call from a number he doesn't recognize he drops the call to Julia and takes the one from a girl named Melanie who needs a ride.

It's almost eleven and Chase is on his way to Bailey's party, driving the Mustang too fast up a winding road called Sweetwater Lane in Summerlin. Hunter sits in the passenger seat breathing into cupped hands, checking his breath, intermittently singing along to the Green Day song on the radio. Chase wears black baggy jeans and a navy Versace shirt, pressed and unbuttoned, with a white tank top underneath. His head is freshly shaved. His face is purposefully not. His skin feels both tight and soft and he smells good. It's the Havana cologne by Aramis that Michele bought him earlier in the day. They went to the Fashion Show Mall so Michele could get new underwear to update the pictures on her Web site. And then Michele gave Chase two hundred dollars because he "deserved it." Chase spent sixty dollars on a small black leather-bound Bosca date book in which he'll keep track of all the girls' names, addresses, and phone numbers. (In fact, he has the date book with him tonight.) Chase slows the convertible as it passes three girls in short shirts and low, tight jeans marching arm in arm along Sweetwater Lane toward Bailey's house. They shriek when Hunter growls at them. They want a ride and Chase stops the car and Hunter mutters "sweet" under his breath and the car idles until the girls get within reach. Then Chase pulls away and leaves them behind.

"Save your money tonight," Chase tells Hunter, almost as if it's a warning.

"I miss Monique," Hunter says, surprising Chase.

"Seriously?" Chase asks. "Julia's friend?"

"But Monique doesn't miss me," Hunter sighs. "That's the way it goes."

Jettas and Jeeps and SUVs and a few Kawasaki Ninjas are parked in front of Bailey's house and inside there are mostly girls. There are also a few guys in their late thirties and early forties—prosperous, buzzed, playing it cool. Jazz-funk fusion is the sound track and dim lighting makes everyone look great. Chase thinks this scene is unusually sophisticated for Bailey and decides that Michele deserves the credit. When Chase turns to ask Hunter if he wants a beer Hunter's already lost in the crowd.

Chase downs a Corona in the kitchen, standing across from three young girls who smoke cigarettes and drink something pale pink from tumblers. Chase is about to introduce himself to the one girl he recognizes from the suite at the Palace. (This is the girl who stood in the doorway and told him that Michele was in San Diego or L.A. and was "totally not worth it." This is the girl who thought Chase was the john.) She wears a tight white T-shirt with the word SWITCH-HITTER on it. Michele suddenly appears and kisses Chase on the mouth and the girl from the suite introduces Michele to her two friends. Michele fails to introduce Chase to the girls but Chase doesn't care because he remembers that this girl is from Centennial. A flicker of regret and then he wonders what difference it makes.

"Where is he?" Michele asks the girls.

"Upstairs?" The girls shrug. "Outside?"

"Have you seen Bailey?" Michele asks Chase.

He shakes his head then looks back at the girl from the suite.

Michele frowns and heads out of the kitchen.

"Bailey's dad owns the Hard Rock," one of the girls says.

"Is that what he told you?" Chase asks.

"Who *are* you?" one of the girls asks, annoyed. "And why are you staring at us?"

"He came up to the suite," the girl says. "At the Palace. He came up looking for Michele."

"You know," one of the girls says, "you don't need to come to the hotel. A lot is happening outside the suite."

"So what?" Chase asks. "Why are you telling me this? I don't give a shit."

"Who the hell *are* you?" she asks.

"I used to be your sister's favorite teacher," Chase says.

"News flash: I don't have a sister, faggot."

"I'm your driver," Chase says. "I'm supposed to make sure you get from your mother's house to wherever you're going and back again in one piece."

And then it happens so fast and unexpectedly that Chase doesn't recognize it at first. Bailey is standing next to the glowing aqua pool. And there is a person standing next to Bailey in an oversize white-and-red-striped Polo shirt, baggy jeans, and a thick Rolex on his wrist. This person is explaining something to Bailey. This person is gesturing with his hands. This person is punctuating certain points with a high-pitched laugh. This person is causing Bailey to nod.

  This person is Rush.

And when Bailey slowly turns his head from Rush and looks at the house his eyes meet Chase's. Bailey is considering things and still looking at Chase through the glass doors of the kitchen when he says something without turning back to Rush. Rush immediately looks over at Chase and then smiles tightly. Bailey nods at something Rush says. Bailey motions for Chase to come outside. Rush becomes surprisingly relaxed. Bailey and Rush keep talking, occasionally looking in Chase's direction, and since the girls have left the kitchen Chase holds up a finger, like *hang on,* and turns away, watching the girls as they head over to Hunter, while he tries to put this all together. Chase considers following the girls but once they get to Hunter one of them whispers something in his ear that causes Hunter to glance around the room. Hunter nods curtly and that's the cue for the four of them to go upstairs. Chase turns and grabs another Corona from the counter and heads outside because there's nowhere else to go.

"It's cool, Chase." This is Bailey thinking he needs to talk Chase down as he moves toward them standing together by the pool. "It is very, very cool, okay? Rush told me what happened between you guys and I wouldn't have invited you if it weren't totally cool now." Bailey turns to Rush for confirmation that things are now totally cool.

Chase plays along and reassures Bailey that everything is fine and, to prove it, turns his attention immediately to Rush.

"I'm so sorry, man. I feel like shit." Chase extends his hand and Rush is easy with the situation and they exchange a hand pound.

"You're a hard-ass," Rush says with a grin. "You were one of the three teachers at Centennial who everyone knew had a sack and would kick your ass if you stepped to them." Rush nods approvingly. "Hey, did they really fire you?"

"They had to," Chase says. "They thought you and your mom would sue them."

"We are." Rush laughs. "They suspended me for two weeks. My father was all *You did what you had to do* and bought me a Yamaha GP800 and took me out to Lake Mead." Rush pauses. "He wanted to come after you. I told him you were cool. I stepped to you."

"Chase is always starting shit he can't finish and he is so not cool," Bailey says. "In fact, Chase is fucking nuts."

The muscles in Chase's shoulders and neck tighten. He realizes he's clenching his teeth. He should be relieved but there's something off about the situation. "Yeah, I'm a mess," he manages.

"But he's leaving," Bailey says and turns to Chase. "Right? You still leaving?"

Chase nods and sips the Corona. He studies Rush. "I'm really glad we got to patch things up. Rachel said you were coming after me."

Rush rolls his eyes and makes an exaggerated gesture with his arm. "Rachel says a lot of things."

"Yeah." Chase forces a grin. "She said you guys were plotting something."

"Bitch just wants someone to listen to her. That's all she wants." Rush shakes his head in disbelief. "And I tell her, maybe someone will listen to you if you shut the fuck up once in a while."

"Well, when she told me you said *I think we should shoot that motherfucker,* it kind of freaked me out."

"She just likes to cause trouble," Bailey says. "She's full of shit."

"Rachel needs to take her meds and stop calling my house," Rush adds. "My stepmom is so close to calling the cops." He grins. "The psycho-bitch is *stalking* me."

"She was so sure you were plotting something. She wouldn't shut up about it."

"It's attention. It's a cry for help, dude," Rush says. "I mean, this girl fucked her mom's boyfriend."

"She's a very naïve little girl," Bailey says, checking his BlackBerry.

Rush continues to detail Rachel's unraveling. According to Rush, after Rachel's mom found out that Rachel had indeed fucked her boyfriend, Rachel stayed with Rush for a month until it got out of hand and she went nuts on him and then she moved in with her brother, Ronnie, at the two-bedroom apartment in the Tropicana Gardens.

"I had to let her go," Rush says. "She was obsessed with me. She'd call me all the fucking time, and my mother, and all of her candy-corn friends a thousand times, insisting someone better listen to her. *Someone listen to me, someone listen to me.* That's all she kept saying was *someone listen to me* and then it stopped. All the calls. Everything. She suddenly dropped it all. Like it never happened. She's fucking bipolar or something."

"Aren't we all," Bailey murmurs, grinning at something he's been texted.

But Chase isn't paying attention anymore. He's watching the house: the living room filled with girls and the older men and he starts running the numbers in his head and trying to remember if he locked the door to his apartment when he left. Chase is brought back when Bailey mentions the 9-millimeter he carries under the front seat of the Impala now.

"They say you live a new life," Bailey says. "They say you, like, become a whole other person every seven years."

"I've heard that," Chase says.

"So we really don't know each other at all when you think about it." And then an odd segue: "Rush is going to help me out for a little while."

"That's, um, great," Chase says, smiling tightly.

"Half the girls here tonight are because of Rush," Bailey says.

"I know a lot of people," Rush says matter-of-factly. "Dude, it's like a Centennial assembly here. You don't recognize any of them?"

"Some of them, I guess." Chase sips his Corona.

"Because they sure as hell recognize you." Rush glances at Bailey and then back at Chase. "Like three or four have already come up to me and they're all grabbing my arm, like, *Oh my God, did you see who's here?* And I'm all *They fired his ass and he's with Bailey now.*"

"So what are you getting out of this?" Chase asks. "Like a finder's fee or something?"

"No, no," Rush says, swinging his head back and forth. "Nothing like that."

Chase considers this. "Well, then what do you get?"

"He gets your job when you leave," Bailey says.

In Bailey's room with the king-size burgundy bed and the African masks, Chase sits on the window ledge and stares out into the backyard while Michele finishes unpacking from her San Diego trip. Bailey figured out when all this started back in January, before other girls were brought in, that it would be so simple for him and Michele (or just Michele) to fly to a few cities and stay at airport hotels. All the appointments would be booked in advance after running their ads on Craigslist and directing clients to their Web site. Imagine it: three-day trips to nice hotels in five or six cities over a few months could net ten thousand dollars. Bailey made an itinerary and constructed the Web site with Michele's picture and a brief biography, complete with fake customer reviews. But Michele never agreed to leave the city and told Chase that her life would have to be in a tailspin if she ever got on a plane to fly somewhere else to do this.

"You smell really good," she says. "I meant to tell you that."

"The girls from downstairs, Brandi's friends, are up here getting high."

Michele nods while rooting through her suitcase.

"With Hunter," Chase adds.

Michele suddenly pays attention to Chase. She walks over to him and touches his lips with a finger.

"It just gets better and better," Chase says.

"You look like shit, Chase." She presses her index finger against his forehead, then gazes down at the pool and the girls mingling with men old enough to be their fathers.

"Does Bailey have this whole thing under control?" Chase asks.

Michele turns away and walks back to the suitcase, where she removes a white envelope filled with cash from San Diego, and she says it doesn't matter whether Bailey has the whole thing under control.

"Since when doesn't it matter?" Chase asks.

Michele counts out a hundred dollars and hands it to Chase. He doesn't ask her what it's for. He just says thanks. He doesn't care what it's for. He needs it.

Chase gazes back into the darkened yard, the glowing blue rectangle at the center of it, and then: Rush. "That's the kid I got fired for." Chase lifts himself from the window ledge and lets himself fall backward onto the bed. "Downstairs. Outside. He's working for your boyfriend." Chase stares at the ceiling fan and watches the blades spin. He tries to key in on one and stick with it but gives up because it makes him dizzy.

"Bailey got Rush because he can control him," Michele says. "And probably to fuck with you a little. Bailey's getting antsy.

Bailey thought you were leaving, but you're still here. For some reason he thinks you're in the way. He's worried about you."

Chase realizes why and his entire body constricts and he asks her, "Should he be?"

"Oh, Chase, don't go there." Michele starts throwing clothes into a hamper. "Bailey stopped asking when you're leaving because every time I tell him, you stay longer. He doesn't believe me anymore. He thinks you'll convince me to screw him over."

"I might. I will. I mean, I would consider it."

"He's panicking."

"Are you?"

"I'm as calm as a ghost."

"Did you get your house yet?" Chases asks softly.

She shakes her head. Michele moves back to the window and watches Bailey and Rush and the girls and the men who have come to meet them mingle in the backyard around the glowing pool. "Bailey's making half of what he should be because he doesn't keep track of things. Girls skim money or work a weekend, then quit. The suite is costing more than he thought because girls and *his* idiot friends just end up partying there instead of working. He's seriously not paying attention. And I tell him this and he's just not focusing." She considers something. "And I just have to get as much as I can before it all goes to hell."

"Why don't you just lose the suite at the Palace and do it here?"

Michele shakes her head.

"Well, Rachel has her own place," Chase says. "She'd let you use it. Just give her brother an occasional freebie." He pauses and reaches out to her. "Like you used to do with me when you'd sleep over at my mom's place."

Michele closes her eyes.

Chase is so tired that he could fall asleep, here, in Bailey's bed.

"Did you know that Hunter told me he's pissed away about ten grand on your little friends?" Chase says dreamily. "Did you know that?" He considers. "Probably."

"Hunter's got plenty," Michele says, reaching for the envelope of cash by Chase's side.

"Hunter had about twenty from his grandmother," Chase says as if he's talking to himself. "Now it's like a thousand." Chase's eyes are barely open and he's trying to focus on Michele. She slides her hand over his face and it's warm and dry and he closes his eyes again.

"Maybe Hunter's the one who should be leaving," she says.

"And you lied to me about San Diego," Chase says. "Isn't there something you're forgetting? Isn't there some step you're skipping?"

"Go to sleep."

"Suddenly you're taking trips alone to San Diego?" Chase starts breathing deeply. "That wasn't part of the summer plan."

"Plans change." Michele leans over and kisses his forehead.

"I know they do," Chase says, falling away. "Now you give a shit."

He remembers: a spot opened up on the couch in the living room. He remembers walking downstairs and looking around for Michele. He remembers the conversation by the pool with Bailey and Rush. He remembers that he had fallen asleep on Bailey's bed. But now Chase is awake and leaning back and drinking Grey Goose, staring at silent black-and-white images flickering on a white wall. It's Bailey's movie: kids careening down a waterslide; kids at a skate park tumbling to the concrete; kids at the mall; kids in a hotel suite half-dressed and dancing to music you can't hear. And then Chase loses consciousness again until he hears Michele calling his name from somewhere. The living room is completely dark, the blackout curtains drawn and the candles burnt out. Everyone has left. He has no idea what time it is. "Chase, come here," she calls out.

"Where are you?"

Chase finds her on the stairs. She has been crying and her breath reeks of Captain Morgan and as she leans closer he can smell her hair and feel the warmth from her skin and Chase wonders if she's going to kiss him and he swallows hard and thinks maybe he'll let her.

"Easy," he says. "Come on."

She presses her hand over his mouth too hard. He pushes it away.

Michele tells him she saw a coyote in the street last night. "I turned a flashlight on it and it froze. Bailey wanted to shoot it."

Chase doesn't want to hear this. He wants her to try to kiss him.

"I thought Bailey would help me," she says. "I was scared and I thought he would help me."

"But that's not the deal you made."

"What about the other night with Julia? I mean, fuck you, Chase. There's an appropriate and respectful way to handle things and treat people you care about."

"There is."

"Telling stories to your girlfriend about me and what I happen to be doing right now or what you *think* I'm doing—which, by the way, is not even one tenth of my life—is completely inappropriate and it's you being a disrespectful asshole."

"Okay," Chase says softly and takes her hand.

"You suck," she says. "You really do."

She tries to pull her hand away but he doesn't let her.

"Look, I'll be around tomorrow," Chase says with a sudden rush of sadness.

"I don't care," she says. "I don't care anymore."

"Let's hang out," he says. "We'll just get lunch or see a movie."

"Leave."

Julia calls in the morning and tells Chase that New York looks like a possibility.

He's confused. "For the summer?"

She pauses. "No. Permanently."

He pulls out into traffic on Boulder Highway.

"Are you still coming this weekend?" Julia asks.

Chase remembers he said he might go see her in San Francisco. But he has seven rides scheduled for Saturday, each noted neatly in red ink in his Bosca planner. It's only Thursday.

JOE McGINNISS JR.

"I've gotten so little done."

"Come for a night."

"I can't hear you."

She raises her voice and asks if he can hear her and he says he can and she tells him not to worry about this weekend. She'd barely be around anyway. He apologizes. And then Julia says that New York is looking good because the San Francisco office may not be the best fit. Again, Chase can barely hear her because the wind is so strong and he's doing sixty-five with the top down and trucks are roaring past and he has to tell her that she's hard to hear and can they talk when he gets home and she says of course and "Isn't it kind of exciting though? New York? I mean for you. I mean I'm excited about New York for *you*."

From a distance his mother looks young. She sits alone in the booth at Denny's smoking a cigarette, watching an older couple at the counter try to calculate 15 percent, handing the receipt back and forth to each other. She looks small in her floral-print sundress with her blonde hair in a ponytail. From across the restaurant she could pass for thirty-five, maybe forty. But now that Chase is across from her in the booth he can see the darkness under her eyes and the two deep creases that run across her forehead like scars.

"You should be in bed," she says after Chase asks the waitress if the coffee is fresh and she says she'll check. "But you know this may be our last breakfast together for a while."

"Mom, please."

"You're not going to fly back once a month to have breakfast at five in the morning with your mother."

"Do you need me to?"

"I like it." She takes a drag off her cigarette and waves some of the smoke away.

Chase hands her seven pieces of paper, monthly balance sheets of her projected income and expenses. "I did it through the end of the year."

His mother studies the pages with a serious expression on her face.

The waitress brings coffee that tastes bitter and old.

"Have you ordered?" Chase asks.

His mother shakes her head, still studying the sheets. "What about my Vanguard?"

"Put a little more in each month. Julia says another mutual fund, too."

"So no trips to San Francisco to see my son?"

"That's covered."

"She looked so beautiful."

"Yeah. I know."

Even in the restaurant with the music piped in through speakers over their heads they can hear the bells and ringing of the slot machines. Chase stares at his mother as she watches the older couple finally figure out the tip. They walk slowly out to the casino floor and disappear.

"I'll be fine," she says.

"What do you mean?" Chase asks. "Of course you'll be fine."

"I can see that look. I can see that expression on your face."

Once a month, on Sunday mornings at five when she finishes her shift at Treasure Island, they meet for breakfast because that's when she's most vulnerable. This is the loneliest time for her. This is the time when she used to gamble. At her worst, his mother would leave work and walk the Strip in the blackness of early morning to the Mirage or Bally's. She played until eleven or noon and as soon as she got home she'd walk quickly to her bedroom and sleep until four or five. She would wake up and take a shower. She ate whatever was left over— cold pizza, KFC, maybe pasta if Carly had cooked it. She would ask them if they had done their homework or heard from their father. She would stare at the television, at whatever Carly and Chase had on, her eyes unfocused, until eight, when it was dark again and she'd get dressed and leave for work.

"You'll have beautiful children," his mother says. "Mixed kids are always so attractive. That singer, what's her name, she's mixed isn't she?"

Chase's phone rings, and since he doesn't recognize the number, he takes the call.

The call during breakfast was from a girl named Aubrey. It's three now and Chase waits in front of the Palace and waves off two different valets who he doesn't recognize. They tell Chase he has to move the Mustang if he's not a guest but then a girl says his name. She is thin with red hair and looks sixteen but because of the orange tan could be older, maybe even twenty.

"Come on." Chases pushes the door open and Aubrey gets in.

They are going to a town house in Green Valley Ranch for a one-hour "massage." (Michele booked it. Bailey knows nothing about this booking. This is the way things are starting to work.) But Aubrey has no massage table—only a huge leather purse and a bottle of baby oil and a vibrator that she shows him. It's blue. Chase decides she's closer to sixteen than twenty. Aubrey is into the rave scene and all her friends spin. Chase didn't even know there was still a rave scene. She says she's from just outside San Diego—a place called El Cajon. She moved to Henderson when she was nine because her mom wanted to be close to her aunt, who had a house near Nellis Air Force Base. She weighs eighty-seven pounds. Her favorite food is an Egg McMuffin. Aubrey smokes two cigarettes and makes three phone calls during the fifteen-minute drive from the hotel to Green Valley Ranch. There is no one at the town house in Green Valley Ranch and Chase asks Aubrey if she's sure about the address.

"Michele gave it to me."

Aubrey calls the client again but gets voice mail and says, "I'm here, outside, waiting for you. Call me back, sweetie."

Ten minutes pass. Aubrey smokes another cigarette. She asks Chase if he has a girlfriend. She asks Chase if he's ever been to L.A.

"Michele says you did some modeling?"

"Web sites," Aubrey clarifies. "This photographer for some architecture magazine paid me ninety dollars an hour to pose, and paid for the hotel, and some are for his personal Web site and the others were for whatever."

"This was in L.A.?"

"Yeah. I'm going again." She flicks the cigarette out the window. "He wants me and a friend to pose for three hundred an hour this time."

"How did you meet him?"

"MySpace," Aubrey says. "We're going to try the beach this time. I keep suggesting it. But the hotel is by the airport so, you know, we never seem to get out."

"Hermosa Beach is nice," Chase murmurs to himself.

"I love to travel. I'm really into ancient civilizations."

Aubrey went to Greece last year, alone. Her friends bailed because they didn't have the money. "I cried when I saw the Coliseum."

"Parthenon."

"People were staring at me like, *this girl's crazy*. But I couldn't help it. I just started bawling right there at the sight of it." She pauses, idly checks her cell. "I want to go to Belize next, but that's harder to do alone."

"Is it?" Chase asks, totally detached from the conversation. He hopes her cell will ring and it will be the guy and the guy will be ready for his appointment and things can get moving. Chase tells Aubrey to call the man again. There is no answer. She leaves another message for him to call her back and let her know within the next twenty minutes if this is happening or—and now the rehearsed line—she's going home because she has a ton of homework to do. Chase can't tell whether or not she pulled it off. Chase glances at her crossed legs and then looks away.

The homework line closed the deal. The man calls back. He's ready. Aubrey leans over and grabs her purse and kicks the door open. She skips up to the house and rings the bell and looks back over her shoulder and smiles at Chase and the door opens and she disappears inside the house. A moment later the door opens and Aubrey skips toward the car.

"It's okay," she says. "He's a magician." She reaches for the pack of cigarettes she forgot. "He has a monkey."

"Call me when you're done," Chase says.

She walks back to the house and Chase sees the silhouette of a man in the shadow of the doorway and watches the door close. In his leather Bosca planner Chase scrawls the name "Aub" and "GVRanch-2235 Sunburst Manor" and the date "6/9."

The sky is pink and orange and the sun is dropping. The wind picks up. The street is empty except for a few cars parked in driveways. There are no people anywhere. Chase closes his eyes. He hears buzzing that grows louder and turns into ringing and then there's nothing: no sound, just a dark, cold sensation and falling, plummeting down.

Aubrey slams the door and Chase jolts awake.

"How much did that add up to?" Chase asks, U-turning, then driving away from the house toward Green Valley Parkway and back to the city.

"It ended up being four."

She couldn't have gotten away with the lie even if she hadn't hesitated. She's skimming. They all do.

"You were in there for two and a half hours."

"Right, four for each hour."

"This is Michele's call, right?"

Aubrey nods.

"Then don't fuck around. Skim all you want from Bailey. Just don't skim off Michele."

Aubrey closes her eyes for a long time and then asks, "Do you know that little girl Rachel?"

"Are you high?" Chase asks. "What are you talking about?"

"A little bit. But do you know her? Do you know Rachel?"

"Why are you asking me about her?"

"Because she talks about you, like all the time, Mr. Chase."

In front of a small apartment building on the outskirts of the Strip, Chase tells Aubrey to give him half the money.

Aubrey smiles lazily as she reaches into her bag and removes her wallet.

"You shouldn't get high with the clients," Chase says.

She hands the money to Chase and as she turns away she says, "And you should be careful."

Chase was sitting in the kitchen on the Fourth of July eating ice cream sandwiches at noon, listening to Carly read his progress report from the summer semester. (Chase had to make up two classes he failed in the spring.) It was all about how Chase had a "keen intelligence" and was "a natural leader" but "his attitude doesn't serve him well" and "he seems convinced that he knows better than his teacher." The progress report wondered if there was "something missing."

"Why are you such an idiot?" Carly asked.

Chase told her that if she went through his stuff again he would talk to Mom about statutory rape laws. "I think they're pretty strictly enforced in Nevada."

"But why are you such an idiot?"

"Do these guys know you're sixteen?"

"The question, Chase, is: do they care?"

"You take too many chances."

"I may not be up here"—Carly held her hand over her head—"with you and all the other C-minus students, but I'm not stupid."

He told Carly to be careful because the UNLV fraternity she liked to go to with Michele was notorious for parties that got out of control.

"We know, Chase." Carly rolled her eyes. "We know."

"But does Mom know?" he asked.

"Who do you thinks puts the condoms in my purse?"

That night they watched the fireworks bloom over the Strip from a suite at Bally's. His sister stood near him, twitching and nervous and scratching her arms because she'd taken too many of the pills Michele had given her and she thought she might pass out. Carly had taken the pills earlier because she had to close Hot Topic—where she worked to get discounts on clothes—and there was no way she'd get through everything without the pills. When she got home from Hot Topic she cleaned her room and then cleaned Chase's room and vacuumed the house and emptied out all the shit from their mom's car and when they checked in to the hotel, Carly told Michele that her heart was about to burst and she was sweating and pale so they put her under the spray of cold water in the shower and wrapped her in a wet towel, and lying there sobbing, Carly promised to never take the pills again as everyone watched the sky explode.

The next afternoon Carly sat in their backyard with her legs in the water, slumped over, hands clutching the side of the pool. She was sixteen and so tired. The bruise on her chin from where it hit the asphalt leaving a party three weeks ago had faded and her skin was as brown as the wall surrounding the yard. The crickets were loud but it was a soothing sound and the glowing aqua water of the pool looked warm enough. Carly wore cutoff shorts and her new white bikini top and stirred the water with her legs, watching the circles she made. It was quiet and calm and Chase liked that.

"You have to let some things go," he said. He was now in the pool, treading water in front of her.

She said nothing but nodded.

"The drug shit goes nowhere. Where are you going to be in five years?" he asked. "Last night was scary, Carly."

"I know where I'm gonna be in five years, Chase. Either dead from a DUI or a senior at UNLV." She paused. "I don't know which is worse."

Chase scowled and swam away, switching to backstrokes, watching the darkness fill the pink sky like a spilled bottle of ink. When he looked back at his sister he saw the orange sun in the reflection on Carly's sunglasses. It was dipping quickly below the mountains on the other side of the valley.

When Chase got out of the pool and reached for a towel Carly asked in a soft voice that surprised him, "Where are you going?"

"Inside?"

She stared at the clear water. Chase wasn't cold standing on the lawn because the desert air was so warm and it kept washing over everything like a narcotic.

"Stay with me," she said.

9

Chase is home, starting and stopping, erasing and starting over the charcoal sketches that will become the paintings for Devon's show. After a few hours his hands are red and raw. Nothing he's completed pleases him. It's hopeless. He walks outside and lights one of the American Spirits that Michele left in the Mustang at some point. His cell rings. It's Julia. He hesitates. Julia would laugh at the sight of him smoking. It might have suited Chase if Julia didn't know him. He just stands there staring at the cell's aqua display—Julia's name and number—and he can't bring himself to answer it. The reason he can't answer the call is somehow tied together with the work he needs to finish for Devon's show but has barely started. And he knows the conversation will end in an argument and he'll snap and say something he may or may not mean about not ever wanting to go back to New York and that wasn't part of the deal and how goddamn condescending it all was: her happiness for him was all about how the art world *is* New York and that moving there together would kill two birds with one stone. This begins to enrage him and he still doesn't answer the phone. He goes back inside and starts again but it isn't any good and by the time he realizes he should just take a break he's sweating and covered in charcoal and it's dark outside. He takes a shower. For dinner: a can of tuna and an orange. He gets dressed. Chase has three rides to give tonight, including driving Hunter to work because the Caravan is shot to hell and Chase knows where the money to fix it went. Chase pulls into the traffic on Boulder Highway. Trash and debris swirl in the air then dive down and tumble across the asphalt. Chase turns up old Dre and leans back a little, letting the loud thumping hip-hop move through him, and soon he is just drifting down the highway and he likes the way it feels. When he hits a deserted intersection on East Charleston he just lets the car roll through it.

Hunter sits across from Chase in a booth at an IHOP on the Strip. He has a show at Treasure Island in an hour and is in costume minus the eye patch.

"Did you tell her you don't want to move to New York?"

"She said she could 'see us' there."

"So—*adios* California? *Hola* New York?"

Michele calls and Chase doesn't answer it and she doesn't leave a message. It rings again and it's Michele and again Chase won't answer. It rings once more and he stares at the display until his eyes cross. Exasperated, Hunter snatches the cell from Chase's hand, flips it open, and calmly says, "He doesn't love you and never will, so get over it."

Chase reaches for the phone but Hunter pulls back.

"You lose, bitch!" Hunter yells into the cell and when he hands it back to Chase Michele is still there. Chase listens for a minute before simply saying, "I just don't think so." He clicks off. He stares at Hunter. Michele wanted a ride to Public Storage to get cash. Michele wanted Chase to go with her to a house in the Lakes where Bailey's dealer lives.

Hunter stares at Chase evenly before speaking. "Dude, I understand. Even for me, it's hard leaving. I want out, but honestly, I've got a rent-free room at home with a private bathroom, a car, central air, and DirecTV. I've got a pool and cash in the bank and free food. I feel like shit when I don't get callbacks from schools and I can't even get an interview for shit teaching jobs like yours. But I'm comfortable. Day-to-day, there's nothing I have to worry about. I mean, I want to get the fuck out of here, too. I just don't know where to go." Hunter thinks things through. "But the Sun King suite at the Palace? Very nice. Hmm. I'd sleep with dudes to live there."

"Michele needs—"

"Michele? Forget it. You can't do anything about that."

"About what?"

"The problem with her plan and why she's not going anywhere."

"Why is that?"

"She likes mints on her pillows."

"Michele asked me to ask you how Brandi was," Chase says. "Why would she do that?"

Hunter suddenly has to stare out the window. He reaches for his glass of water and takes a very small sip and returns the glass to the table but doesn't let go of it. He sighs. "What did that bitch say?"

"It doesn't matter what she said Hunter—"

"Oh fuck that fucking bitch—"

"That girl is still in high school, Hunter," Chase says.

"She's seventeen, dude. So? What does that make me?" Hunter asks defensively. "Age of consent."

Chase sucks on an ice cube. "How much have you spent?" Chase asks this but knows the answer. According to Michele, Hunter is one of Brandi's most lucrative clients. According to Michele, Hunter spends at least four or five hours a week with her. Most of this is paid but some of it is not, which suggests to Michele that there actually might be something more going on: the hint of an emotional attachment.

"Brandi is what she is."

"And what is that, Hunt?" Chase asks.

"A girl who doesn't make me feel like shit about myself."

"Don't you think there's a reason why?"

"I don't think about things like that. I can't look at it that way."

"Do me a favor," Chase says, sucking on another ice cube, then spitting the ice cube back into the glass. "Don't call Bailey. If you want to see Brandi just do it through Michele instead."

"You of all people shouldn't get judgmental on my ass," Hunter says. "I might use Bailey's services but dude, you're driving them around—"

"But I don't *do* anything with them, Hunter."

"No, you just deliver them."

Chase can't sleep but he's too tired to sketch so he watches KLAS news: seven dead coyotes hanging from a clothesline in the backyard of a house in Henderson. A man tells the reporter that he's doing his part to keep the children safe. Chase sips a

Corona and turns off the television during a story about teenagers assaulting tourists at the MGM Grand. With the TV off
there's only the sound of the air conditioner humming as Chase
spends hours online. He Googles the name of the artist he read
about last month in *The New York Times* because sometimes
reading about him motivates Chase, though more often than not
it overwhelms and depresses him, which automatically pushes
him toward porn sites, and while masturbating to the stuff he
downloads, he wonders why these girls are doing this and why
are they all so young? Sirens wail outside. A couple has a brief
fight next door. It's after two when Chase checks the Vegas
forecast though he knows what it will tell him. Chase calls Julia.
She doesn't pick up. He leaves no message and waits for the
phone to ring. He's sad, though not surprised, when it doesn't.
He sends her an e-mail:

Jules,

   7-Day Las Vegas Weather Forecast

   Monday 110
   Tuesday 110
   Wednesday 112
   Thursday 112
   Friday 113
   Saturday 114
   Sunday 114

Heat Alert and Air Quality Advisory until further notice. WTF
am I still doing here??? This is June. Summer in Paradise. Think
I'll take their advice and stay inside. Lots of painting to get done

for The Show that I hope you want to come to. Are you foolish or
brave enough to come back? Have I scared the h*ll out of you yet?
I'll understand if you've got laundry to do or a headache. I could
use a small farmhouse in upstate New York or Montana right about
now. All trees and hills. God I miss you. Wish me luck!

Before logging off, Chase checks MySpace. Michele told him
Brandi and Rachel and some of the other girls have pages and
their sites are monitored to make sure they're not disclosing
anything about Michele or Bailey or the business. Brandi's page
is a blur of pink with red and blue hearts. She has 445 "friends."
The reason: her pictures and home videos. Chase can't down-
load any of the videos but the pics are accessible. The pics are
all of Brandi and her friends, mostly at a party of some kind,
holding bottles of beer and smoking cigarettes, Brandi in a string
bikini, Brandi in her underwear. A column of various messages
runs down the left side of the page. Inside a small black square
icon it reads "Fuck With Me and I'LL FUCK WITH YOU" and
below it "don't hate me cuz you ain't me, BITCH!!!" and then
some personal note in her own words to all of her "peeps" and
"niggas" and "gangstas," and she thanks God and her mom and
pop and steppop and cousins for "everything." And on the right
side, where Brandi's 445 friends have left messages and pics,
there is one from Rachel: *"Omg Bran!!!! I luv u soooo much*
Bitch!! This summer's off the hook—cha-CHING!!! met sum cute
guys and they wanna take us to Tabu l8tr and smoke a little 420
b4. And u r so right m's a nasty lil slut and you can't trust the
bitch. But as u say—we got that all figgered out. Call u l8tr—luv
ya lots <3."

*   *   *

Chase attaches the page to an e-mail, which he sends to
Michele. Michele is online, too, because before Chase can log
off he gets an immediate response. Michele says it's old news
and under control. And she also needs a ride tomorrow, early,
and she booked it, not Bailey, and she wants Chase with her.
In bed, before he falls asleep, Chase masturbates to images of
Michele in her low-rise jeans but they don't work and only
Brandi naked, on all fours, by a pool, her ass pushed up in the
air, her body dark (except for that one place) and glistening with
oil is what finally makes Chase come.

Chase just lies awake in his bed the next morning. In the cool
quiet of the apartment he stares at a crack in the ceiling over his
bed. He's been following its progression for months now. The
symbolism was alarming and made him tense. He would be unable to fall back asleep if he woke up and saw the crack in the
ceiling. (He was also afraid of what was in the crack.) And for a
while he was convinced the crack, thin and meandering, was
growing. But now he doesn't care. He would call someone about
it if he were staying in Vegas, but since he's not, there's no point.
    The pounding on the door is Michele.
    It is just after seven and the orange light from outside seeps
through the venetian blinds. Chase lies still, following the crack.
    Michele starts calling his name. "Charles, open the door."
    Last night Chase promised to go with Michele this morn-
ing for the "wake-up" at Mandalay Bay. She's been filling her
days with more appointments that Bailey doesn't know about.

This is the money that Michele can keep for herself. She wrote in the e-mail last night that the transition would be easier if Chase were staying for the rest of the summer. "Transition to what?" Chase said the words out loud as he typed them.

When Chase lets her in this morning Michele has to tell him to get dressed.

He pulls his shorts off and walks naked across the room to his dresser to find something to wear—a defiant gesture that makes him feel sexy, even though Michele is not paying attention.

Michele complains that Chase never returns her calls since Julia visited and if he wants to officially dump her as a friend, just do it.

Chase tells Michele that he's been painting a lot and then asks how the after-hours party was last night and if Hunter showed up.

Michele startles Chase when she shouts, "Why are you *avoiding* us?"

But she doesn't wait for a response. She types a message on her new Treo and mutters to herself, calling whoever she's texting a fool. Michele talks to herself as she types: "Because Bailey, you fucking dipshit, she's fifteen years old and we don't need any more girls and this is your fucking problem and besides you got her from a Craigslist ad and the tweaked-out Goth look isn't working. So no, I won't fucking train her. You should feel free though."

"And last night in the suite?" Chase asks lightly when Michele looks up.

"What about it?"

"How was it?"

"Tense."

Chase asks what made it tense.

"Bailey."

"How did he make it tense?"

"He got drunk and accused me of stealing from him."

"Well, can you see how he could define it that way?"

"It's not stealing if it's mine. They're my girls and my appointments and it's my time." Michele sighs. "Anyway, he was wasted and accused two other girls there of stealing. And threw you in for good measure. Then he kicked everyone out. Except Hunter, who got a bloody nose and bled all over the white comforter, then slipped Bailey five hundred dollars for the room for the rest of the night with Brandi."

"That sounds like so much fun."

"I think that may have been the last party for a while."

"I am not sorry to hear that."

"Hunter is." Michele turns to him. "Hey, I liked your idea."

"What idea?"

"The idea of running it out of Rachel's place. I think you're right. I think Rachel and her brother would go for it if we made it worth their while."

"Jesus Christ," Chase says, whirling around. "I wasn't serious, Michele."

While Chase sits in the sun waiting for Michele he calls Julia. Their conversation is brief. It revolves around her ideas about New York and Chase's "stubborn" and "irrational" resistance to moving there. Chase regrets making the call. Then he tells Julia that he regrets making the call. Julia says the feeling is mutual.

Julia asks why he even bothered. Chase doesn't give a reason because he doesn't have one. Sometime around ten o'clock—after Michele is finished with the oncologist from Denver—Chase calls Julia back at a red light on Tropicana.

"Why do I call you when I'm like that?" he asks tiredly.

"I don't know."

The light turns green. Julia says something Chase can't hear. He's barely listening.

Chase is thinking of Michele in the Mustang after the appointment this morning. He's thinking about Michele trying to count out loud and losing track and then counting a third time. He's thinking about Michele saying, "Fuck this" and jamming a handful of twenties that turn out to be $320 (Chase will immediately re-count the money when he gets home) between his legs and saying nothing else. Chase is thinking of that drive all the way to Bailey's house in Summerlin because there were too many people in the suite. Michele had simply muttered "thanks" at the house in Summerlin when Chase dropped her off after the silent drive. Gray mornings in the Mustang with nothing to say were not unusual for them now.

"I shouldn't have called you like that," Chase says to Julia while steering the car with a hand resting in his lap. He's making his way home.

"You exhaust me."

"I'm sorry."

"Why do you do that? Why do you call and tell me those things? That you can't do what couples do? That you can't move forward? That you can't make commitments? That New York is impossible?"

"I don't know" is all Chase wants to say.

"What am I supposed to *do* with that? You tell me we're rushing things. That you can't see yourself in New York. That *I'm* the one who's misguided?"

"I said it was a potentially misguided *move*."

Julia exhales loudly.

"Don't, Julia. Just don't sigh, as if the whole world is—"

"Handle it, Chase, please," she says. "That's all I want. I just want you to respond the right way. It's not complicated. But I really need to know that you can talk to me."

"I'm getting some good work done here." It's a lie but it's all he has.

She says her orientation was fine. She says she was surprised when he didn't ask how it went the last time they spoke. She sounds agitated. Chase starts to mention his show again, and being preoccupied, and he apologizes but the words come out sounding defensive and petty.

After a long silence Chase asks, "Hello?"

"I'm pregnant, by the way."

Chase pulls into a CVS parking lot and lets the engine idle. He doesn't say anything. Morning traffic rushes past on Maryland Parkway. The sun is burning through the low gray clouds. He sinks into his seat. A faint ringing begins in his left ear and then moves to the right.

He swallows. "Okay," he says.

"Okay? Okay what?"

"Nothing. I said okay." He's trying to piece things together. "I mean, what do you want me to say?" He clears his throat, trying to loosen the tightness in his voice. He sits up straight. "What are you thinking? Is there something you want me to say?"

"Not really." Her voice is softly condescending.

"Do you seriously think we can handle this now?" he asks.

"Yes," Julia says. "I do."

"But not really," he says. "You don't really think that."

"Yes, I do," she says. "And it's fine. *We'll* be fine."

"It makes no sense."

"What doesn't?"

"This happening now. You can't *want* this."

"We'll be okay."

"You're so sure about things, Jules. You think things always work out. How are you so sure this will work out?"

"Why are you so sure it might not work out?"

"Things don't always just *work out*. Okay? Life doesn't just work out, Julia. Not *everyone* can handle everything just right."

"We can," Julia says. "If we're together, we can handle everything."

He falls into a dazed silence. He'll hate the baby. He'll hate Julia. He'll feel smaller and pettier than he does now. He'll be cornered. He'll drown in New York. "Where, Julia? Where are we going to do this? In a one-bedroom apartment? Where the hell will it *sleep*?"

"Some people can handle this, Chase."

"Some people can't handle *half* of it, Julia," he finally says.

"I don't know what that means."

The air conditioner broke and Chase is awake most of the night. He lies on top of the sheets in his basketball shorts, running through the same cycle of thoughts. He tells himself Julia really doesn't want this now. It's too soon. How can she be doing this? She's just start-

ing her career. Chase tries to think of ways he will guide Julia to the
appropriate decision without appearing to do so. He sits up in bed
suddenly, agitated but clearheaded. He writes a long e-mail to Julia
explaining everything. During the typing of this letter his cell rings
and he checks the call and it's a girl who needs a ride and after a
brief flash of hesitation Chase writes this detail to Julia. He writes
about all the calls coming in from teenage girls who need rides to
hotels or houses or apartment complexes so they can fuck men for
money. He feels an adrenaline rush as he types this. He doesn't
judge himself. He poses open-ended questions about the situation as though there's something ambiguous about the truth, as
though what is going down is actually open for interpretation. He
rereads the e-mail and spell-checks it. It's better-written than he
first thought and he now feels that he has control over everything
between them. And once he sends the e-mail events will unfold
as they were meant to. Nothing will be held back. Nothing will be
hidden. It feels good to express it all. Chase tells himself: this is
the truth and this is real and this has to be done. When Chase
finishes the e-mail (he prints it out because he's that proud of it),
it's nearly four pages long and single-spaced. When he rereads it
again he realizes that a page and a half of it is about Michele. And
that isn't the point. So he deletes the entire thing.

"They want to discuss my options," Julia says.

"I thought it was New York."

"That's what they want to talk about. It's up in the air. I'm
flexible because I know you want to be here." She pauses. "It's
still a possibility, I guess."

They don't say anything for a long time. There's a loud crash outside—the sound of glass shattering—and Julia asks what that was and he makes a guess, telling her it was the wind.

"But New York is better for you," he says quietly, clenching his teeth. "New York is two hours away from your family."

"I can barely hear you," she says.

Chase sits up in bed, exhausted. "We don't have to do this now. Any of it."

"Why don't you want to go to New York?" Julia asks. "Just be real with me, Chase."

An image: a one-bedroom apartment with mismatched furniture and piles of books and newspapers and all those blank canvases and a crib next to a futon and the stark plainness of it all and a baby and there's Chase staring out a small and grimy window overlooking a sea of brown and gray buildings.

"I don't know if I'm ready for New York again." Chase walks to the window and pulls back the blinds. The sun is blazing and he can feel the heat radiating out from the glass. "I don't know if I'll ever be ready."

"For New York?" Julia asks. "Or for—"

"For everything else." Chase cuts her off. "No, I'm not ready. I'm so far from ready you have no idea. I have no plans. I have no ability to make plans. I see today and tomorrow and that's it. I'm regressing. And you see it happening to me but won't say anything. You're either hoping it goes away or turns around or whatever, but you don't want to face it."

"It's less complicated than you're making it."

"Suddenly you're ready? How does that work? Spell it out for me. What makes sense about doing it this way?"

"What way?"

"You're just starting out. I'm nowhere. And we're going to be parents?"

Julia keeps saying: "Nothing is decided."

Chase drives out to the Hills, the unfinished development in Summerlin where Michele's house will be, not far from Spring Mountain and the house where Chase grew up in Green Valley. Michele's parcel has become a wooden skeleton on a concrete foundation. There are no signs of life: no grass unrolled or saplings planted. Chase parks at the end of an empty street and sits in the Mustang listening to the radio while looking down at the valley and the Strip bisecting it. When he turns the engine off everything is quiet except for the palm trees rustling and all the sharp edges get dulled for a moment. He smokes a cigarette and turns off his cell phone in case Julia calls. He watches the red and white lights from an airplane as it drifts silently toward McCarran. Chase walks to the edge of the asphalt where a red stone column stands—the entrance to a new development that was put on hold. Carved in it are the words SUNRISE MANOR. And then Chase looks for his apartment on Boulder Highway and after he finds it his eyes move north to the Strip and then west to the Palace and then over to Wyoming Avenue where Devon's gallery is and then to a small road you can't see just behind the Sahara—Beverly Way—where his mother lives, and it all looks so easy from up here. Sometime later, he feels relieved when he checks his cell and sees that no one has called. Sitting in the Mustang looking out over the lights of the valley, he makes a call.

*   *   *

"So?" Julia says, still on the phone an hour later. They're both exhausted. There was disgust in his voice, she tells him, when he asked her repeatedly how she could let this happen. He says he was only arguing that it was wrong for them. And then Chase switches tactics and tells Julia he cannot see a way that he would ever be okay with it but if she wanted to go forward with something like this it was her choice. It had been a couple of days and already it was killing them.

"Tell me something," Chase says.

"Like what?"

"Anything," he says.

"I read that it's twice as safe as having your tonsils removed," she finally says.

10

Hunter and Chase are sitting outside in the heat by the back-yard pool. Chase is here to pick up Brandi. Hunter wanted to come along. The house belongs to Brandi's mother and stepfa-ther who are, apparently, away. The house is a mess: empty bottles of Absolut and Corona and red plastic cups scattered everywhere. Jessica Simpson blasts from speakers the girls have dragged onto the patio. Brandi and her friend smoke Marlboro Lights and drink the Starbucks green tea Frappucinos they demanded Chase bring. They're waiting for a ride to a town house in the Mesas for a two-girl/schoolgirl special. Chase and Hunter were on their way to get ice for Hunter's father's party when Michele called Chase to tell him where to go. Brandi is one of their best girls and loves to get high so Michele asked Chase and Hunter to be cool and let her share Hunter's weed. But Chase and Hunter arrived too early and decided to take a swim and hang out by the pool until it was time to head for the Mesas.

The four of them are on chaises by the pool, stoned. Melted whipped cream drips off the sides of the Starbucks cups onto the concrete. A procession of black ants drown themselves in the sugary white puddles that have formed around the cups. Chase's thoughts drift to Julia and between songs he hears the sound of chain saws and a motorcycle revving and he closes his eyes and hopes to just drift off into nowhere. But the music is too loud for Chase to lose himself and the girls talk over it. When Chase opens his eyes again it's to turn his head to the side and stare at Brandi's tan skin slick with oil. Both girls have their navels pierced and their bikinis are pink and pale yellow. Brandi's friend is the one in yellow and though Hunter told Chase she's younger than Brandi it's hard to tell because of the silver eye shadow and the fake breasts and the cigarette. She has a notebook open on her lap and is copying a homework assignment from Brandi. They're both attending summer school at Centennial. Chase is too high to follow the conversation, just catching fragments.

"I so want your tits," Brandi says to her friend. "How much?"

The girl, barely paying attention, says, "*Free*-ninety-nine."

"Bailey better send some of that my way."

"Bite his nipples when he comes and he'll give you his gold card."

"But fucking Cabo again? I don't think so."

"Like there's something special about it."

"And he doesn't tell you you're there to work."

"Drunk sunburned fags who sweat all over you."

"*It's by the ocean*," Brandi says, mocking Bailey's lazy voice. "*Listen to the waves crashing.*"

"Yeah, but some fat man is passed out on my bed and he's snoring and farting."

"Those look really good though," Brandi says, checking her Nokia.

"Who is it?"

"The Spaz."

"Is she not a complete dyke?"

"With those glasses? With that hair?"

"She wants to transfer to Meadows next year."

"She dropped out?"

"Rush's dad's getting her in."

"Is she fucking him, too?"

"She was at the graduation."

"For Rush?"

"Rush's dad had all these limos lined up waiting to take them to the parties."

"I heard Russell Crowe spoke at the ceremony."

"You know that bitch got into the VIP at Ice on Thursday."

"Rachel did?"

Hunter reaches out and nudges Chase's arm and mutters, "Ice, ice, dude, remind me to get ice for tonight."

"Her mother's a paraplegic," one of the girls says.

"Or a paralegal," the other girl says, their voices a blur in the afternoon heat.

"Rachel was paid like eight hundred dollars by Rush's lacrosse friends."

"For what?"

"To go with them to a room at the Hard Rock."

"Oh God."

"When they were done, she was totally passed out and they stripped her down—"

"Stop—"

5

"And they shaved her head and wrote Eminem lyrics on her ass and—"

"Oh God, stop—"

"And took a shit on her and left her out on the Hard Rock beach."

"I so wish that was true."

"And Bailey says *we're* mean drunks."

"Someone's going to fuck her up for real."

"She's going to get her ass kicked."

"You know Rachel stole three thousand dollars from the suite."

"No way."

"Bailey just keeps it in a drawer."

"And she stole it?"

"Not all at once," one of the voices says. "Over a period of a few days."

"How did the Spaz accomplish this?"

"By replacing fifties and twenties with dollar bills—"

"What a genius. Who's dumber? The Spaz or Bailey?"

"—and always keeping a fifty or a twenty on top of the stack."

"Why did she do it?"

"Rush put her up to it. At least that's what the girls say."

"What a thieving little bitch."

The girl copying the homework tosses the notebook to the ground and the wind ruffles the pages and a few pieces of paper tumble into the pool and neither of the girls notices. As Chase shifts on the lounge, eyes closed, his bathing suit damp from swimming, it occurs to him that either one of these girls could be dead tomorrow. They could simply go to yet another party and trust the wrong person and take the wrong drug and pass out in an empty bedroom and never wake up. This causes something icy to move through Chase.

Brandi straddles Hunter. He wakes up, yawning. "Where is it?" she asks, playfully.

Hunter says, "The blue bag."

"But it's not there," the other girl says. "We already checked."

"Then I don't know where it is," Hunter says, closing his eyes.

"Well, where *else* could it be?" she presses.

"Maybe you've smoked enough for one morning," Hunter says. "Do your homework or eat a sandwich or something. You're blocking my sun."

The girl reaches inside Hunter's shorts and removes a tiny cellophane bag and tosses it to her friend.

"But that stuff is shit," the girl says.

"No kidding," Hunter says.

The girls go inside anyway and Hunter again asks Chase to come with him to the party his dad is throwing tonight and when Chase tells Hunter he can't Hunter rolls his eyes.

"What else are you going to do?" Hunter says. Then adds, "I can't survive it solo."

"I have to drive them to the Mesas in thirty minutes." Chase hesitates and looks over his shoulder toward the house the girls just went into and then back to Hunter. "I don't know what I'm going to do."

Hunter's cell has a Chewbacca ring tone that roars a few times and as he reaches for it, Chase realizes that if he adds their ages together—the girls—they are thirtysomething.

Hunter squints to see the number and answers it and says, "Ice, dude. I got it, Dad. I know, ice, ice, ice," and then he hangs up. Hunter drops his hand to his crotch and adjusts himself. "How do you think this all looks?" he asks, stretching. "I mean, being here and the summer?"

Chase nods. "It is what it is, right?" and then, "Does it matter?"

"Well, you brought me here," Hunter says. "I was just curious what you felt."

Hunter stands and hesitates for a moment as though he can't decide about following the girls inside. He says nothing to Chase. He just walks toward the house, leaving Chase alone and staring into the clear blue water, the notebook paper floating on the surface, the black ants reeling in the melted whipped cream. A chain saw rips through a dying palm, its sound carried by the wind up, and over the wall that surrounds the backyard and then the white glare of sirens wailing somewhere down in the valley reminds him it's time to take the girls to the Mesas.

Inside, Chase follows screams of laughter upstairs. He follows the laughter down a carpeted hallway to a girl's bedroom. He pushes the door open. No one notices him. The girls are still in their bikinis. The three of them are sitting in a stuffed pink chair. The girls are climbing around on Hunter's lap. Hunter isn't wearing his bathing suit. An HP desktop monitor is in front of them while they play to the black eye of a webcam. One girl types and the other pulls her hair up into a ponytail. Chase moves close enough to smell the coconut oil. He reads over their shoulders as they update a MySpace profile. Brandi is now

straddling and dry-humping Hunter's thigh as he buries his face
in her neck and cups her breasts, then slides his hands inside
her bikini top. The other girl slides a hand over Hunter's erection and pulls Brandi's top completely off as, with her free hand,
she adjusts the webcam. Chase turns away, heads downstairs,
and waits until they're finished.

Hunter's father is having a party in the enormous pink house
in the gated section of Summerlin for a comedian he signed to
headline at the Stardust, and Chase wonders if it's the same
comedian Michele went to see the other night. Hunter's father
is an executive at the Stardust and may own part of it—even
Hunter doesn't know, or at least doesn't talk about it, and Chase
vaguely doesn't care. Hunter's dad is too tan and wears a gold
Tank watch and his teeth are bright white from his Zoom sessions and he has been too recently Botoxed: faint red blotches
dot his forehead. Hunter's father calls Chase "Charles" and likes
to squeeze his shoulders and rub his back whenever he says
hello. Hunter once told Chase he thought his father might be
gay (which may explain his mother and the young Italian) but
Chase never asked what made Hunter think that and Hunter
never brought it up again.
    "Leonard Warren just came back from Telluride with an
orange tan and his leg in a cast." Hunter's father is speaking
to a group of thin middle-aged people and he's loud enough
so that Hunter can hear him from across the living room. He
actually looks over at Hunter and Chase just to make sure
they're listening over the soft strains of Mariah Carey. "Lenny
Warren. Leonard. My son's childhood playmate who used to

stick firecrackers up the asses of dead animals—or at least I
hope they were dead." Hunter's father goes on to explain that
Leonard Warren was a disturbed and abused child who was
destined for a life of Disney World vacations with a whale of
a wife and Ritalin rats for kids until Leonard Warren went in
on a real estate deal with a partner of Hunter's father and made
two million dollars last year. The two million helped Leonard
Warren hook up with a gorgeous model-bartender from the
Palms, and when they got married Leonard Warren's father
bought them matching red Hummers.

"And what does my son do?" Hunter's father asks, glancing at Hunter. "You want to tell them, or should I?"

Hunter raises his Corona in his father's direction. "Ativan,
Welbutrin, and Zoloft—it's all working out for you, huh, Dad?"

"I guess I'll have to tell everyone what my son does," Hunter's
father says. "And really, it's nothing to be ashamed of. I mean,
I'm his father and I'm not ashamed. In fact, it's quite impressive.
My son gets set on fire and thrown overboard from a fake pirate
ship four or five times a night and then gets wasted with some
wetbacks at the casino and stumbles in around three while his
friends make small fortunes and marry beautiful women."

Hunter's face is blank as he brings the bottle of Corona
he's gripping to his lips.

"That's what five years at UNLV gets you," his father sighs
theatrically.

"And you still can't figure out why I won't work for you?"
Hunter asks.

His father suddenly walks over and apologizes loudly and
tries to hug his son but Hunter stands stiffly, waiting the scene
out.

"You want to get in on the action?" Hunter's father turns to Chase, grabbing him by the shoulders and holding on.

"What action is that?" Chase asks.

"I could use a sharp mind like yours." Hunter's father laughs and slides his hand up the back of Chase's neck. "What do you do these days, Charles? Last I remember you were painting walls in the ghetto. No one shot you over there I take it?"

"I'm still painting."

Hunter's father takes a deep breath and stares at Chase too long with his glassy eyes. "Have a lovely girlfriend, too, I hear."

Chase glances over at Hunter, who simply shrugs.

"That's admirable." Hunter's father sips from a large glass of warm gin. "I hear she's very beautiful. A businesswoman? Is that right?"

Chase nods.

"Does she have any friends who would hook up with my son?" Hunter's father laughs, and when he brings his hand up to wipe the sweat from his face, Chase notices that the thick gold class ring on his finger is from USC. "I've always had a feeling about you, Charles. That you were the one friend of Hunter's who would do something special and not just run a car wash or manage a nightclub. I always knew that you'd do something real, you know? Something *tangible*."

"It sounds like Leonard Warren's making out." Chase shrugs.

"Leonard Warren is a fraud." Hunter's father closes his eyes and waves a hand around. "He'll be broke and in jail within a year." He starts grinning and then makes a grab for Chase again. "Thank you for being such a good friend to him . . . I'm

referring to Hunter, by the way. He gets so much out of knowing you, Charles." Hunter's father has placed a moist hand on
Chase's cheek and is staring at him lovingly until his fingers
locate the scratches and he snaps out of it.

Michele's wearing shorts and a bikini top and mutters to the
valet as Chase pulls up to the Palace in the Mustang. She says
nothing when she gets in the car so Chase just sits there with
the engine idling.

"Go," she finally says.

"Where am I taking you?" he asks.

"I'll show you."

Chase is staring at her and soon she's staring back. Her
brown eyes seem darker and she's pale; white flakes of dry skin
ring her nostrils and scale her chin.

"Do you want to help me or not?" she's asking.

"I don't know that this is helping anybody."

"I need you with me. I'd like you with me."

"For what?"

"I'm not doing this alone."

"Doing what?"

"Does it matter?"

Chase drives to Tropicana Gardens where Rachel lives. There is
a deserted security booth at the entrance that he doesn't remember from the last time they were here. The asphalt in the parking
lot is sticky and soft from the heat and the tires make a tacky

sound as the car slows in front of the building. Chase tells Michele that he'll meet her upstairs but she tells him to just park the car. When he hesitates, Michele glares and says, "It's all about you, Chase. Right? It's always about you, isn't it?" After Chase parks the Mustang Michele gets out and slams the door and he follows her up three flights of exposed stairs to apartment 317.

Michele keeps knocking on the pale blue door where the 7 is scratched off—there's just the outline of where it used to be.

"I can hear the TV," Michele says, knocking again. "She's in there."

From inside, barely audible: "Who is it?"

"It's me, sweetie. That's me knocking."

The door opens a crack. Rachel peers out.

"What do you want?"

"Hey there," Michele says cheerfully. "Is Bailey around?"

"Later, okay?" Rachel starts closing the door.

Michele blocks it with her foot.

"You said Tuesday, Rachel, and now it's Saturday." Michele's tone is no longer falsely sweet. "We made a deal and we've been very patient."

"It's actually Sunday," Chase corrects Michele but she ignores him.

"Can we do this tomorrow?" Rachel asks.

Michele stares at her through the crack in the door and after a long silence Michele says, "Open the fucking door, Rachel."

*   *   *

The apartment is dark and messy. There are three people in the living room slouching on the leather couch: Rachel's brother, Ronnie, another kid about his age, and a heavy older guy. Wrestling is on the gigantic flat-screen television. There are bottles everywhere: Corona, Courvoisier, Bacardi. The room feels like the third day of a three-day party. Michele leads Rachel down a hallway to a bedroom and the door closes behind them and Chase hears it lock. "That's the move I'm talking about!" the heavy guy wearing a black Raiders jersey yells and grabs Ronnie and pulls him to the floor where they start to wrestle. Bottles are knocked from the glass coffee table.

Suddenly light floods the room. Then a door slams and the room is dark again.

"Oh Jesus, fuck, dude, are you *ever* fucking leaving?"

This is the first thing Bailey says when he lets himself into Rachel and Ronnie's apartment. He's talking to Chase and instead of responding Chase is and is not wondering exactly how and when Bailey got himself a key to Rachel and Ronnie's apartment. The fat dude stands and leaves Ronnie gagging on the floor.

"Is Michele here?" Bailey asks.

The fat dude points in the direction of the hallway.

Bailey nods and surveys the apartment. His eyes fall to Ronnie. "Are you ready?"

Distracted, Ronnie pulls himself up from the floor. Ronnie isn't wearing a shirt and is too skinny.

Bailey stares at Ronnie. "You want to put something on?"

Ronnie digs a red tank top out from behind a couch cushion and pulls it over his head and his arm gets caught in the wrong hole. Bailey sighs. The fat dude is standing now, too, and

suddenly everything centers on Ronnie and his struggle with
the shirt. Bailey reaches out, pulls the shirt from Ronnie, turns
it inside out, then back again, and tells Ronnie to put his arms
up over his head and Bailey puts the shirt on for him.

"Now you go and don't come back until tomorrow," Bailey
says and hands Ronnie a key card. "It's the twenty-second floor
and do not order any fucking porn or room service. Just chill.
There's some weed in a blue Tumi bag."

"What are you going to do to her?" Ronnie asks.

"What makes you think we're going to do something?"
Bailey asks, cocking his head like the curious monster in a hor-
ror movie.

"Dude, I know she fucked up."

"Did she?" Bailey asks, mock-mystified. "Did your sister
fuck up?"

"She's been stealing from you guys." Ronnie's now actively
whining.

"Go, Ronnie," Bailey says.

"She's just a kid," Ronnie says in protest.

"She's your sister, Ronnie," Bailey explains. "And you were
the one who sold her out."

"I changed my mind."

"You sound like a bitch when you talk like that. Go."

Before Ronnie leaves he looks over at Chase standing away
from it all.

Ronnie could stay, Chase thinks. He should but won't
because it's easier to leave. Chase turns away. The door closes.
Ronnie and his friend are gone.

"Everyone's taking advantage of me," Bailey says to the fat
guy in the Raiders jersey. "I mean: what the fuck?"

Bailey wears cargo shorts and a charcoal tank top, and puka shells are strapped around his neck. His eyes are bloodshot. He looks at Chase head-on. Chase notices this because it's something Bailey used to struggle with: those years when he was unable to meet Chase's eyes after what happened.

"Hungry?" Bailey asks.

The kitchen is too bright and Bailey puts four Eggos in a toaster oven. The timer makes a ticking sound as they stand across the room from each other.

"Hunter has this thing for Brandi. It's like a compulsion or something. And I think he's feeling just a little bit guilty that she's, well, not of legal age. Yet. Keep an eye out on that one. Right, matey?" Bailey winks like a cartoon pirate. "He's starting to freak her out a little. All the money he's throwing at her— Jesus, what a tool."

A long silence: the toaster oven keeps ticking.

Bailey stares into the middle distance of the kitchen. Chase wonders what Michele is doing and tries to think of something to say to Bailey, who takes a carton of orange juice from the refrigerator and pours Chase a glass, then drinks from the container. The timer makes a buzzing sound and Bailey removes the Eggos and Chase realizes how hungry he is. Bailey says, "Crispy" and smiles but then he's opening and closing cabinets and he can't find any maple syrup and he curses as he slams a cupboard door. Bailey stands perfectly still in the middle of the kitchen.

"I can't eat this shit without syrup. These fucking kids. Want them?"

Before Chase can answer Bailey tosses the Eggos into the sink, then leans against the counter, seemingly dazed with disappointment. Bailey scans the floor and finally mutters that he's tired, something about too much blow. Chase is gripping the edge of the counter tightly. He shifts his weight from one foot to the other and back again.

"What's she doing in there?" Chase asks.

"She didn't tell you?"

"No."

"Rachel needed a little pep talk from someone she trusts." Bailey shrugs. "I tried but no go."

"About what?"

"Stick around."

Bailey's cell rings. He checks the number and leaves Chase alone in the kitchen. The smell of the waffles triggers a wave of nausea. He tries to hear what Bailey is saying and it sounds like he's giving directions because he mentions I-15 and Tropicana and Chase keeps wondering what Michele is telling Rachel. But the fat guy in the Raiders jersey comes into the kitchen, blocking Chase's exit, and hacks up a mouthful of mucus and spits it in the sink. The fat guy stares at Chase. Chase doesn't look away. The fat guy asks, "What's your fucking problem?"

A stupid grin appears on the fat guy's face.

Chase notices the USMC tattoo on his forearm.

"Wait a minute," the fat guy says. "You're here for the show, right?"

*   *   *

"Dad's such a tightwad," Bailey says. He's back in the kitchen, holding the container of orange juice again and offers Chase a sip even though he never drank from the glass Bailey poured him. "He says nothing good ever happens on East Charleston. He says that no one goes there. Just white trash and wetbacks for dollar drafts. He says opening a club there would be a moronic decision. I wish he was dead." Bailey shrugs his shoulders. "Fuck him." Bailey belches, then dumps the last of the orange juice into the sink and tosses the carton into the trash. "You still painting?"

Chase shrugs. "A little."

"You have a show or something coming up?"

Chase nods.

"And then you leave?"

"That's the plan."

Bailey rubs his face with one hand, processing something. "Hey, did you see my movie?" he asks.

"When I was over at your house for that party."

"Wasn't much of a movie, really," Bailey says. "Just experimenting."

"Yeah, filming Michele?" Chase asks. "Not exactly a movie, I guess."

"Dude, she's a train wreck. She's her own special effect. What else do I need?"

"She needs to be watched," Chase says.

"I know," Bailey says. "She'd disintegrate if people stopped paying attention to her."

This is not what Chase meant but there's no point in explaining it to Bailey. "What's going on in there?" Chase motions toward the locked door in the hallway.

Bailey squints at Chase like he's trying to figure out if Chase is serious, or if Chase really doesn't know.

"She's clarifying things."

"What things?"

Bailey shrugs. "Making sure Rachel knows what *bring half the money the day after you get it and not a day later and not a third of the money or twenty-five percent but half the fucking money because that's the agreement and if you're not comfortable with it fucking quit and we'll find someone who is* means."

Chase can barely nod.

"Let's just say her business model is flawed," Bailey says. "She spends too much. But then her role model does, too." He laughs spitefully. "That suite is fucking killing me." Bailey lights a joint and takes a drag. He offers it to Chase. "It's been like a month now," Bailey says, exhaling. "But it's all the extras that cut the profit: the room service, the movies, manicures, these idiot chicks run up all kinds of bills. That's what's fucking everything up. That's what I didn't take into account and it pisses me off. But it's partially my fault. I need to keep a tighter rein." Bailey manages to locate where Chase is through the haze. But then the bedroom door finally opens and Michele sticks her head out.

Chase follows Bailey into the room. Michele closes the door and then—after a beat—decides to lock it. Rachel sits on an unmade bed with pink sheets, her knees to her chest. The room is dark because the blinds are drawn. A ceiling fan slowly turns. Michele sits on a faux-leather chair in the corner of the room. She doesn't take her eyes off Rachel. Bailey leans against a white wall with his arms crossed.

"I can get it," Rachel says.

"But can you get it today?" Michele asks.

"I can get it in a couple of days."

"How are you going to get that much cash in a couple of days?"

Silence from Rachel before she says, "Let me do a few more like we used to do."

Bailey sighs. "Did you think we wouldn't notice?"

Rachel doesn't move.

Bailey snaps, "Speak, bitch."

"I didn't say anything."

"Well, you better fucking say something," Michele says.

Rachel chews her lower lip.

"If you're screwing him, you're screwing me, idiot." Michele glances over her shoulder at Bailey.

"I can't do it," Rachel says.

"You don't have a choice," Bailey says.

"I don't want to do this anymore."

"Then pay us back the money you owe."

"But I can't now."

"Round and round we go," Bailey says.

"Look, what I've been trying to propose to you, Rachel, for the last fucking hour, is that our idea is easier," Michele says. "A couple of these and you're free."

"But I don't want to do it like that. I thought you knew me. You know I tried that one night with those guys and . . . " Rachel starts breaking down. "You were so fucking cool, Michele. You told me—"

"That's your big mistake right there, bitch," Bailey shouts. "Michele's fucking nuts."

"You lied to me," Rachel is sobbing at Michele.

Michele sighs. "I thought you had fun that night. I thought you eventually said it was okay."

Rachel is shaking her head back and forth like a child. "When those guys came to the room I told you and you knew I didn't want to do it and you lied—"

Michele stands up. "You called me for a month begging me to let you hang out with us. You said you needed cash. You were the one, Rachel, who told us you were willing to do what it took for that cash. You took advantage of me."

"You took advantage of me, too," Bailey adds.

"I am so tired of your shit," Michele says.

Rachel clamps her hands over her ears—her face red—and screams, "I'm not ending up like you, bitch."

Michele whips her cell at Rachel and it cracks the oval mirror over the bed. No one says anything. Michele calmly reaches into her purse and removes a cigarette and lights it with a steady hand. She takes a long drag and exhales out the side of her mouth and sits back down and crosses her legs. It's a studied look, like she's seen this pose recently in a movie: legs crossed, arms folded, cigarette burning. She doesn't take her eyes off Rachel. Chase begins to think that there is nothing Rachel will be able to do or say to get out of this. But then something breaks and Michele is smiling at Rachel.

"You're beautiful," Michele says. "Isn't she, Bailey?"

Bailey smiles, too. "She's a fucking hottie."

"I don't feel good," Rachel pleads.

Michele's gaze falls on Rachel's tan thighs. "Your legs look awesome. You've been doing the Pilates I told you about?"

Rachel nods.

Michele leans forward. "Don't make this such a big deal. It's just an hour. It's just a couple of jobs. It means nothing. And we're back to square one when it's over."

"A couple?" Rachel asks.

"A few," Bailey corrects. Rachel looks at him. "How much is the rent here? Like a thousand? Eight hundred? That's three nights in the suite, right Chase?" Bailey turns to Chase. Chase is clenching and unclenching his jaw. "I mean, we could clean this place up and it would be perfect. Right, Chase? Isn't that a great idea?" The way Bailey says this—menacing, aimed at Chase—opens up something festering and alive.

Chase can barely control it. He wants to hurl himself against Michele.

Rachel looks at Chase. Chase is forced to look away first.

"Fucking psycho dick," Rachel screams, shaking. "What the fuck are you even *doing* here?"

"Enough," Bailey snaps.

"What about Cabo?" Rachel asks in a small voice.

"What about it?" Michele glances over at Bailey, who just gives a quick nod.

"We're still going?" Rachel asks.

"First-class tickets and your own suite," Bailey says.

"You can even bring a friend," Michele says.

"Can I bring Rush?"

"Of course," Bailey says.

Chase feels himself sinking into the wall.

Michele hands Rachel a roll of toilet paper. "Clean yourself up."

There's a knock at the door. Bailey walks over and opens

it a crack. The fat guy says something and peers inside. Bailey
nods and closes the door.

"Who are they?" Rachel asks.

"It doesn't matter." Bailey says. "Nice guys."

"Friends," Michele says. "Friends of ours."

"They're from Riverside," Bailey says. "They're from nowhere."

Rachel reaches for her cigarettes. Michele grabs her arm.
"Later," she says. "After."

"What time do you want me there?" Rachel asks.

"Where?" Bailey asks, suddenly confused.

"The suite," Rachel says. "What time?"

"They're coming here," Bailey says.

"Where? Here?" Rachel asks, her face crumpling again.

"It'll be okay," Michele says.

"But what about the suite?" Rachel asks, sobbing.

"Here is fine," Michele says.

Rachel is shaking her head. "Not here. Not in my bedroom.
Let's go to the Palace."

"But here is better," Bailey says and looks over at Michele
who nods, her eyes locked on Rachel.

"You gave them my address?" Rachel asks, choking. "You
gave them my fucking address?"

Bailey looks at Michele, then at Chase. "That's the plan.
Right, Chase? Here, and we start today."

"I'm tired," Rachel says. "I'm tired. And I'm feeling really
sick, too."

"You're fine," Michele says.

Rachel is sobbing again. "I have my period."

"Bullshit," Michele says.

"They don't mind," Bailey says. "That's okay."

"She doesn't have her period, Bailey," Michele says.

"I do."

"Show me," Michele says.

"What?" Rachel wipes her eyes.

"Let's see it."

Chase clears his throat. "Michele."

"You're still here?" Michele asks but doesn't look at him. "Get up and show us. If you do, fine, we'll postpone."

Rachel's shivering. She says nothing.

Chase notices how small Michele's eyes are. Michele tucks her hair back behind both ears.

"Michele," Chase says again.

"What are you still doing here?" she asks.

"Because you wanted me to be," Chase says lamely.

Bailey moves to the window and pulls back the blinds. Sunlight floods the room and Michele moves into its path but her face is hidden in the remaining shadow as she stands over Rachel. She reaches down and gently touches the girl's chin, lifting it. Rachel turns away, causing Michele to mutter something. Michele grabs Rachel's face and squeezes it and Rachel tries to push Michele away but then Rachel makes a horrible squealing sound as Michele forces something into her mouth and says, "Trust me, it's better this way."

A sunburned man in his late forties who wears a thin mustache and has his blow-dried hair combed back. The man is naked and has an erection. The man tells Rachel to stand up. He wanted it this way. He wanted to be in the middle of the room. The man wanted to be nude. He wanted to have the girl on the bed. He wanted the girl to be in pajamas like she was getting ready for bed. He wanted to share the girl with a friend of his but the friend is late. The sunburned man has decided to start anyway. He starts to masturbate. The man tells Rachel to watch him. The man wants Michele to say, "Do it." Rachel opens her eyes. Rachel leans forward on the edge of the bed. The man laughs at something Bailey, now shirtless, whispers to him. The man wants Chase, also shirtless, to stand over Rachel. The man wants Chase to pull the hair back from her face. The man wants Chase to ask her if she brushed her teeth. The man asks Rachel if she ever walked in on her daddy doing this. The man says he always wanted a daughter so he could fuck her whenever he wanted. Whatever Michele gave Rachel has kicked in. Rachel, trembling, is so wet her thighs are slick with it.

The spotlight from a police helicopter zigzagged randomly back and forth across the neighborhood. His mother sat on the porch smoking a cigarette and sipping gin on ice and staring at the huge Sahara marquee, its enormous burnt-orange digits alternating back and forth between 9:02 and 100 and 10:08 and 98 and 11:11 and 97. Once she had drunk enough to get to sleep Chase helped his mother to her bedroom and then locked all the windows and doors. He then went to his room and called his father in Malibu but nobody picked up. Carly was listening to Pink Floyd and had a joint going and her bedroom was dark except for the flickering light from candles. She sat in front of the vanity that once belonged to their grandmother, putting makeup on in the dark. Carly took a drag off the joint and asked Chase if he was coming out with her tonight. "Where?" he asked. She smeared dark eye shadow over her lids and grinned and mentioned Michele and the new outfit she'd be wearing. Chase asked her if she really wanted to go out because the past few months had been tough and most nights out ended badly: Carly drank too much and passed out in strangers' apartments and got into fights with girls. "Bailey's not a stranger," she said and their eyes met in the mirror and Chase sighed and Carly said that he should come, too, and all Chase remembers is that he smiled at her as Pink Floyd crashed into "You Better Run."

11

Julia is asking Chase again because he tells her he wasn't listening the first time she said it. But that's not the truth: maybe he was simply too tired to process the information. They have been on the phone for three hours. Chase walks to the window and looks out over the parking lot. Two little girls race their bicycles from one end to the other, the orange sky all around them and a heavy woman drinking a beer and watching her daughters.

"What do you think is going to happen?" Julia asks. "If we don't have it."

"I want this to work. This can work."

"You're not here," she says. "Why is that?"

"Being there would help?"

"It might."

"How would that help, Julia?"

She says under her breath, exhausted, "We've been on the phone for almost four hours."

And then Chase says it.

"I don't want to be a father."

* * *

Michele calls from Brandi's house. Michele went there this afternoon to collect. Michele went to Brandi's house unannounced. This is what Michele did today because she also needed to know if the rumor was true: that Brandi had new breast implants and that Bailey paid for them.

"You're surprised?" Chase asks. "Are you really surprised?"

"Brandi's turning the girls against me."

"What would you like me to do about it?"

"I'm alone here and she's not."

Chase knows how to get to Brandi's house in Summerlin. Michele has forgotten that Chase has already been there many times and when she started giving directions he cut her off. Chase parks next to a massive black Ford Excursion attached to a trailer with four Jet Skis on it. In the intense heat, Chase's feet stick to the driveway's asphalt. He follows the screams of laughter through an open gate at the side of the house. In the backyard Brandi sits in the sun just outside the shade from a gigantic umbrella situated between the pool and the house. She wears sunglasses and pink cotton shorts. A cigarette burns in an ashtray next to a can of Diet Coke and copies of *People* and *Star*. She doesn't turn her head to look at Chase when he walks past because of the iPod and he can hear her groaning and what he thought was a towel is actually bandages—sheets of thick gauze wrapped around her chest. Michele materializes.

"Brandi's sweet sixteen," Michele whispers into his ear. "They're hideous. She got them two days ago with guess who?"

Brandi keeps moaning, her head shifting from side to side.

"Is she okay?" Chase asks.

"She's been doing that all day" is Michele's only answer. "It's the Vicodin."

Michele takes his hand and leads Chase around the pool to where Brandi's brother and his friends—teenage boys, tattooed, muscular, highlights in their spiky hair—surround a large metal crate. There's an animal inside the crate. At first Chase mistakes the animal for a dog but it's too skinny. And then Chase realizes what it is.

"They caught it two days ago," Michele tells him.

"You look awful," Chase says suddenly.

She just stares at the terrified animal and her words come out slowly. "Rachel called me."

"Why?"

Michele doesn't answer. Chase asks her again.

"She said her brother—charming Ronnie, you remember him, right?—wanted to kill me and Bailey and yes, you, Chase, were also included on his list." Michele contemplates something, her expression changes. "But then she said she understood what we made her do and that maybe she deserved it."

"I think she's fucking with you. I think that change of heart is bullshit, Michele."

"I know. I have to figure out some things." Michele pauses and closes her eyes for a long time. "My fucking head's about to explode."

"Rachel is totally fucking with you." Chase pauses. "She's in on it with Bailey."

Michele is staring at Chase and asking him, trying to get his reassurance that Bailey doesn't know what Chase is doing.

She insists that the whole point of that day with Bailey and Rachel in Rachel's apartment was to prove to Bailey where their loyalties lay.

"It clearly didn't take," Chase says, flinching.

"And then there's Brandi," Michele murmurs. "She brings in so much money. And it's hard to find someone that young who's reliable."

"Don't you think it's clear now where her loyalties are?" Chase spits out.

Michele is looking away while Chase points out the obvious: all the girls do is talk to each other. It doesn't matter if they swear to God they won't tell Bailey a thing.

"Watch your fucking back with that chick," Chase says. "She's unhinged."

His anger turns to exhaustion so quickly he almost starts weaving.

"I have to get a handle on this quickly." Michele is shaking her head. "There's no one I trust now. Do you know that? No one."

Someone screams. The boys curse. They point at the crate.

Chase watches the animal cowering. Its fur is ruffled by the hot wind and it makes sick whimpering sounds. The coyote is small and curled up, terrified. It tries to hide its head under its paws but is shaking too violently to accomplish even that.

"Look at its teeth, dude," a boy says. "Those fucking fangs rip through your flesh."

"Tim said he saw a pack of them tear some neighbor's dog to shreds."

"Look—it's pissing and shitting, dude, it's so scared," another boy says, excited.

Another boy holds his cell phone up and points it at the animal.

"I can't watch," Michele says. "I'm going to be sick." She turns her head.

One of the boys holds an aerosol can and a lighter and when he approaches the animal Chase makes a connection and finally notices the matted, blackened fur and the singed flesh near the coyote's hindquarters—its tail has been burned completely off. The boy flicks the lighter and a long orange flame dances in the wind. Chase turns away and looks at the house instead. A little girl watches from an upstairs window. The coyote makes a sound Chase has never heard before. And then an older man appears in the doorway of the house. He is wearing a white button-down shirt and khakis. Chase assumes the older man is Brandi's father. This relieves Chase, but only for a moment. An explosion causes Chase to whip his head around. The boys are throwing firecrackers at the coyote.

The man stares out at the yard and brings a glass to his lips.

Michele is shivering in the heat. Michele tells Chase that they never should have come here. Michele says they should leave.

The older man hands the glass to Brandi. He kisses her head. He walks toward the boys. Chase's eyes are fixed on the unlit flare in the older man's hand as Michele starts to walk away. Chase wants to be in the car before the boys do anything else to the coyote. Brandi mutters something to Michele that causes Michele to stop. Chase moves toward them but can't make out what they're saying. Brandi gestures at Chase. Michele shakes her head. Brandi turns away after Michele slaps her.

*   *   *

In the Mustang Michele keeps shaking. There is something about her eyes that Chase has never seen before. She keeps asking him if anyone is following them even as she continues checking the rearview mirror and looking over her shoulder. When Chase slows for a yellow light at Summerlin Parkway Michele screams, "No!" and presses her foot down on the accelerator and the Mustang speeds through the intersection and she screams, "Are you fucking serious? Keep going." And then when Michele's cell rings and she checks it she says one name: "Bailey."

"Don't take it," Chase says. "He's going to play along like he doesn't know a thing. He's going to play it like you two are still working together."

But it's too late. Michele answers the call.

Michele tells Bailey that she can't right now. Michele tells Bailey to send someone else. Michele tells Bailey to send anyone. After this she's quiet for a while, listening. Over the roar of a passing tractor trailer Chase can hear Bailey shouting.

"Because I'm bleeding," Michele says and clicks the phone shut.

"What in the fuck is going on?" Chase asks. "Where in the hell are we going?"

"I don't know," she mutters. "I don't care."

"What was Brandi saying to you? Why was she looking at me?"

"Because she heard you were there."

"Where?" Chase asks. "She heard I was where, when?"

"At Rachel's," Michele says. "That day in the bedroom at her apartment."

The memory of what happened in that bedroom silences Chase.

"Just drive."

"Where should I take you?"

"I don't know," she says again.

"The suite? Bailey's? Where?"

"Keep driving," she says. "Just keep driving."

Chase's apartment is hot. The air conditioner is still broken. He tries to turn it on but nothing happens. Michele's cell rings. It's Bailey again. She doesn't answer it. She leaves the phone on the bed. She pulls her shirt off and drops it on the floor. She trudges into the bathroom. Chase hears the water running in the shower. He opens all the windows after trying to turn on the air conditioner yet again. Bailey calls and leaves a message. Chase listens to it. Bailey asks Michele to do two hours in the suite. The cell on the bed rings endlessly. Chase changes into basketball shorts and nothing else. He sits on a stool in the bedroom listening to the calls come in. Chase tries to look through slides for the show at Devon's gallery but can't focus. Michele walks out of the bathroom wearing only underwear. She looks at the cell phone, which is ringing again. Her hair is wet and water drips from it onto the hardwood floor.

"Just take the call," Chase yells. "Maybe they canceled and you can go see a doctor instead of doing two guys from L.A."

"Do you have a hair dryer?" Michele asks. "And stop yelling at me."

She pads into the bathroom and comes back with a towel wrapped around her head. She lies on the bed and stares at the ceiling.

"Michele."

"I won't stay long," she murmurs.

"Why would you even consider doing this?"

"It will look bad if I don't?"

"Is that where we're at now? At things looking bad?"

"Yes," Michele says. "That's where we're at now."

"What the fuck are we doing, Michele?" Chase shouts.

"Are you going to let me sleep or should I leave?"

She lies with her eyes closed tightly, curled up on the bed. Her left leg shakes. She's sweating. "I never sleep anymore," she says. Chase ignores her. He's arranging the slides for the show at Devon's gallery, ranking them from best to worst. There are eight and most of them are terrible except for two, which are just okay. Then there are the handful that got Devon's attention and Chase considers simply showing those: his mother, Michele, Carly, the Strip on a rainy Friday afternoon. The prospect of hanging work that is five years old and passing it off as new depresses him. Chase tries to remember the time when his slides seemed better and can't and this thought triggers a wave of fear: the show won't be anything special, the show won't lead to anything that will help him, and after the show is over he'll still be in Vegas with Michele and he won't have anything to take to Julia in California and he'll be no closer to becoming that smug white boy profiled in *The New York Times* with a model on his lap.

"Do you care what happens to me, Chase?" Michele asks.

He doesn't say anything, fingers a slide.

"Bailey does," she says. "Despite everything, I know he does. But do you?"

He remembers her lying on his bed in the Green Valley house on Saturday nights.

"Do you care what happens to me?" she asks again.

"It already happened to you," he says.

12

The apartment is cool again and the air filled with the vanilla incense that Chase has been burning all morning. A paint-splattered drop cloth covers the floor and an easel sits empty between the red leather chair and his bed. He sips strong coffee from a blue mug and gazes at the collection of slides fanned out across the drafting table. There are forty of them and they're mostly oil on canvas, a few prints, some charcoal sketches. He completed the majority of them after college—his first year teaching in Vegas—and those are the ones that are better, Chase tells himself; those are better than anything that came before, better than anything he did in high school or the first two years back east at NYU or in his last two years at UNLV. He tells himself there is every reason to be optimistic. Chase calls Devon and leaves a message about the show and asks whether there will be space for him to work off the canvas—to incorporate some of the room itself: the wall, the floor, the ceiling. He's not sure how or what he'll even do and will likely feel foolish tomorrow when Devon calls back because by then the buzz will have faded and

Chase will back off his request for more space because he knows that these bursts, these highs, are short-lived and superficial. After Chase hangs up he stretches a new linen to replace another he wasted on a rushed self-portrait. He likes the physicality involved in doing it himself. He uses a paring knife to trim the excess fabric and lightly slices a finger but it requires only some cold water and a Band-Aid. His apartment feels like a studio again. Julia needs to see this when she comes: Chase working, focused and hungry; the boy she fell in love with in New York; maybe it will resurrect her optimism.

"It didn't take," Julia says flatly when she calls three days later.

Chase hasn't slept in what seems like days and asks Julia to say it again.

"It didn't work," she says.

"What didn't work?"

"I got the injections and I was supposed to bleed and it was supposed to come out and it didn't so I have to try again."

"You went?" he asks.

"It didn't take. I just want this over with."

"Jesus, Julia." He swallows. His throat is dry. He takes a deep breath and exhales.

"I'm going to do it there."

"Wait." Chase pauses. "Just . . . wait." But no more words come until he says, "I'll find somewhere—"

"I already know a place," she says.

"What do you mean you know a place?"

"On East Charleston," she says. "Do you know where that is?"

* * *

It's Tuesday morning and the traffic is bad on East Charleston. The top of the Mustang is down and the sun is white and huge and they're breathing in exhaust fumes and hearing only the other cars and horns and parts of songs coming from the radio. Chase keeps adjusting the vents and trying to point the teeth of them in Julia's direction so that all the air from the air conditioner is aimed toward her but it's not making any difference because the air seeping from the vents is warm. Julia wears sunglasses and the same orange long-sleeved T-shirt she slept in even though it's at least ninety degrees outside. When Chase asks her if she's hungry Julia reminds him that she can't eat anything for twenty-four hours before the procedure and Chase apologizes because he keeps forgetting this, which infuriates Julia. At a red light on Bonanza it suddenly occurs to Chase that he did not bring cash and that his American Express card won't work. "I'm sorry," he says. "About what?" she snaps. He doesn't answer, just signals and pulls into the left lane and at the next intersection makes an illegal U-turn and heads back in the direction of the Strip and then turns onto Sahara and then right onto Beverly. He leaves the engine idling and runs inside his mother's quiet, empty house and takes a single orange-and-white $500 Stardust chip from his dresser, one he hadn't been able to part with because it was the last one given to him by his grandmother. He drives fast back to the Strip where he stops at the Stardust and walks quickly inside and stands in a slow-moving line until he changes the chip so he can pay for the procedure.

* * *

The waiting room of the clinic is crowded with maybe a dozen young girls. When they sign in the receptionist tells them they're backed up today. They wait ninety minutes. Julia makes eye contact with various girls in the waiting room. She watches them carefully as their names are called. They all seem to walk like they have been through it already. Chase is the only man in the room.

Julia stares at Chase impassively across the yellow table at California Pizza Kitchen. The restaurant is too bright. The sun pours through the sweeping windows. He has to squint to see her. It's three o'clock and crowded but Chase isn't hungry and they just sit in a booth not drinking the two iced teas they ordered. The pain, Julia says, is nearly gone, though it was bad last night. Last night: standing behind a couple arguing in German at Badlands Liquor and Spirits, the woman's mascara streaking down her pale cheeks; Chase driving back to the apartment through the warm wind with a bottle of Ketel One and a liter of 7Up, looking at the billboard with the male model asking "What Kind of Man Are You?" Chase drank most of the vodka before he passed out at dawn while Julia slept in the bed, moaning in her sleep.

"We never even tried," she said when they both woke up and looked at each other.

The sheen of sweat on Julia's forehead looks metallic beneath the fluorescent lighting in the restaurant. She keeps staring at Chase.

"What is it?" he asks.

Julia says nothing and continues to stare at him.

Chase pours another packet of sugar into his iced tea and watches as the grains fall to the bottom of the glass. Once they settle he looks back at her.

"You've been in my life for a long time and I feel nothing," Julia says. "I spent too many hours thinking about us and planning our lives together and right now I feel nothing. I'm not angry. I'm not even sad. When I look at you it's like you're not even there."

"We can get past this." But the words come out with almost no conviction.

She laughs, exasperated. "Don't talk like that. You sound like a zombie."

"I mean it."

"It's just sad when you talk like that," Julia says. "You sound like your hooker friend and there's nothing to do but cringe."

"I'm sitting here with you now," he says. "I'm not running from anything."

"Maybe," she says. "Or maybe it just looks like you aren't."

Chase stares at her, his chest tightening. "Nothing is easy, Julia."

"Don't defend this. Not with me. Not now. Don't defend how this ended up."

"Maybe you should figure out why you kept me around as long as you did."

The Mustang speeds toward McCarran where Julia's flight leaves in an hour. Julia tells Chase to slow down. Chase ignores her. Julia says it again. Chase brakes too hard. Julia lurches forward in her seat. He apologizes. She shakes her head as he pulls up to the terminal.

"Do you really think anyone here cares about you?" she asks.

"I don't know."

"I cared about you," she says.

"I know."

"Did that mean anything to you?" she asks.

He nods.

"What did it mean?"

He loses it. "It meant everything." He begins to cry uncontrollably.

Julia gets out. She reaches into the backseat for her bag. "Don't get up," she says.

It was two a.m. when Chase finally fell asleep after coming home from the party. It was Michele who called and woke him. Her voice cracked when she told Chase to come to Bailey's house. Chase, groggy with sleep, asked Michele what was wrong and Michele finally just said, "Everyone's gone." Chase got to Bailey's before the ambulance did (later, he found out that the driver had gotten lost). The night before—when Chase told Bailey he wanted to go home—Bailey promised that he would look after Carly. There were so many people in the house when Chase left: people he knew from school, kids who knew Carly, kids who would come by the house on Beverly in their new Jettas to pick Carly up, kids who would take Carly to Wet 'n Wild and the Fashion Show Mall and the Desert Breeze Skate Park where they would get high with all the cute skater boys. The place was teeming with her friends and it all seemed safe. Chase left Michele and Bailey and Carly in the master bedroom. They were sitting on a king-size bed in a circle, their score of meth in tiny blue cellophane balls spread out between them like some kind of treasure they had found and were about to split up. There was an eagerness on that bed that was almost infectious, that almost made Chase stay. But he said goodbye and walked through the house and into the night.

On his way back to the city Chase is thinking: it's the end of June. It has been six weeks since he moved Michele into the Sun King suite on the twenty-second floor of the Palace. Chase doesn't know how much he's made but he has $6,000 in cash at the apartment on Boulder. And he tries not to think about the clinic on East Charleston, the smell of the pale green waiting room or the way Julia looked at him when she disappeared into McCarran. He just wants to make it to his bed in the air-conditioned apartment and cry until he falls asleep and then he'll figure out what comes next. He passes the billboard, the male model in red underwear asking the question Chase can't answer. It's still only June, he thinks.

Bailey's white Impala is parked in the gravel lot outside of the complex on Boulder. Chase glances back at it twice on his way up the exposed stairs to his second-floor apartment.

"Why are you staying?" Bailey is asking. He has a large red welt on the left side of his face and scratches on the pale underside of his forearm. "There's nothing going on here. I don't understand why you haven't left yet."

"What makes you think I'm staying?" Chase asks casually.

"Because you're still here," Bailey says. "But there's nothing here for you."

"This doesn't have anything to do with me, Bailey," Chase says. "This has something to do with you, not me. What do you want?"

"She says I'm abusive and insecure," Bailey says. "Do you think I'm abusive and insecure?"

Chase walks to the window and peers outside at the Impala and recalls nights riding shotgun around the valley. Michele would be in front between them on the red leather seat. Chase is about to ask Bailey to leave when the phone rings. Chase wants it to be Julia. He wants to see her name and number on the caller ID screen and tell Bailey he's got to take the call and to get the hell out of his apartment. When Chase sees who it actually is he doesn't pick up. The phone finally stops ringing, then starts again, another call.

"Answer it," Bailey says, glaring at Chase.

Chase glances back at the display.

It's Michele for the second time. Michele knows Chase always checks his caller ID before answering. The third time it rings Bailey walks over to the phone and looks at the caller ID and answers it.

"He's busy," Bailey says and hangs up and looks at Chase. "She's sorry she can't talk but she's feeling a little shaky right now. She's not herself."

Bailey scans the apartment. The kitchen is spare: a microwave, a toaster oven Chase never uses, red and blue plastic cups. An old Sony nineteen-inch color television he's had since college. The only thing relatively new is an HP desktop.

"How much has she given you?" Bailey asks.

"Not enough."

Bailey takes another look around the apartment. "You really don't have shit." Bailey considers something. "So you probably banked it. So you probably gave it to your girlfriend to invest. You probably told her you won it. Or maybe you lied and actually told her you sold a painting. When is that lame show you're in?"

"Tomorrow."

"And after the show?" Bailey asks. "Will you be leaving then?"

"I don't know."

Bailey's eyes are small and bloodshot. "There's this theory that says every seven years—" he starts.

"You already told me." Chase closes his eyes for a long time and asks, "How is Rachel's place working out?"

Bailey gazes at the floor. He makes a noise that is noncommittal. After a long pause he asks, "Did you think it wouldn't matter whose side you took?"

"I don't know what you're asking me."

"You drive girls in your sister's Mustang because I offered the job to you," Bailey says patiently. "I chose to give you money to tide you over because we have a history. And then you try to convince Michele to fuck me over. Is that your role in this thing?"

Chase shrugs.

"I love Michele," Bailey says. "I'm serious. I love her."

"That's funny," Chase says. "I assumed you thought she was a thieving bitch and made you feel like shit because you're not me."

"That hurts, bro."

"It was supposed to."

"How many girls do you and Michele have?" Bailey asks. "Which ones are on your team?"

"Five," Chase says immediately. The directness surprises Bailey. "But now she doesn't know because they're all playing games and Michele doesn't trust anyone."

"What do we do about this, Chase?" Bailey asks. "Don't you think we have to straighten some things out?"

Chase stares at Bailey.

"Don't put me in this position, Chase."

"Go, dude. Leave. I want you out of here."

"Take it easy," Bailey sighs. "I just wanted to make sure that one of my oldest friends isn't stealing from me."

"I'm not stealing from you, Bailey."

"I want to clarify things," Bailey says. "The girls are booking appointments behind my back and then they're giving Michele the money, right? That's all I want to know."

"I think that's happening. Yes."

"You've got to stop this with Michele. You have to cease and desist."

"Or what, Bailey?" Chase asks. "Or fucking what?"

"I've known you a long time, Chase."

"Jesus, that's so tired, Bailey. Yeah? And? What does that mean?"

"I don't know if this is something you really want to start heading into," Bailey says. "I don't think you want to go where this road is heading. I'm making you an offer to get off the road."

Chase smirks. "I'll give it some thought."

"You really don't have a fucking clue what you're dealing with."

"Are you dangerous now, Bailey? Should I be worried about you?"

"You are not paying enough attention," Bailey finally says. "You are not seeing the bigger picture here."

The way Bailey says this makes Chase's chest tighten. He is suddenly certain that Bailey would tackle him if he moved toward the door.

"You have not been paying attention, Chase."

It's a clear day and Chase lays five unfolded cardboard boxes flat in the backseat of the Mustang and drives across the sun-baked valley to Summerlin where Bailey lives. A black Silverado pickup truck with massive tires is parked in the driveway. Chase doesn't see Bailey's Impala. The front door is unlocked and inside the house it's cool and dark and all the blinds are drawn. Two girls watch *TRL* on a plasma television. Neither one acknowledges Chase. The girls are wearing bikini tops and shorts and when Chase asks if Bailey is around they shake their heads.

"Is Michele here?"

But they're laughing at the shrieking audience on *TRL* and when Chase is about to head upstairs a huge guy comes in from outside wearing bathing trunks and a thick rope chain around his neck. A girl is screaming something in Spanish from the backyard and when the heavy guy slides the door shut behind him the screaming continues but becomes fainter. The heavy guy, whom Chase recognizes from Rachel's apartment as the guy in the Raiders jersey, ignores Chase and walks into the kitchen. The guy holds a bloody rag and tosses it on the counter and grabs a bottle of Clorox from the cabinet under the sink and pours the bleach into a dish towel. When the guy turns to leave he looks directly at Chase and a shadow creeps across his expression, making his eyes seem endlessly black.

"Want to see something wild?" the guy asks.

When Chase shakes his head the heavy guy leaves.

Outside the kitchen window three girls are gathered around two halves of a massive sidewinder snake, a machete tossed next to it, blood on the concrete.

Chase has to pass Bailey's bedroom to get to Michele's. Bailey's door is closed and Chase slows down to listen. He leans against the door but hears nothing. He tries to open the door but it's locked. Michele's bedroom is dark and smells of cigarette smoke and perfume. In the dull light from a rice paper lamp: piles of clothes, ashtrays filled with butts smoked to the filter, melted candles, magazines, shoes, unopened mail, compact discs, and Rachel's Tasmanian Devil bong. Wrapped in plastic and stacked on top of one another are four thick accounting textbooks. All of the furniture is black leather and dark oak, and African masks are everywhere. A framed floor-to-ceiling Elvis poster seems out of place. There are Post-its on the mirror, by the door, on books, on her bedside lamp, on a laptop's screen. An enormous black astrological chart, marking the return of Saturn with a series of yellow dots and intricate patterns of white and red swirls, hangs from another wall opposite the window.

Chase starts tossing Michele's clothes and shoes into the boxes he carried in. He unplugs her laptop and packs it, along with a photo of a dark, haggard woman—her legs crossed, a cigarette in hand, wearing a faded pink Care Bears T-shirt. This is Michele's mother. In a drawer Chase finds the photos of Michele that he took years ago. There are a few with Carly as well. He pauses at one of Michele and Carly at Wet 'n Wild standing at the top of the tower, the sky above them a brilliant contrast of charcoal and bright purple and the wind whipping hair across their faces, half hiding their smiles. Chase gets most of Michele's things into his car. The sun is orange now and the houses cast long black summer shadows. When Chase passes Bailey's bedroom on his last trip inside, music is coming from behind the door. He tries the knob again and this time he's able to slowly push the door open.

A shirtless guy wearing a black skullcap points a camcorder at the two girls from the living room making out naked on a futon. The guy is Rush. 50 Cent is playing and the room smells like marijuana and no one notices Chase standing in the doorway. One of the girls slides her hand inside the other one and Rush, holding the camcorder, starts to touch himself while steadying the camera. He slides across the carpet on his knees until he's in front of the girls, who are now sweating and writhing on the futon, fingering each other. Rush grabs a bottle of baby oil and sprays it over their bodies.

Even though the sun is setting Chase has to squint when he walks outside for the last time, all of Michele's things now packed in the Mustang. A little girl races down the street carrying a lacrosse stick and then disappears into the shadows. A blonde real estate agent gets out of a yellow Hummer with a middle-aged white couple and two small boys, who follow the agent into the house next to Bailey's. Against the orange sky three massive vultures make lazy circles over something nearby.

It was dawn and Bailey's house was silent and warm and Michele was sitting on the floor of the master bedroom with her shirt off. She faced a wall. Sunlight flooded the room. Bailey sat on the bed with his head in his hands. On the burgundy carpet, lying under a single white sheet pulled up to her chin was Carly, her face the color of ash, and the first thing Chase wondered was why they didn't cover it. Chase thought it was blood that was smeared across her mouth, but when he knelt next to her he realized it was lipstick from someone trying to resuscitate her. Chase touched Carly's neck. It felt cold and waxy. Michele kept shivering. She was talking to herself. "Everyone left, you know, everyone left and it's not like anyone tried, I didn't leave, I just watched her and everyone else, they just left . . . " She soon trailed off. Bailey kept his head between his knees. Chase took his hand from Carly's neck and he closed his eyes for a long time. When he opened them, he reached for the sheet and pulled it from her chin. She was naked. Her skin was so pale it made the birthmark on her hip as well as her nipples and her pubic hair seem unusually dark.

"She was like that," a voice said when Chase asked where her clothes were. They didn't know. That's when he saw Michele's T-shirt on the bed. That's when Chase realized that at one point they were going to dress Carly but decided the sheet would be easier. Bailey said that when people overdose they get so hot that they'll strip off their clothes to try to cool down. Bailey was

explaining this as Chase slid his hands carefully under Carly's thighs and lower back and started to lift her. Bailey stood to help. Michele tried to keep the sheet over her while Chase and Bailey clutched Carly's arms and legs but the sheet just draped over her torso and slid below her breasts and eventually, halfway down the stairs, fell off completely.

"Where are we going?" Bailey asked, walking backward down the carpeted stairs of his parents' house, his hands wrapped around Carly's ankles.

"Call an ambulance," Chase said to Michele, who followed, the sheet in hand, still wearing only her jeans and a bra.

"Why?" Bailey asked, his eyes bloodshot from the drugs.

Chase didn't respond. They stood in the entryway to the house. Chase caught their reflection in a sweeping gold-framed mirror on a wall. Chase had been only partially convinced that this was really happening but the mirror told another truth. He was cycling through bursts of incomplete thoughts that took no real shape.

She'll breathe. We'll pound her chest. A closed fist to jump-start. But we have to cover her face. We can't touch her. Mom.

His ears were ringing and the tightness in his head made his skull feel like it was in a vise. He cleared his throat, he found his voice.

Michele walked past them to the kitchen and called for an ambulance.

"Outside," Chase said.

Bailey agreed because he was worried that his parents would be "culpable" if Carly were found inside the house. Michele joined them and was still wearing only her jeans and the bra (it was all she could manage) while she sat next to Carly, the sheet draped over Carly except for her face, on the front lawn outside the house. The grass was thick. The sprinklers had been on throughout the night so the lawn was still cool and wet. The sun was pouring down on everything. They waited for the ambulance. A car drove past and slowed, the driver staring at the scene on the lawn. When Chase stood up the car kept going. And then they heard the sirens in the distance. Michele threw up on the sidewalk. The medics moved quickly even though Chase kept telling them she was dead. They followed procedure. They pressed her neck and held her wrists and lifted her eyelids. They did not attempt CPR. They said "Triple zero." They moved her body onto a stretcher and lifted her into the back of the ambulance.

No matter how many times Chase told them she was dead they didn't seem to listen and so he stopped saying it, and when he rode with her to the hospital they seemed relieved that he wasn't talking anymore. Chase noticed there weren't sirens and the medics no longer moved with any kind of urgency. No one spoke to Chase or even looked at him. The driver spoke to someone at the hospital and told them again "triple zero" and described Carly's condition as showing "no cardiac electrical activity" and in early stages of rigor mortis. Chase slid his hand under the sheet and wrapped it around Carly's head. He felt her hair and it was soft. He spread his fingers like a comb and ran them through it once before they took her body away on a high gurney, its wheels squeaking as they pushed it slowly down a bright hallway.

Chase found himself at a pay phone underneath a television that was bolted to the wall he was leaning against in order to keep from falling. (He had left his cell in the bedroom on Beverly.) He realized it was only eight hours ago that they had sat together in her room. He could have reached out and touched her shoulder and told her to stay home with him and watch a movie instead of going to the party. But she never listened to him when he said stuff like that. And then Carly was sitting on Chase's bed and they were children and it was Christmas morning before anyone was awake and their father was back living at home after moving to California for the summer because he and their mother were going to try to make things work. Carly said it felt weird having him back in the house and in a hopeful tone asked Chase if he thought their father would stay. Chase lied to her that Christmas morning and said of course he thought their father would stay. He knew Carly saw through the lie. This happened after they opened presents, when their father took pictures of the three of them outside in the backyard and never once joined them in a single photograph. He left on New Year's Eve. Alone in the emergency room Chase suddenly felt so cold he was afraid he might freeze.

He opened his eyes and stared at a vending machine and watched as a woman put money into it, causing a bag of Doritos to detach itself from a hook. The woman reached down and grabbed the Doritos from the vending machine's black mouth. Chase picked up the plastic receiver of the pay phone. It felt greasy. He slid two dimes in and pressed the buttons, getting them wrong once, hanging up, fishing the dimes out, and trying again. The phone rang on the other end of the line as the woman opened the bag of Doritos and returned to her seat and stared at the television above Chase's head. On the other end of the line the phone stopped ringing and Chase heard his mother's voice and then he told her where he was.

13

"So where's my shit?" Michele asks tiredly when she calls later that night.

"I thought you were going to Cabo."

"No."

"I've got your stuff."

"And your point is?" Michele asks.

Chase tells her to meet him at the Public Storage on East Charleston at eleven, after his show. Michele agrees. When she doesn't offer to come to the show at Devon's gallery Chase considers inviting her. He suddenly realizes how badly he wants someone there with him.

"You should come to the show tonight."

There's a pause that Chase can't deal with.

"Julia left," he says. "Why don't you come with me tonight?"

"Julia left? I don't get it. Aren't you supposed to follow her to California?"

"Come with me tonight and we can talk."

"I'm sorry she left."

"You shouldn't be," he says. "Or maybe you should be. I don't know."

"Oh Chase, what did you do?"

"Can I pick you up?"

"I can't," she says.

"For like an hour, Michele. You can spare an hour."

"You sound so sad."

"I'm not sad."

"She's better off in the long run anyway."

"Why do you say that? What about me? Am I better off?"

"There's a different answer to that question."

"Come with me tonight."

"That was a really stupid thing you did. All of my shit? What were you thinking?"

"Just come to the show and we'll talk about it."

"Bailey was very impressed, by the way. He's drunk. Don't worry though. He knows I didn't know you would pull something like that."

"He cares, Michele?" Chase asks. "Does he really care?"

"Cares?" Michele thinks about this word. "Well, he's totally predictable with his little choke holds and pulling my hair." She pauses. "People who don't care walk away."

"He had to know this was coming," Chase says. "He had to know that I was going to try to do something for you."

"That was for me?" she asks. "You sure?"

"Yes."

"Connect the fucking dots for me, Charles. Julia's gone and you have all of my stuff and you're on the phone with me now and somehow you don't have the answer."

"What's the question?"

"Bailey is still in the house."

"Do you need me to come over?"

She hangs up.

Chase walks alone into a red-lit room in a white stucco store-front gallery on a bland stretch of Wyoming Avenue. There are only about fifty people but the room is small so it feels crowded. He regrets that he didn't devote more time to this show. The work looks old: his mother's ranch house and the yellow lawn on Beverly Way, Michele nude with knees held to her chest, all legs and arms and black hair, and *Carly*. The canvases hang in the far corner of the room, ignored. The Beastie Boys are play-ing and a tan girl in overalls and a baseball cap carries around a tray with little plastic cups of white wine. Chase guzzles a couple of them. He calls Michele three times and gets voice mail. The gallery is too warm and the ceiling is too low. Chase makes his way to the corner where his canvases hang, clutching his third glass of wine. His bio is handwritten on a blue index card next to the painting of Carly: *Vegas Native, Teacher, Attended NYU and UNLV. Gained notoriety as a high school junior when he was fea-tured in the* Review-Journal *and* LV Weekly *for multicultural mu-rals he painted on the city's west side. This is his first show.*

Chase stares at one of the other featured artists: a thin, plain-looking blonde girl wearing a black T-shirt and cargo pants. Her face is flushed and her cheeks look strained from smiling. Her work is a collage of colored broken glass dangling from filament wire. Chase notices that the shards of glass hang only a few feet from his section of the wall and no one wants to deal with making their way through it to get to his work, but the warmth from the fourth cup of wine courses through him and it's all momentarily okay. He locates the two other artists: a black dude with Elvis Costello glasses and an Asian girl with pigtails and multiple facial piercings handing out pink postcards for her next show. Chase resents them both. He stands alone with his hands shoved deep in his worn olive cargo pants, feeling sorry for himself, getting drunk, wondering just how long he'll stay, why he even bothered to come at all, why he's still here now. He calls Julia. He closes his eyes and ends the call before it goes through. When he opens his eyes another tray of little plastic cups passes by. He manages to lift one from the tray before it disappears. He downs it and feels sick. He stares into the colored broken-glass collage and becomes dizzy. When the nausea passes Chase is still standing there, alone. He had known this night was coming and he had known what he wanted it to be: four or five new works anchoring the wall, Julia here for the weekend in a suite at the Hard Rock, his mother and maybe even Edward at the show with Michele and Hunter and even Anthony and Isabel from his Centennial class, who would have their parents with them, and the night would be his, and he'd spend most of it fending off compliments and thanking everyone for everything and confirming his plans: to leave Las Vegas and continue painting in San Francisco. But none of that matters when his cell vibrates and he sees that it's Michele. She won't answer Chase's questions about where she is and what happened with Bailey. Suddenly it's eleven and Michele demands that he meet her. But Devon is motioning to Chase, raising a bottle of Red Stripe in his direction. Devon wears black jeans and white Chuck Taylors with no laces and a paint-splattered denim shirt.

He's tan and has spiky bleached-blond hair. Chase considers pretending he didn't see Devon and turning away and moving out into the hot dry night unnoticed. But it's pointless. Devon apologizes to Chase for the arrangement. "If you'd gotten it here sooner we could have done something about that."

Michele wears no makeup. There is a red handprint on her neck (this is the outline of Bailey's fingers). There is also a purple welt on her forehead. This can all be seen clearly under the fluorescent light inside the Public Storage building on East Charleston. Chase brushes her neck with the back of his hand. He's surprised that she lets him.

"I went to Bailey's house," Chase says. "Before the show. I drove by. Were you there?"

"Yes," Michele says. "We were there."

"His car wasn't in the driveway. All the lights were off. I knocked and knocked."

"He insists on curling up in the dark with me after a fight."

"Where is he now?"

"He's waiting for you."

"To do what?"

"Nothing. Don't do it. Don't do anything."

It's hot inside the warehouse. The elevator carries them to the third floor. The sound of huge fan blades grinding against metal becomes louder when the doors open. They get off and make their way down the narrow hallway. At the end of the hallway the sound is unbearable. Michele covers her ears with her hands. They don't bother trying to talk over it. Locker number 3114 is secured with the same heavy combination lock it had last time Chase was here. Once inside, Chase pulls the door closed behind them. Michele is on her knees. She's digging through a pile of clothes. She finds the red canvas bag. She counts the money. It's all there.

"Eighty-one," she says, looking up at Chase.

"Take it," he says. "Take it all. All of your shit's downstairs. It's all boxed up. Take everything. Take it now."

She just stares. "What are you doing?"

"You're leaving. Take the money. I've got all your shit in a locker downstairs. Just take it and leave. Go to Sedona. Go to Santa Fe. Go anywhere."

Michele tucks a strand of hair behind her ear. She stares blankly at the money.

"I can't believe I thought I was going to buy a house," she murmurs.

"Just start over," Chase says. "Do this for me. I'll take you."

Michele tells him to shut up.

When Chase asks her why, she says, "Because I'm thinking."

This is what Chase did when Carly died: zipped up the back of his mother's black dress and drove the two of them in her Subaru—because she could barely grip the steering wheel—to the funeral at Green Valley Presbyterian where Chase held his mother's dry, cracked hand the entire time. After the service Chase found his father sitting alone in a rented black Mercedes, sobbing uncontrollably. Later, Michele and Chase drove out to the hills in Green Valley that overlooked the city and got drunk while sitting on the hood of Carly's Mustang. Chase asked Michele to sleep with him that night and she did. And the next day Chase checked

in to Bally's with the money his father gave him before he went
back to Malibu. Chase stayed in the hotel room at Bally's for two
weeks, most of which he spent drinking because at the time that's
all Chase wanted to do.

Michele calls and hangs up. It's eight in the morning. When
they left the Public Storage on East Charleston with all of
Michele's things, Chase drove Michele to her cousin's house
in North Vegas. They both decided she would be safer there
instead of at Chase's apartment or in a hotel room somewhere
along the Strip. When Chase calls Michele's cell and asks,
"Where are you? Why haven't you left?" Michele answers, her
voice dragging, "I don't know. I don't know why I haven't left."
    There's a long pause during which Chase can hear her
breathing into the phone.
    She says she needs to see him. Her voice is so soft that
when he asks her when, he can't even hear her response.
    "Where in the *fuck* are you, Michele?"
    "I'm at my cousin's . . ." Michele stops. "I put everything
back, Chase."
    "What do you mean? No. Michele, no. Please tell me you
didn't."
    "I put it all back."
    "But don't you realize what's going to happen?" Chase
cries out.

Bailey sits in Rumjungle in a dark booth eating oysters and sipping a Corona. Occasionally he glances at his BlackBerry. His

thick, tan arms are lined with scratch marks. He's sitting across from Chase and Michele. This is how Bailey wants it: Chase and Michele next to each other and opposite him. It somehow confirms something for Bailey. "I was watching your movie again tonight, before coming over here, and I realized that there's something not working with it," Bailey says to Michele. "I don't know if it's the way it's cut or the way I shot it, but there's something that's off. Maybe I'm not director material."

Michele shrugs. "Maybe you should have gone to film school."

"Then again it may have been the subject matter."

Bailey slides a black leather carryall across the table toward Michele. He swallows another oyster and then gazes at Chase.

Michele looks inside the carryall and then back at Bailey, confused.

"What's the problem?" Bailey asks innocently.

"What is this?" Michele asks back. "This is like— Are you fucking kidding?"

"It's your share."

"My share of what?"

"Your share of everything." Bailey makes a sweeping, all-encompassing gesture with one arm.

"There was two hundred in the accounts."

Bailey shakes his head. "There was two-twelve."

She looks down at the money in the carryall, then back at Bailey.

"We've reached a point where this little cunt is holding twenty-five thousand in cash and it's still not enough." Bailey sighs. "You basically have to take this. This is all I'm offering you."

"You're shit, Bailey," Michele whispers.

"Was it his idea?" Bailey asks, motioning to Chase.

Michele is shaking her head. "What idea?"

"Was it Chase's idea to try and fuck me?"

"No one's trying to fuck you, Bailey."

"So it wasn't Chase's idea?" Bailey asks. "I was so sure of it."

"It was no one's idea," Michele says. "It's just something that happened."

"How much did you take?" Bailey asks. "I just want to know. You can keep what you made. It's yours, I guess. But I do want to know how much you made using my suite, and my girls, and my idea."

Michele reaches for Bailey's hand and for a moment he lets her take it. Then he pulls the hand back.

"You've had a thousand cocks in you and I've felt every one of them." Bailey says this so tonelessly he could have said anything. "Including his." He points at Chase. "A thousand cocks," he says, shaking his head in disgust. "You're all used up. And since Chase has already done me the favor of moving your shit out of my house, I don't see what else there is to discuss." And then he turns to Chase. "And what is playing out no longer involves you."

"I never really was involved, Bailey."

"You can't be surprised at this," Bailey says, turning back to Michele.

"What do you want?" Michele asks.

"I'll never understand how you do what you do," Bailey says. "I will just never understand how you can be this kind of person."

"I made a mistake," Michele says.

"Shut up. That's not my problem anymore."

"What do you want, Bailey?"

"What do you think you'll do now? Back to school maybe? Are you staying with him?" Bailey doesn't even look at Chase. "Is he finally going to take you away from all this?" Bailey tries to conceal the emotion of the moment by sucking down another oyster.

"What the fuck do you want me to do, Bailey?"

"Oh, that's the nasty backstabbing cunt I'm used to."

"Fuck you."

"I want you to stay in the suite for the next week. It's paid through the end of the month. You were talking about getting an MBA, remember? When his girlfriend was here you were saying you could see yourself doing that and maybe business was something you could pursue because—how did you put it— you had a 'knack'?" Bailey fingers the lip of his beer bottle. "Or maybe you want to compete with me. Go head-to-head instead of acting like one of your skimming, cheating skanks. We can do that." He pauses. "No? I didn't think so. Take the money and clean yourself up. Put this behind you. See a real thera- pist. Find out why you crave cock so much."

Michele is still staring at the money Bailey has offered her. "This isn't enough for anything. What about the house?"

"You mean that house you and your astrologer picked out?" Bailey laughs. "Who did you suck off to get on the list? Who was your inside man?" He pauses. "Do you know what I heard?" He turns to Chase and leans forward. "I heard it was Ted. The fag who stripped at Olympic Gardens and took guys in the back for a hundred a pop. Ted, the meth addict who worked for KB

Homes for like a month and convinced you he could get you a house. We're talking about him, right?"

Michele realizes something and her expression changes. "Have you seen him?"

"Why are you asking? Because he won't return your calls?" Bailey shakes his head slowly. "What did he tell you he did for them that made you think you could trust him with twenty thousand dollars?" he asks. "Ted drove a fucking golf cart for them. Did you eat idiot toast for breakfast? You're such a stupid fuck, Michele."

"Look, what's the point of this, Bailey?" Chase says. "What do you want?"

Bailey ignores Chase's questions and continues addressing Michele. "You don't owe me anything. But if you ever want to make it up to me I need some shit done. Think special favors. Think Rachel. Because right now all you have to show for all the shit you've done to yourself is in that little tiny bag, bitch. All of it. You earned it, Michele. Every fucking dollar. I know it's not what you were hoping for. But it's what you deserve."

14

In the Sun King suite on the twenty-second floor of the Palace, Michele takes a shower and snorts two lines. She has a week to get this off the ground and she is determined.

Michele is sitting on the bed, surrounded by room service trays and candles, and she's going back and forth between her Treo and her laptop. A girl who looks vaguely familiar to Chase sits cross-legged on the carpet, staring at the television. Chase sinks into the massive pillows of the couch and waits.

They had gone to Public Storage on East Charleston. They had opened the locker. As Bailey promised, all the money was gone. Chase asked Michele why she brought the money back to Public Storage after they left with it that day. She didn't respond. Chase asked Michele why she didn't leave. He asked her why she didn't take his calls. "I got high," Michele said. "I was scared." Chase asked her why she didn't accept his offer to drive her anywhere she wanted to go.

"You already do that for me," Michele said.

The girl in the suite with Michele and Chase is seventeen. She's from Henderson. She needs the money. She has a baby. She has day-care bills. She helps pay off her stepfather's gambling debt. She laughs when she says this. The new arrangement is explained and the girl, who was originally hired by Bailey, swears that she will never talk to Bailey again. Michele explains that the new arrangement will be better for everyone: simpler, safer, more profitable. There are four other girls, not including the girl from Henderson, who echoes Michele and agrees that a smaller operation is better. The girl from Henderson keeps taking tiny sips from her soda.

Michele takes a shallow drag off her cigarette. Studying the laptop, she asks the girl from Henderson, "Can you do an eleven? It's out-call."

The girl nods and shrugs.

Michele looks at Chase. "Ten-thirty?"

"Ten-thirty," Chase repeats.

When Chase wakes up it's a little before ten p.m. Michele is typing a message on her Treo. The girl from Henderson is in the shower. Ten minutes later the girl from Henderson blow-dries her hair. She applies too much eyeliner. She spreads body glitter across her chest and neck. At 10:25 the girl and Michele do two lines of coke off the glass coffee table. They kiss each other on the mouth while Chase watches, his eyes glassy and bloodshot. Chase opens the door for the girl from Henderson.

"Come back after?" Michele asks.

* * *

The week is over. It's Michele's last day in the suite. She is pale and patches of acne are breaking out on her chin and forehead. Bailey will not return her calls. Michele wants another week in the suite and she's willing to pay him for it. Also, Michele and Chase are both considering the same question: what should they do about Rachel, who is here in the suite, flushed and shaking, curled up on the sofa, crying for help, streaks of black mascara smeared down her face. Rachel says she wants to work for Michele. Rachel says that Bailey and Rush put too much pressure on her to take the nasty appointments.

"What do you want me to do?" Michele asks.

Rachel wants to stay with Michele. Rachel wants to work with her again. Rachel wants it to be like it was in the beginning.

"I want to level with you," Michele says. "It won't be like that."

"I don't care."

"You can't stay here."

"I know you're doing your own thing and I can totally help."

"You're a mess."

"I have so many cool friends who are totally up for it."

"Rachel, you're a mess and I don't trust you. You shouldn't even be here."

"We can get a place. We can get our own place and do it from there."

"Where? Your brother's apartment?"

"The apartment's gone," Rachel says. "My mother came down to move us out and she took Ronnie to Salt Lake with her. She would have fucking taken me but I disappeared until she left."

"You should get out of here."

"I have nowhere to go."

"What are you going to do, Rachel?"

"I want to go with you."

Michele seems to be considering this. Chase stands up.

"We'll get a place," Rachel says. "Right?"

"And until then?" Michele asks. "Until we find a place?"

Michele looks at Chase before asking Rachel if she can stick around tonight. Rachel nods.

Michele picks up the house phone. She extends her stay in the suite for two more weeks.

The first of the two additional weeks in the suite, Chase is busy. All he does is drive the Strip and 215 and East Charleston and Summerlin Parkway. He takes the girls to houses in the Lakes and Green Valley Ranch and to hotel suites at the Venetian and the Palms. Chase does this without thinking. He takes the money from the girl when she returns to the car. He counts the money out. He slides half of it into his pocket. He takes the girl home or he takes the girl back to the suite if Michele says it's okay. Chase gives Michele the money after each appointment. Michele gives Chase his cut. They order room service. They schedule more sessions. They respond to calls. They interview girls. Chase takes pictures to keep the Web site fresh. He poses them. He leans them over and with an open hand presses gently on the small of their back where they should arch more. He is not paying attention to his new role. He finds himself watching Rachel. He starts smoking weed again. If he wants to fuck any of them he can. Chase does not care what he does anymore. They are teenagers and he starts to wonder what they taste like.

During the last week in the suite Michele disappears. When Chase finally reaches her she says she's at the Travelodge on Bonanza. A young girl opens the door when Chase gets there. Chase asks for Michele. The girl lets him in. The girl doesn't speak. It occurs to him that the girl might have started working for them. Her skin is dark. Her hair is black. It's neatly combed and falls to her shoulders. She wears a pink T-shirt and low tight jeans. The girl smiles easily. She averts her eyes when Chase asks her if she's Michele's cousin because Michele mentioned that her cousin might be moving here from San Salvador. Chase wonders why this girl is in a Travelodge with Michele in the middle of the afternoon. The girl just smiles shyly and then points toward the bed in another room where Michele sits staring at a soap opera. Michele is at the Travelodge on Bonanza trying to clear her head because she's barely breaking even on the suite and of the five girls working only Aubrey is reliable. Rachel skipped two appointments in one week and each time broke down and apologized to Michele and promised she'd get it together. Michele can't afford to give up on Rachel because her picture is the reason most men call.

*   *   *

Chase tries talking to Michele about harmless things. He tells her that Hunter is planning to go to Oregon. He tells her that Hunter is going to stay with his brother who has work for him cutting down trees (Chase does not tell Michele that he has been thinking about joining him). This activates something in her. Michele sits up and reaches for a cigarette. "When you talk to the pirate remind him that he still owes me two thousand dollars." She says this slowly, her eyes trained on the television. "And I thought the pirate was going to Hawaii. I thought he was going to Hawaii because he wanted to surf."

"No, it's Oregon."

"Oh," she says, still staring at the television. "I thought it was Hawaii."

"Michele, are you okay?" Chase asks.

Michele doesn't answer, just stares blankly at the TV.

"I want to tell you something," he says. "I drove Rachel last night. Did she tell you?"

Michele's response comes slowly. "No."

"She's setting up her own appointments."

"I didn't know." Her voice is thick and drugged.

"We need to figure this out."

Michele just nods. "I was thinking we could go to your father's house," she says at one point. "We could drive across the desert to California. We could start over there."

Chase begins to back away from her. She notices.

"Where are you going?"

"Aubrey needs a ride."

"Oh."

"Someone's got to run this thing."

"We could drive all the way to Malibu." She pauses. "Would you ever want to do that?" she asks. "With me?"

"He sold it."

From the driver's seat of the Mustang Chase watches Hunter leaning against the railing at the edge of the Desert Breeze Skate Park, talking to a girl who is nearly as tall as he is. Thin dark clouds reach across the sky like fingers on a giant hand. Hunter is surrounded by guys riding waves of concrete and girls in tiny shorts and pastel tops. Hunter leans in closer to the girl. When he turns toward the parking lot and pulls his hair back from his face, he is looking directly at Chase sitting alone in the Mustang. Hunter raises a hand and lowers it. He walks over but doesn't get in the car.

"Are you going tonight?" Hunter asks.

"I don't know. Are you?"

Hunter sighs. He runs his fingers through his tangled hair. He stares out across the scorched asphalt and says he needs a challenge, though after a pause, he adds that he'll likely end up at the suite because he always seems to.

"I'll see you there," Chase says nonchalantly.

"Where, the suite?" Hunter asks, surprised. "You're still fucking around with that? Dude, enough."

"Michele is so out of it she thinks you're moving to Hawaii," Chase says as they watch a boy tumble off his skateboard and fall hard onto the concrete. "She says you owe her money."

Hunter asks Chase to come with him to Oregon.

"Why?"

"We'll get a place in Eugene. It's a college town. There'll be tons of women."

"Oregon?" Chase asks. "What the fuck would I do in Oregon?" But he realizes that in asking the question he has answered it.

"Come with me, dude, seriously." Hunter stops when he sees the expression on Chase's face. It's hopeless.

"Michele says you owe her two grand," Chase says.

"So you're collecting for her now?"

When Hunter sees that the expression on Chase's face hasn't changed, he grimly turns away. "She's killing you and you're letting her."

"I'm doing fine."

"You really think so?"

"I sold three paintings," Chase lies. "That's something."

The girl behind the desk at Bally's asked Chase how long he'd be staying and since he didn't know he simply told her a week. She asked him if he had proof that he was eighteen and warned him that she couldn't give him a room unless he was. Chase was sixteen but his fake ID said he was twenty-one and from Arizona. The girl behind the desk told him it was a pretty bad fake ID but Chase must have looked so tired and worn out that she felt sorry for him. The sympathy turned to flirting and the girl told Chase she could get fired for doing this so don't trash the room. She asked where he was really from and Chase said Green Valley. She told Chase her cousin lived in Green Valley. Because Chase was from around here the girl gave him a suite for the single-room rate. He was shaky from not eating and needed to lie down. He didn't want to be alone. He asked her where she went to school because she looked so young. She said UNLV. Chase told her she looked like his sister. The girl blushed, flattered. "She's dead," Chase said.

It's the Fourth of July. It's the last night. The suite is crowded and dark. Chase has to wait for his eyes to adjust. He looks around for Hunter but can't find him. The entire room is filled with young girls. Michele is in the bedroom on her cell. When Chase walks in she clicks it shut. Rosa, the dark girl from the Travelodge who turned out to really be Michele's cousin, sits next to Michele, smoking a cigarette and staring at the laptop. On the screen is a photo of Michele sitting on a chair wearing a sheer black body stocking with her head thrown back. Michele is twenty-one on her Web site. Michele and Chase exchange a look. His expression says: you promised me you would get it together, you promised me that you'd use this night to turn the corner. Most of the girls in the suite know Michele and they say hi as Michele leads Rosa around by the hand. The music has gotten louder and the vibe is less relaxed than when Chase first came in. When Chase spots Bailey from across the room he realizes that everything is pointless and the world is wrecked.

Bailey throws his arm around Chase, drunk, and gestures across the room. "She wanted me to see this. She thought it would intimidate me." Bailey considers a cluster of girls in the corner. "It's impressive," he says. "Let me get your opinion. Right there, her, with the hair—the black chick?" Bailey keeps motioning into the darkness of the party. "Sixteen. Goes to Durango." Bailey pauses. "What do you think?"

"About what?"

"Would you do her? I mean, I know you've had a thing for that." And then Bailey leans in and says carefully, "By the way, Michele told me what happened and I'm with you."

"You're with me on what?" Chase backs away.

"Hey, there's no way *I'm* having a kid at twenty-five," Bailey says. "I'm just saying I'm sorry how that turned out." Bailey wraps his hand around the back of Chase's neck. Chase is not afraid of Bailey but the fact that he knows about Julia and their lost child scares him. Bailey keeps asking him about the sixteen-year-old black girl from Durango. "I mean, you're a good judge. Would you do her?" Chase is tense and when he starts to pull away Bailey tightens his grip.

"I'm actually glad you're still around," Bailey says. "Forget all that drama." Chase feels so weak that he can't help but let Bailey pull him even closer. "Forget all of it," Bailey says into Chase's ear. "You're still a bud. You're still my friend. You can stay as long as you want."

Chase could hear the cold air pouring through the vent over the bed and the muffled hum from the generators and fans below the window, which vibrated when helicopters passed too low. He could hear a maid in the hallway singing to herself in Spanish and the clang of silverware and dishes from room service trays being collected. When someone knocked on his door he just stayed where he'd been frozen for the last hour: on the edge of the bed, elbows on his knees, hands clasped as though in prayer. Whoever knocked always went away. Carly had been dead a week.

Michele came over and spent days in the suite, watching movies and drinking brandy. They promised that they'd take care of each other no matter what happened and they both cried and Michele told him how protective Carly was of her when they ran away. When Michele and Chase fucked she kept her eyes open the entire time. She sat over him and said nothing. She barely moved her hips. She just stared at his face and they stayed like that for a long time until he was able to come and then she collapsed on his chest and he fell asleep crying. When Michele woke him up she said she was scared for him and Chase told her he was scared, too. All Chase wanted to do was wait for the sun to set and drive the Mustang convertible across the desert and listen to the mix tapes Carly had made and read through her old notebooks and the letters she wrote to some guy in the marines she dated who dumped her and all the bad poetry she wrote about drugs and rock stars.

Bailey came over once to see Chase at the hotel. He didn't stay very long and was uncomfortable the entire time. He sat on the bed where Chase was watching TV and whenever their eyes met Bailey had to turn away. He twisted the thick silver ring on his thumb and when Chase's head wasn't down Bailey stared out the open window at the lights of the Strip. Bailey looked tan and more muscular than Chase remembered him being the night of that last party and Chase suddenly resented that Bailey was probably working out the same as before, as if nothing had happened. Soon they were staring at a movie about teenagers trapped in a house with a man who liked to cut them open and position their corpses doing mundane things like showering or watching television. Finally Bailey stood up.

"She seemed okay," he said.

"At what point, Bailey, did she seem okay?"

"You're too hard on people," Bailey said.

Chase was drunk and wearing only boxers and asked Bailey, "Am I being too hard on you now?"

Bailey said he understood Chase's anger and that he'd been stoned every day since. Bailey told Chase that he should get out of the hotel room. When Chase didn't respond Bailey sat back down next to him.

"Let's go, man," Bailey whispered.

"That's not a good idea right now." Chase wasn't even aware that he was crying.

Bailey rested his hand on Chase's chest. His palm was open and cool and Chase didn't move. Bailey's face was too close. Chase could smell marijuana and hair gel, and when Bailey's face moved closer to his he felt the warmth of his breath. And then they kissed. Bailey urged him back against the headboard, clumsily. He slid a hand around Chase's neck. Bailey said, "It's okay." His other hand moved to the front of Chase's boxers and eased them down until they were off. Chase kept his eyes open. The light on the smoke detector blinked. It went from red to black to red again.

Chase's apartment is cool and quiet tonight. The only light in the room comes from the computer on the drafting table. Chase reads Julia's e-mail three times before printing it out and carefully sliding it into a manila envelope. He places the terrible thing in his nightstand drawer. He lies awake staring at the television: endless episodes of *COPS* with the volume down. His eyes keep wandering to the drafting table where he sat a couple of months ago and asked Julia to marry him.

15

Chase has a headache when he wakes up. The apartment is dark even though it's just after nine. He showers and puts on cargo shorts and a black Killers T-shirt and drinks half a carton of orange juice. Hunter calls and asks if he wants to go with him to buy new tires for the Caravan before he leaves for Oregon. Chase asks Hunter when he's leaving and Hunter pauses, then says, "As soon as I get the new tires." When Chase arrives at Hunter's father's house he's surprised to find that Hunter already has the Caravan packed and is sitting on the front steps drinking a Corona. Chase struggles to keep his voice level when he asks, "Is this for real?" He motions for Hunter to move over so he can sit down. Hunter slides over and sips his beer. Squinting in the sunlight at the dinged-up Caravan, Hunter offers Chase a Corona.

"It's eleven in the morning" is all Chase says.

"Exactly." And then Hunter asks Chase, "Will you please reconsider going with me?"

"It's tempting,"

"What's stopping you? And don't say Michele."

"No." Chase pauses carefully. "It's not Michele."

"And don't tell me Carly."

The name startles Chase. His face feels hot. There is nothing else to say. After driving Hunter back from the Tire Emporium he simply drops him off and pulls away. On an empty stretch of Summerlin Parkway heading back to the city Chase presses down on the accelerator so hard that the steering wheel shakes. The wind screams beneath the white sun.

It's night and Michele is sitting on a chaise longue at the deserted end of the Palace pool. Heat rises up from the concrete. Next to Michele are a pair of pink cotton shorts, a pair of leather and cork high-heel wedges, a pile of magazines, an iPod, two packs of American Spirits, and a tube of suntan lotion. Chase breathes in the scent of coconut and cigarettes and barely glances at the red blotch on Michele's inner thigh. Chase has to focus on the blue water in the pool, rippling in the wind, in order to keep it together. Michele says the pills only make her feel a little less bad. This could have been done on the phone but he couldn't help himself: Chase wanted to see her. He asks her where he's supposed to go tonight.

"Century Suncoast." She doesn't even look at him.

Chase is supposed to meet Rachel at the Century Suncoast 16 in Summerlin. She isn't where she said she'd be when they spoke. He drives the Mustang in circles around the vast multiplex, his eyes adjusting to the darkness, and then he sees her:

Rachel with a group of girls her age. She spots the Mustang and waves. When Rachel gets in the passenger seat she asks Chase where Michele is. Chase says at the pool at the Palace. Rachel mentions how cool it is that Bailey and Michele worked things out. Chase doesn't bother correcting her. Rachel is staying with a friend in Green Valley Ranch who wants to work for Michele. Rachel says her friend is off the hook and that her YouTube video gets more hits than Kari Sweets. All Chase wants to tell Rachel is that nothing she says matters next to what she is doing and that she will probably be dead soon. But when Chase coolly shrugs, this moves Rachel to grab the hand in his lap and she stares at him, glossy lips slightly parted, almond eyes narrowed, and he's thinking about her in a way that not too long ago he wouldn't have. He suddenly feels both apologetic and younger. He wants to be soft with this girl. Rachel is psyched about the appointment because the guy is loaded. Chase asks her what time the appointment is booked for. Rachel says, "It's at eleven-thirty or midnight. He's supposed to call to confirm." She checks her cell. "But I want to be there early," she says.

"Why?"

"Just to be on the safe side."

"There isn't one, Rachel."

It's now after eleven and Chase is waiting for Rachel in front of her friend's house in Green Valley Ranch. He lets the Mustang's engine idle. He watches the traffic pass along the highway. Rachel has changed into a checkered schoolgirl skirt and a white blouse tied in a knot at her waist. She's wearing black-and-white saddle shoes. Rachel trips coming down the

stairs. She sits splayed out on the second-to-last step of the staircase, laughing. When Rachel gets in the car she kisses Chase.
She insists she's not as messed up as she looks. She grabs his
hand and presses it to her chest. "Does it feel real?" Her breast
feels unusually firm and full. Rachel places her hand on top of
his and presses down. "Feel it for real," she says softly. Chase
gently squeezes it and as he keeps squeezing Rachel he reaches
inside her bra—he has an erection, he wants to kiss her—but
finds a clear gel breast enhancement that Bailey bought for her
when she was working for him. "He thought I needed new boobs
but fuck him." She removes the other one and shoves them into
her purse. "I like my boobs, but by the time you're butt-naked
the guys really don't care. I'm the little girl. Bailey wanted to
cut me open. Bailey's all *I know someone who'll do it right*. I'm
so glad I paid them back. I'm so done with his shit." She pauses
and for once the patter turns somber when she says, "Cabo?"
She sighs. "Yeah, right."

"What's tonight?" Chase asks, adjusting himself.

"I know this guy," Rachel says. "He's cool. A comedian.
He was on *Jimmy Kimmel* once."

Chase is driving fast along Summerlin Parkway toward the house
where Rachel has her eleven-thirty and even though he thought
he was paying attention—winding through smooth dark streets
lined with houses that seem to get larger with each block—Chase
realizes he has no idea where they are or how to get back to where
they came from. He turns the car in to a development named
Canyon Terrace. The wind gusts and shifts suddenly and it keeps
changing directions like it does before a storm. After driving

deeper into the development Chase turns onto a road marked No Outlet. Rachel checks her cell and mutters the address: 13237 Bella Vista. Chase keeps peering into the darkness, driving slowly. "There it is." Rachel grabs his leg.

Chase stops the car.

Before Chase can turn the ignition off Rachel hops out and walks quickly to the front door of the house.

The man who lets Chase and Rachel in is about thirty. He's sunburned. He has a shaved head. He wears a black wifebeater. His arms are sleeves of tattoos. Chase wonders why there is no furniture in the house. The man keeps grinning at Rachel. The fact that Rachel seems oblivious makes it even worse. "Hi, I'm Sleater."

"Where's Van?" Rachel asks.

The man's grin moves to Chase when he answers. "He's upstairs."

"Cool," Rachel says. "This is like a huge house. Is there a pool?"

Sleater says, "Yeah, there is." But when he says this he's looking at Chase.

"I'm going to check out the pool," Rachel says.

Sleater doesn't stop her.

When Rachel passes the kitchen Chase notices another man.

It happens quickly: the three of them standing in the empty living room.

Chase fights the urge to leave by digging his hands in his pockets.

"You guys just move here?" Chase asks.

The man who joined Chase and Sleater has a gut stretching out a Toby Keith T-shirt. He has a long ponytail and a bright red face. Sleater introduces him as John but seems to pause before naming him.

"Where are you from?" Chase asks casually.

"Boulder City." Sleater steps toward him. "Got a light?"

Sleater produces a cigarette when Chase tells him he doesn't.

"Well, let's get the party started," Chase says. "Van's upstairs?"

Sleater nods.

"Are you guys, like, part of his posse, or what?" Chase asks.

"Relax, dude." John grins but it's fake.

Sleater keeps staring at Chase with an expression that doesn't change.

Chase wants to know why they're standing so close to him.

"We're just hanging out, bud. What about you?" John asks. "What are you doing here? Sorry to disappoint you, but you're not our type."

Rachel comes back in from outside.

"You like the pool?" Sleater asks Rachel. "Nice, isn't it?"

"Yeah," Rachel says. "It's really big."

"It's heated, too," John says. "We can all go in later."

When John looks at Chase there's the understanding that Chase is not invited.

Chase realizes that the only way to move through this is to keep everything cool since everything feels wrong.

"So what brought Van out to Summerlin?" Chase asks the

guy with the unlit cigarette. "Does he have a contract with one of the hotels?"

"No. He moved here because of the weather."

Rachel is already halfway up the stairs.

Sleater and John both notice Chase creasing his brow with concern.

"She'll be fine," one of them says.

"No problem," Chase says and it's a bluff. "She has my cell and I want it back."

"But who's going to call you?"

Sleater asked this, his thin lips dry and cracked. Chase realizes that this was a serious question. But before he can answer Rachel calls Chase's name from upstairs.

Chase finds Rachel standing next to the window at the far end of a bedroom lit with track lighting. The window looks out over the blackness of the backyard and the shadowy palm fronds weaving silently in the warm wind. When Chase sees that the pool has no water in it he realizes that this is a setup and that they need to go. Rachel notices the moment that Chase sees the empty pool and her expression is briefly sympathetic. She bites her lower lip and stares out the window. "It's okay," she whispers.

"Let's just get out of here," Chase says. "This was just a bad call. That's all."

Rachel laughs nervously and takes in a deep breath and holds it.

"Rachel." Chase puts his hands on her thin shoulders and she flinches. "We need to go. We have to get out of here."

She's trembling when she says, "You should have known better."

"Rachel," Chase says tonelessly. "Rachel. Rachel."

"You're fucking dead," she gasps, backing away from him. "Oh, dude, you're so fucked."

Chase forces himself to take a step toward the door.

But the guys from downstairs stand in the doorway.

And behind them are three others.

They let Rachel through.

The lights go out. Everything is black.

Chase hears the bedroom door slam shut.

And then Chase hears Rush's high-pitched laughter.

Chase had no idea how many of them were in the room. His stomach dropped as adrenaline soared through him and "Please" was all he managed to say. He was frozen. His legs simply wouldn't move. His jeans quickly became warm and wet. The blackness was dizzying. He could barely breathe as he raised his shaking arms and held them in front of his face. There were flashlights. There was a sharp blast of heat. Everything was suddenly white and ringing. Chase felt the entire right side of his face shatter. Falling, the deafening reverberation in his right ear echoed through his skull. He choked on blood and mucus that poured from his nose into his open mouth and directly down his throat—he was coughing up so much blood that he couldn't breathe. Then: the fleshiness of an arm around his face. He was being dragged across the carpet. Aluminum bats landed with such force that Chase could hear his chest crack open. He involuntarily raised his forearm to fend off another blow but someone grabbed it and snapped it, turning it into a wet and splintered thing. When Chase started screaming a gloved fist plugged his mouth with an impact that ripped his front teeth from his gums. The last thing Chase thought before the blackness swept over him was this, and it was very simple: you brought yourself here and that's how you found yourself here. And as his clothes were being torn from his body Chase lost consciousness and was free.

Michele found another tooth on the floor of the Mustang. She placed it on the nightstand next to the others. It has been eight days since the attack. Chase spent four nights in the hospital, though he never found out how he got there. He was told that he was left ("dumped" was the actual word used by one of the staff) at the entrance of the UNLV medical center in the backseat of the Mustang. For some reason Chase thought this was a clue. When he regained consciousness he wrote Michele's phone number down using his left hand and had someone on the staff call her. Michele came immediately with his mother, who wept when she saw what had happened to her son. The two of them picked Chase up from the UNLV medical center when he was discharged. Chase did not want to recuperate at the house on Beverly and his mother said that she understood but she wanted him to come with her and stay at Edward's place in Montana at the end of the summer. After a trip to the apartment on Boulder to collect some of his things, Michele put Chase in Bailey's Impala and drove him to the Strip. She turned right in to the long U-shaped driveway at the Palace.

*   *   *

On the twenty-second floor, in the Sun King suite, Chase drifts off to sleep for an hour at a time. The headaches are so relentless that not even the Norco or Oxycontin manage to dull the pain. Because his arm is splinted and in a cast and his torso is wrapped tightly—to protect the four broken ribs, the smashed clavicle, the cracked sternum—it's impossible to find a comfortable position to sleep. The situation with his eye was described by the doctor as a "blowout" fracture, meaning the bone shattered and slipped down into the sinus cavity "like a trapdoor." The surgery corrected this and stabilized what was left of his cheekbone with titanium plates and screws. His jaw is wired shut and will remain so for five weeks. Michele slips a straw between the wires that fill his mouth. She holds his head forward with one hand while Chase sips the chocolate protein shakes. Soon he relents and begins taking the Vicodin every three hours. This is what registers: Michele with her legs crossed on the red leather chair adjacent to the bed, reading aloud in a soft voice from various magazines; Michele on her cell phone; Michele praying in Spanish; Bailey standing in the doorway.

At one point when Chase is lost in the Vicodin, he asks Michele if she has seen Rachel. Michele moves her head so imperceptibly that Chase can't tell if it means yes or no. When Chase is about to tell Michele that Rachel was responsible for what happened to him his head gets light and he has to stop talking because when he's talking, he starts sweating, which makes

the stitches tingle until they burn. On two occasions, in his
early-morning half-sleep, Chase scratched them so hard that
he pulled the stitches out and woke up to find his face stuck
to a soaked pillow matted with blood. When Chase asks
Michele again about Rachel and about Rush and about the
setup and what Bailey knew, Michele is sliding her soft warm
lips around his cock and her shirt is off and he can't move
anything and just has to lie still watching the pale line on her
scalp where her hair parts as it moves up and down. He's so
high on the Vicodin that he's surprised he can even come, and
when she pulls her mouth off him she slowly makes a circle
with her index finger around the skin just above his pubic hair
the way she used to when they were sixteen and he was a boy
staying at Bally's.

Chase wakes up to find Bailey sitting next to him. Bailey is leaning forward, staring intently at the horrible injuries. Nothing is
said for about a minute as Bailey just stares with a kind of sick
wonder at Chase's wrecked face.

"Stop it," Chase finally has to stay.

"I know who it was," Bailey says. "And when you're ready,
we'll take care of it. However you want to handle it."

"Of course you know who it was, Bailey." Chase closes his
left eye.

"When you're better—"

Chase raises a hand to cut him off. "Stop it."

"We'll all work together again," Bailey is saying. "Like we
started out." Bailey rests his hand high on Chase's thigh. "I
cleaned up your ride, too. You could eat off that shit now."

"I can't be around you anymore, " Chase says. "You have to go. You have to never come back."

"But everything's happening perfectly," Bailey says. "We've still got half the summer left."

When Michele is not taking care of Chase or booking appointments she stays with her cousin in North Las Vegas and not with Bailey. But Michele goes back to Bailey's house one afternoon. Michele begs for the money that is hers. Michele says she is leaving for good. Michele mentions going back to El Salvador. Bailey calls her a whore and rips a patch of hair from her scalp when he drags her out of the house and leaves her on the street bleeding from her nose and mouth. That night she accepts his apology. A day later she agrees to Bailey's terms. One: to let the money situation go for now. Two: they will resume working the business together again.

According to the surgeon the procedure involves rebreaking Chase's face to allow for the precise positioning of the bones so he'll look normal again, at least in theory. Exposure to direct sunlight will trigger severe headaches for months, if not years, and Chase may walk with a limp for the rest of his life because his femur was fractured in three places. Chase tries to explain this to Michele when they leave the hospital for the fourth time that week. He walks with crutches. He may eventually switch to a cane. The sun is brilliant and white and though the sight in his left eye hasn't been restored, the brightness—even with the prescription sunglasses—makes his eyes water and burn, and the headache gets even worse. Explaining the procedure to Michele seems to be a distraction that works.

"They'll bring my left eye up even further so it'll be in line with the right one. Then they'll remove the wires from my jaw and in two or three weeks I can go ahead and get my teeth done." Chase is speaking to Michele through his clenched mouth. His jaw is still wired shut. "I'll look like a monster."

"No you won't," Michele says, sounding like she's trying to reassure herself.

"They made an incision around my skull and pulled the skin down so they could insert the steel plates and screws. That's what they told me today when they took them out. They showed me the picture. Your face really does peel right off."

"They'll fix it," she says in an even voice as tears spill from her eyes. "It'll be like nothing ever happened."

Michele undresses him when they get back to the suite. She tosses his clothes on the cream-colored couch and his black Killers T-shirt falls to the paint-splattered drop cloth she brought from his apartment. He can stand for only a moment before the first surge of nausea. The room is all easels and blank canvases and CVS pharmacy bags and little brown bottles. It's his for now.

Chase says something to Michele the next morning while he's still in bed. Michele smiles weakly. "You say that because I'm the only one here." She turns away. Chase lies in his underwear as Michele slides a warm wet towel along his neck and chest and gently over the part of his rib cage that isn't wrapped in a cast. He flinches and she apologizes. The soap she's using smells like apples. Her hair is pulled back in a ponytail. When her finger-nails graze his skin he shivers. Holding the corner of the warm towel she slides her hand under the waistband of his underwear. He breathes in sharply and holds it. They've been doing it like this for a couple of weeks. She moves her hand slowly and he tells her that she's beautiful.

Chase watches her pack: first her things into the Tumi bags and then all of his things into a duffel bag. Then she stands at the window and looks out over the Strip. It is the last day in the suite. Michele doesn't seem to mind. She simply shrugs and laughs at the fact that Ted from KB Homes actually came through and put Michele's fifteen thousand dollars down on a place in a glossy brochure that lands on Chase's lap: the Paseos, a Phase IV development in Summerlin. And though the house isn't yet complete (the grass will arrive next week) Michele al-ready started moving her things in. And Chase will move in with her. This is the newest plan that Michele has devised. She doesn't look at him when she speaks. If she did she'd see that Chase has closed his good eye as a flash of panic seizes him. Room service arrives. Egg-white omelets and blueberry pan-cakes and coffee and fresh-squeezed orange juice. Chase will watch Michele eat and he will sip orange juice through a straw. Michele tells him she has an eleven o'clock booking. When he offers to leave he realizes he doesn't have to. It's an out-call.

* * *

When his headache isn't so bad Chase staggers down the hallway of the twenty-second floor in the Palace, past a family
whose two young daughters stare at him. He imagines how
he must look to them: a scarred gimp with exposed purple
stitches and staples running down the back of his shaved head.
The valet is a kid whose movement—an easy jog—Chase
envies. Chase cracks a smile when the kid helps him into the
taxi and doesn't wait for a tip from the monster. And even with
the oversize sunglasses the sun is blinding on the Strip. The
taxi heads northwest to Summerlin. Chase squints. The cab
is moving too fast. Chase is an old person now   he considers
asking the driver to turn back but he needs the prescriptions
refilled and the new meds are at the Albertsons and the near-
est one is in Summerlin. He's thinking about Montana and
maybe going up there once he's able to drive again and then
maybe he'll head west to Oregon to see Hunter. Those are the
plans Chase is devising.

At the Albertsons on Rampart Street Rush has dropped the hip-
hop look and is now a surfer. He wears long shorts and a beige
shirt unbuttoned, Oakleys on his head, skin tan but peeling, a
coral necklace. He slides his flip-flops along the floor behind an
older blonde woman with huge breasts and a Prada bag who
Chase assumes is his mother. They have two carts filled with
groceries and as Rush carefully places a six-pack of Budweiser
into the cart he sees Chase and turns away. Two aisles over Rush
and Chase make eye contact again. Rachel is now standing behind him. Her hair is blue. She covers her mouth with her hand

when she sees Chase. Rush's mother is confused: this battered man and her son are staring at each other but not saying anything. Rush is transfixed by Chase's face: the trail of stitches from his scalp to his jaw and the yellow bruises around his eyes.

"Hang loose, dude." Rush waves his thumb and pinkie.

"You're next," Chase says.

Acknowledgments

Morgan Entrekin for believing. Jofie Ferrari-Adler for making everything better, as well as Andrew Robinton, Eric Price, Deb Seager, Amy Hundley, and the rest of the incredibly talented and supportive staff at Grove/Atlantic. My two wonderful agents at ICM: Katharine Cluverius and Josie Freedman. For their generosity: Roland Merullo, Craig Nova, Jim Shepard, Jill Eisenstadt, John Katzenbach.

The graduate fiction workshop at American University who let me sit in and learn . . . Jim Porter, Stacy Evers, and professor/author Richard McCann.

Scott Dickensheets at *Las Vegas Weekly* for giving me a chance to write for him and get to know his city. And special thanks to all the Vegas kids and families who took the time to talk and share a little bit about their lives to help me better understand their hometown. And Marybeth: for showing me how it works.

Friends who always cared enough to ask about "the book" and everything else along the way: Jon Craig, Chris Hadgis, Stacy Weibly, Mason Branch, Anna Riggio-Rosen, Matthew

Guyer, Bruno Neeser, Ian Mishalove, Ako Mott, Matthew Sanger, Don and Jacqueline Easley, and to the DC basketball crew at Balance Gym and the Jelleff court, keep pushin' the rock.

My sisters and brothers: Christine Marque, Suzanne Boyer, Matthew McGinniss, and James McGinniss (you're next).

Al and Phyllis Ford—for their kindness and love.

Especially for Nancy Doherty, editor extraordinaire, and for my father, Joe McGinniss, who inspires me.

Most of all for Bret: your generosity astounds me. Thank you.

And to Jeanine and Julien: This is our golden age . . . let's take our time.